Are You a Bushranger, Mister?

The Tale of a Wildlife Ranger

Bob Pietsch

Illustration by Robert Ulmann

First published by Busybird Publishing 2017

ISBN
Print 978-1-925585-71-1
Ebook 978-1-925692-15-0

Design & production:
Busybird Publishing
2/118 Para Raod
Montmorency Victoria 3094
www.busybird.com.au

Today, departmental policy and the realities of OH&S, simply mean most of the stories in this book could not happen.

Kirby Wellington is based mostly on the author, partly on a few fellow officers and a bit on fantasy and imagination.

Murray Stephens is based a bit of the author, partly on a few fellow officers and mostly on fantasy and imagination.

MT Morrison and the other villains and civilians are fictional and any resemblance to real persons, alive or dead, is coincidental.

This means you cannot believe much of what you read, but you can smile at the characters and their antics, and try to see that humans have a unique place among the animals.

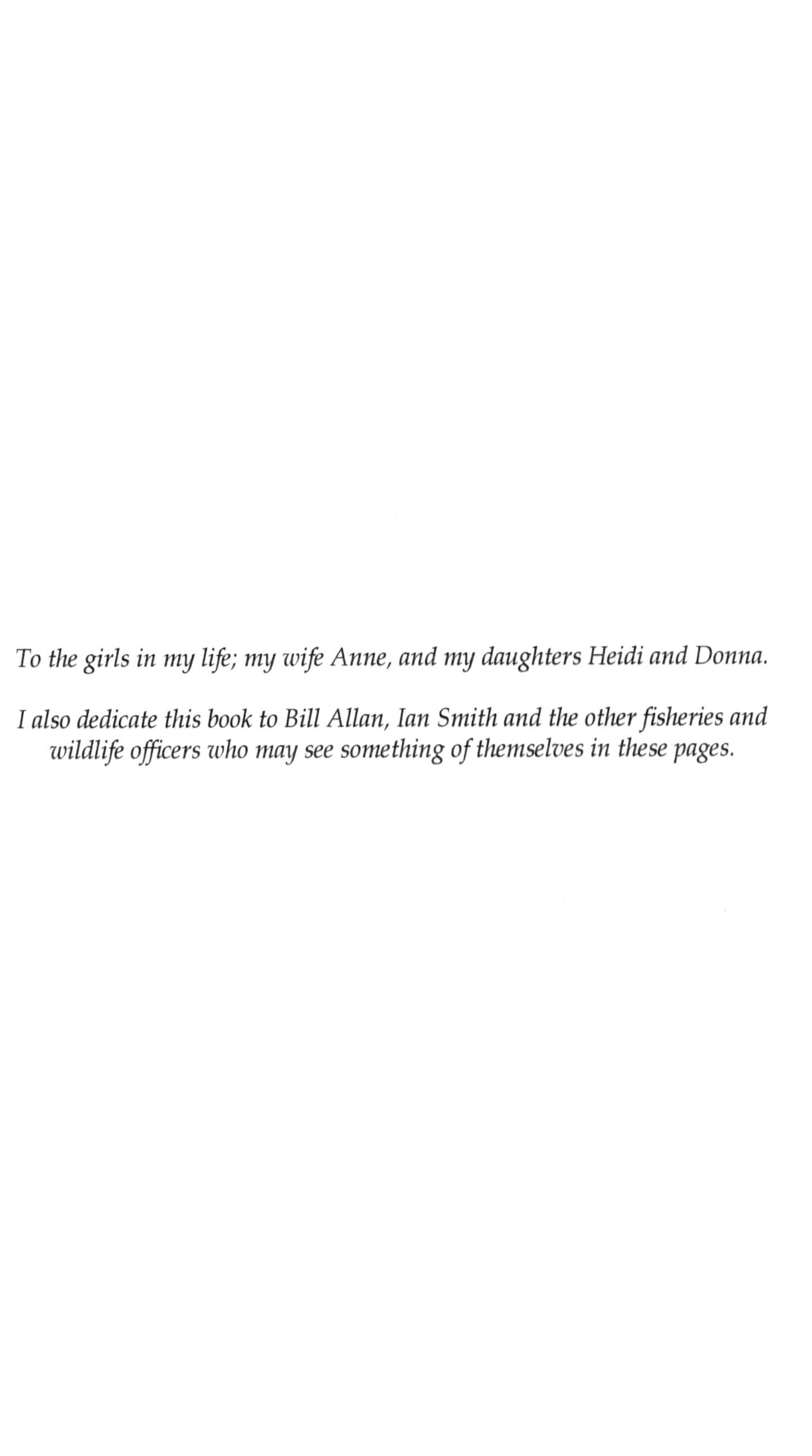

To the girls in my life; my wife Anne, and my daughters Heidi and Donna.

I also dedicate this book to Bill Allan, Ian Smith and the other fisheries and wildlife officers who may see something of themselves in these pages.

Contents

PART 1

IN THE BEGINNING
– AT HEAD OFFICE

Robert Ulmann

Chapter 1

MT MORRISON

'There's no such thing as spare time in this office,' Murray announced. 'It takes a lot of time to keep legislation up-to-date.'

The senior fisheries and wildlife officer leaned forward and looked directly at the two recruits standing nervously in front of his desk.

'You've got to know the law, and to do this you've got to keep your Acts and Regulations amended. You also have to know the department's compliance policy.' He produced a massive text and handed them one each. 'This manual contains the lot – well nearly everything you need to know about policy. If you want to be any good in this job you'll need to read the manual, then read it again.'

Kirby Wellington and Martin Hamilton, the new chums, had just been introduced to every person in the building. At the end of it all Kirby only remembered two of them. Lola—he owed her money for the coffee club—and the boss who had taken them on the introductory tour. Everyone remembered Murray Stephens and it did not take long in his company for you to realise he was boss!

Next Murray escorted the recruits to the store where they collected their uniforms and other items of personally issued equipment. As Kirby looked with pride at his new uniform, he thought back to the job interview. Murray had been on the panel but the only thing Kirby really remembered about him was the uniform. Murray's uniform trousers were a camouflage-green and there were epaulettes, bearing the words Senior Fisheries and Wildlife Officer, on an army-style dress shirt. The creases in his trouser and down the sleeves of his shirt were immaculate and the shine on his shoes brilliant. The only differences in his uniform to the one now issued to the recruits were the titles on the name badges and the absence of the word "senior" on the epaulettes.

Details of the diaries, note books, pens, clip board, overalls, rubber boots, waders, torch, binoculars and rucksack were all filled in on a Requisition for Stores Form, then signed by Murray. Bert, the storeman, duplicated the details on two Materials Issued Vouchers. One required Kirby's signature and Martin signed the other. There was a green copy, a yellow copy, a pink copy and a white copy of everything. Bert's great pride in his work was obvious – he admired every letter of every word as he penned the details in immaculate handwriting.

With their new possessions safely stored in individual lockers, filing cabinets or desk drawers, Kirby and Martin spent the rest of the day amending legislation – and reading the manual.

The next morning the senior officer called the recruits into his office again. Murray was not tall but he held himself erect despite a waistline that advertised his age. Streaks of grey, emerging through dark brown hair, and a totally grey beard, were confirmation of Murray's years. As they stood waiting for their boss to speak Kirby guessed he and Martin were about the same age – twenty-four. Martin was tall, dark and well built. Kirby was tall and blond and could have played basketball.

'Our intelligence tells us MT has recently shifted to Melbourne and is illegally selling protected birds at the trash and treasure markets,' Murray confided. 'We're going out to have a bit of a look at his place.'

'Empty?' Kirby questioned. 'What's Empty? Who's Empty?'

'MT is a nickname,' laughed Murray. 'It's a reference to the space between his ears. He's really Maxwell Thomas Morrison and that's where the MT comes from, Maxwell Thomas. In reality I think the only person left in the world who'd use his real name would be his mother, if she were still alive. Come to think of it, I doubt she'd even admit knowing him.'

'I can't wait to meet him,' said Kirby. 'He sounds a bit lamentable.'

'That's an understatement,' agreed Murray. 'He's recently moved to Melbourne from Costerfield where he's been in trouble with Martin Stein for years. Martin's the officer from up there. MT's not just into wildlife though. One time he was using an illegal drum net to catch fish and when Martin jumped out of the bushes and nabbed him on the riverbank things went a bit haywire. Martin ended up in the water in place of the net! MT reckoned he was innocent but every officer who's ever met the man gives more credence to Martin's side of the story. All our staff have heard of MT and a good many of 'em have nabbed him. He's like a bad penny, keeps popping up everywhere. Seems to specialise in protected birds but he'll have a go at anything. A couple of years back he was supposed to be the supplier of most of the wild-caught parrots, especially the smaller ones, that ended up in the aviculture trade. A few times Martin raided his joint and found mist-nets and book-traps but he's never been done for trapping birds. That'd be a good pinch but unfortunately we just don't seem to be able to get a big one on him. One of these days though he'll get his comeuppance.'

MT rented a rundown old weatherboard house. There was a rusty pedestrian gate in the middle of a dilapidated wire mesh fence along the footpath out the front. The gate was off its hinges and hung on the ground in a half open position. Weeds had over grown the cement path leading straight to the middle of a veranda that ran across the front of the house. The fence posts, once painted, were now just grey weathered timbers. The house was dirty with dust and cobwebs. Grass grew out of the spouting in several places. Even under the shelter of the veranda roof the wall paint flaked and peeled badly. On the left a vehicle driveway led to a single car wooden garage with double doors that opened outwards from the centre. At the side of the garage, between it and the house, was a water tank on a stand. The tank and its stand actually formed the greater part of the dividing barrier that separated the front and driveway areas from the backyard.

When the officers arrived they approached the front door and Murray knocked loudly, urgently and for ten seconds longer than necessary.

'Don't be frightened to show 'em who's boss,' Murray explained when Kirby frowned at the aggression. 'Sometimes you can take control of a situation just by a simple demonstration.' He knocked again, almost as violently as before.

That's enough. I get the point, thought Kirby.

As the three officers waited there were no signs of the bird prisons they had come to inspect. MT eventually answered the door.

'Yeah, yeah, I know who yer are,' MT interrupted as Murray began official introductions. 'I can see yer uniform. Come in, come in. I'll make a cuppa. Do yer wan' tea or coffee?'

'No thanks,' Murray insisted. 'We're here to do an inspection of your premises and it's best to do it now.'

He walked off the veranda, down the driveway, past the garage towards the back yard, and, as it turned out, past some of the evidence he was seeking. MT and the two recruits followed, the trash and treasure man protesting loudly.

Kirby whispered to Martin. 'He looks like Mr Bean!'

'No he doesn't. Mr Bean is a lot fatter. Anyway MT would need three big feeds a day for a month to get anywhere near as good looking. He'd need a shave and a good bath in disinfectant too.' Martin also whispered, holding his nose.

'You're right,' conceded Kirby. 'He'd never double for Mr Bean – he can't shut up.'

Before Murray reached the water tank MT positioned himself in front of him, blocking the pathway defiantly. He had his arms crossed and stood firm.

'There's a killer dog in the yard,' MT announced. 'You hang on a minute while I tie him up. You'll 'ave to wait here, wait here.'

The four men were in single file. MT was facing away from the yard, toe to toe with Murray. Behind Murray came Kirby. Martin was at the rear. Kirby only just avoided bumping into Murray because his head had been turned towards Martin during their private chatter.

Even from his position near the front of the procession Murray could not see into the yard because the tank and high gate prevented both access and inspection. On the tank stand to his left, Murray saw a piece of 25 millimetre water pipe, about a metre long. On one end was an elbow and he picked it up and poked it at MT – the elbow on the business end.

'If that dog comes anywhere near me I'll dong it,' Murray threatened. He waved the pipe out to his right – like an opening batsman practicing a cut shot.

'It's a trained killer,' responded MT. 'Trained by ASIO – an Alsatian trained t'go for the throat. Yer wouldn't 'ave a chance. It's a trained killer, a trained killer.'

'Get out of my way,' Murray said putting on a brave front.

Kirby was impressed. He and Martin had only been two days in the job, but already Murray seemed like the right kind of bloke to have as a boss. Kirby wondered if he could ever be so bold – or even if he could ever hold such a position.

Murray, on the other hand, was glad to have Kirby and Martin behind him. He hoped, however, that neither MT or the new officers would hear or detect that his confidence, like his legs, was just a little wobbly as he pushed open the gate.

In the middle of the yard stood a rotary clothesline and tied to this, by a length of chain, was a mongrel black and white dog. It snarled aggressively at the intruders and began to growl menacingly when MT spoke.

'You'd fix 'em if I let yer wouldn't yer boy? I oughta let yer orf, just for sport, for the fun of it.'

Kirby saw the dog on many occasions after that and whilst he never trusted it, the dog gave no real reason for fear that day — it remained on the chain — or on any other occasion.

There was no Alsatian but across the greater width of the back fence was an old chook run. Along the fence on the far side of the yard was an assortment of run-down birdcages and aviaries. Halfway between these and the clothes line was a rusty two-hundred-litre drum incinerator surrounded by piles of charcoal and ash.

Kirby and Martin had hardly looked away from the dog but Murray had already taken in the yard and the area over the back fence. This was open and grassed, about the size of four house blocks.

'Come on you blokes,' Murray commanded. 'Have a look around now – in the chook house and cages. Look close, there's a fair few birds here. Mostly canaries and budgies but we'll find something amiss, I bet.'

Doesn't he realise MT will hear? Kirby's thoughts were interrupted as the senior officer continued.

'Look over the fence in the vacant block too. That'd be a good place to hide something you didn't want the inspectors to find wouldn't it Mr Morrison?'

Kirby looked over the back fence and saw the area contained a small dam where a goose and a dozen domestic ducks swam around happily. There appeared to be no place where anything could be hidden.

Murray suddenly realised MT did not answer his question.

'Hell! MT's disappeared,' Murray announced. 'You two stay in the yard till I find him.'

What a mess, he thought. *I shouldn't leave the new blokes by themselves but I have to find MT in a hurry.* Murray also knew it was unwise to leave the birds in the backyard unguarded, but he had no choice other than to trust them to Kirby and Martin.

MT was in the first place that Murray looked – the garage.

Murray entered through the right-hand side of the front double doors. What he saw made him both pleased and disappointed. Pleased that he had found MT and pleased that he had caught him out. But Murray was disappointed because his pleasure was at the expense of MT's defenceless, innocent native birds.

The garage was unlined, the eaves uncovered and the floor

an unbelievable mess. There were tea chests, cardboard boxes, assorted canary and budgerigar ornaments and pet accessories lying everywhere. Banks of small cages lined the right hand and rear walls. The disarray was so bad the only clear space was a passageway, from the front to the rear, in the middle of the chaos. MT was at the rear of the building with his back to the door when Murray entered. The air was alive with the fluttering of little wings and Murray knew MT was trying to get rid of the evidence. Many of the cage doors along the right hand side were open and the little prisoners were free, flying around inside the garage. It did not take long for them to see their total freedom was up, over the wall and away, via the open eaves.

'Mr Morrison,' Murray announced loudly, 'I strongly advise you not to open any more of those cages. If you do, you will be charged with obstructing a wildlife officer in the execution of his duty!'

MT obeyed instantly. What else could he do? The doors on every cage containing illegal birds were already open. MT looked around blankly, then with his head down like a mad bull, charged for the only door. Murray had nowhere to go. He stood, flat-footed, directly in MT's path as the bird dealer ran towards him. The force behind the collision surprised Murray and MT struggled furiously as the two rolled around on the dirt floor. Boxes and pet accessories flew in all directions. Murray had an enormous weight advantage and soon had MT in a headlock. The struggle stopped as quickly as it started and when Murray released the pressure, MT walked back into the yard as if nothing had happened. The senior fisheries and wildlife officer followed.

'We've found half a dozen pinioned wood duck in the chook house,' Kirby announced proudly, unaware of the wrestling match that had just taken place. 'And we found some more dead ones. He's been burning them in the incinerator.'

Kirby pointed to several charred carcasses now lying in a heap in the yard. The burned feathers on one or two were so black it was difficult to recognise them as wood duck. As the search of the yard continued Murray kept quiet about his ordeal. Kirby climbed the fence and walked around the dam and the vacant block. He found nothing and, apart from the ducks, three Stubble Quail that did not escape from the garage were the only illegal birds they found. Murray handed the quail to Kirby.

'They'll have to be locked in the car,' he directed. 'And while you're there bring back that big cage for the ducks, will you?' He had the situation back under control, and everything was now to be done by the book. 'You'd better bring one of those plastic bags for the dead ducks too,' he called after Kirby.

Murray began to interview MT. *This is a good clean pinch*, he thought as he recorded the date, time and place and made a few notes about the incident in the garage. After MT gave his name, address and date of birth Murray expected three or four more questions, and the opportunity for MT to explain himself, would see the officers on their way. Murray Stephens had a few things to learn about MT.

'Now what can you tell me about the ducks, Mr Morrison?' Murray continued.

'Well,' MT began. 'See them power lines up there? See the dam out the back? See the ducks on the dam? Well I can't help it if wild ducks are attracted to the dam and the domestic ducks can I? I can't stop birds flyin' into the power lines can I? I can't help it if they drop dead or fall wounded into me yard can I? Look, some even got their feathers singed. None of 'em can fly.'

As he spoke MT waved his arms about erratically. He pointed to the dam, a large transmission line overhead, the ducks in the chook shed and the burned carcasses, but not in the order that he spoke of them.

'That's ridiculous and you know it. The ducks can't fly because you cut their wing feathers. Ah, tell it to the Magistrate.'

The note taking concluded. All that remained was to seize the ducks and get out of there.

'Where the hell's Kirby?' Murray asked Martin when he realised the young officer had not returned. 'It doesn't take ten or fifteen minutes to get a cage. Go and find him will you?'

Martin went to look and returned a short time later, with the cage, a plastic bag and Kirby. Kirby's uniform was now like Murray's – dusty and scruffy, but no one seemed to notice.

'Mr Morrison, here is a receipt for the ducks and quail we've seized,' Murray said to MT. 'These matters will be reported and you should expect to receive a summons to attend court.'

As he spoke Murray handed MT a seizure receipt. It was for:

"3 Stubble Quail, 6 Pinioned Wood Duck (live) and 4 Wood Duck (deceased)."

'Them ducks weren't mine – I already told yer that. I ain't takin' this.' MT crumpled the paper and threw the receipt on the ground. 'I'll fight yer in court. I'll get compensation for embarrassment, defamation of me character – and false accusations!'

'Let's go,' Murray said. He led Kirby and Martin out to the car.

Kirby climbed into the back seat and sat quietly. Martin and Murray secured the seized birds in the back of the station wagon.

'What was the hold up with the cage?' Murray asked Kirby as he pulled the car out into the traffic. He looked at Kirby in the rear-view mirror with Martin half turned around from the front seat to face his peer.

Kirby was silent, sitting with his head bowed. He was convinced his career in the best job in the world was in tatters, only two days after it had begun. He knew he had to make a confession but did not know how to begin. It was bad enough having to tell the boss, but Martin would tell every other officer in the state. Kirby would go down in history as the shortest serving fisheries and wildlife officer.

'I've lost the court exhibit,' Kirby confessed quietly.

'What are you on about?' asked Murray. 'Court exhibit? What court exhibit?'

'One of the quail got away,' Kirby conceded. 'I'm sorry. I'm terribly sorry, but it was hard to manage three quail while I unlocked the car. I've only got two hands. We need the quail for the court case don't we?'

Kirby's confession contained an excuse and Murray knew the quail escaping had been partly his fault – he should not have given three birds to an inexperienced officer in the circumstances.

'Where are the other two?' Murray asked, not answering the question or giving an apology.

'In the cage in the back.'

'That's not too bad,' said Murray. 'I'm not saying it's a good idea to let domesticated birds go, especially ones we've seized. They'll either get eaten by a cat or die when they can't find food, water or shelter. But don't worry too much about the court case. We wouldn't usually take live birds into court – or smelly dead ones for that matter. Sure we'll need to give evidence of their identification. A good photo or two always helps. You know what sort of a quail it was?'

'All three were Stubble Quail,' said Martin.

'I wasn't asking you,' said Murray. 'What do you think, Kirby?'

'Yes. They were Stubble Quail. There were two females and one male. The male got away.' Kirby was not going to let Martin out-score him in the bird identification contest. 'I've seen hundreds on the farm.'

'Good. If Martin can't sex Stubble Quail tell him how.' Murray tried to relieve Kirby's despair, but was still using the experience as a training exercise for the two recruits.

'Well the male has a black patch on his chest and the female has a buffy-white breast. The males are a bit darker in colour.' Kirby's Stubble Quail sexing lesson was confident, but very quiet. 'But that's not all,' he continued. 'I'm afraid there might be some trouble.'

'What sort of trouble?' Murray asked.

'Well, when the quail got away I tried to catch it,' Kirby explained. 'It flew across the road and down a driveway. It only flew low to the ground and I ran after it. It went into a backyard, then flew over the fence into another yard. There was this vegie patch, and the quail landed there. I could see it from over the fence. It tried to camouflage in the straw around some lettuces but I kept my eye on it. I got over the fence and stalked it – I thought I could grab it. I didn't think about the lettuces and I didn't think about anybody watching. Unfortunately the owner saw everything out his kitchen window. He couldn't see the quail and said he thought I was trying to play rugby with his lettuces. He got pretty bloody mad. I suppose I didn't do a couple of his lettuces much good and he wrote down my name. He said he was going to lodge an official complaint.'

Kirby sat there wondering what would happen.

'Let's see if he does,' comforted Murray. 'If he does we'll worry about it then. Today should be a good lesson for you both. There are a couple of things I want you to remember.' As they drove Murray continued with his instruction.

'It's very important not to get distracted,' he said. 'Sometimes it's a bit hard not to, but you shouldn't ever get into an extraneous conversation. You're there to do a job not to be chummy buddy with the crooks. Watch for body language – that's so often the real give-away.' Murray continued with a brief account of the wrestling match in the garage but came quickly back to the lesson he wanted to convey.

'That crap about inviting us in for a cuppa is typical of someone who's got something to hide,' he explained. 'It's just not normal for a crook to give us a cuppa. Think about it. That sort of thing isn't in the policy manual but it's common sense when you think about it. You've got to keep your wits about you. Then that bull about the killer dog. That was just another way to buy time and space, and I don't mind admitting it was a bit of a worry. Don't ever let 'em know you're frightened though. You've got to keep control all the time. When I saw MT had gone I knew we had a case. But we should've been working as a team and seen him leave.'

'What would've happened if it had been a killer dog?' Martin asked.

'We'd have found out how good I was with the pipe,' Murray said as they pulled up in front of the office. 'Your next lesson is how to write a witness statement for court.'

Chapter 2

THE PET MAGPIE

'I've got an echidna,' an unknown voice announced the moment Kirby picked up the duty office phone.

There were no introductions and the statement was so abrupt Kirby had to ignore the telephone protocols he had learned in the few weeks he had been a fisheries and wildlife officer. In that time he and Martin Hamilton had been to court and listened to a departmental court case prosecuted by Murray Stephens. Through that experience the young officers could see how their statements of evidence would be used, and could understand a little better, how to avoid the trap of hearsay. With this knowledge, and a lot of coaxing from Murray, Kirby finally finished his statement about MT and the ducks. With that task out of the way Kirby found he had a lot of time to read his manual and amend his legislation. As the days passed Kirby's responsibilities begun to include answering the duty office telephone and manning the departmental radio. On this Monday morning Kirby was rostered in the office.

'Is the echidna injured?' he asked.

'No, it's fine.'

'What suburb are you in?' Kirby inquired completing the phone log as he spoke.

'Boronia.'

'Yes, well,' Kirby had begun to explain. 'Echidnas used to occur all over what is now suburbia and it's possible the echidna has wandered in...'

'No. It came from Barmah Forest.'

'Barmah Forest?'

'Yes,' the caller explained. 'We went camping up at Barmah on the weekend and found it lost in the bush. We brought it home and don't know what to feed it. Can you come and get it?'

I can't believe there are so many fools out there, Kirby mused.

He was beginning to expect the unexpected, but was still shocked at the frequency of virtuous calls made by people who were so ignorant. Half an hour later Kirby answered another call.

'Are you allowed to keep magpies as pets?' a female voice demanded.

'No, magpies are protected and it is not legal to keep, cage or kill them,' Kirby answered confidently.

'Well,' Valarie Lucas challenged instantly. 'What if you've got one and you keep it in the house but not in a cage? It's got its wing clipped but goes out in the backyard sometimes.'

This last question and statement had Kirby on guard again. *I've got another one*, he thought. *All the nutters even sound the same.*

'That would be not be allowed either,' he said flatly.

'Well,' the caller rambled in explanation. 'The woman next door has a magpie like that and it sometimes gets into our yard and it's vicious, it's dangerous. Yesterday it was over our fence again and it attacked my daughter and I had to take her to the doctor to get stitches in her face and head. It pecked her real bad. The doctor said she was lucky she didn't lose her eye. She had seven stitches and I want you to do something about it. That woman should be prosecuted.'

Kirby recorded the complaint made by Valarie Lucas. This included the address where Dorothy Sampson allegedly lived and kept the magpie. Kirby relayed the details to the boss and Murray assigned Kirby his first solo operation.

'Seize the magpie and book the woman up,' the senior officer instructed.

Kirby grabbed a cage, pen and notebook and, armed with a street directory, drove to the address. It was a hot day and the front door of the suspect house was ajar. After knocking and receiving no response, Kirby knocked again. There was still no answer so he ventured down the side path towards the rear of the house. He entered the back yard through a wooden gate and found himself looking across a neat little lawn and garden.

Dorothy Sampson was small, elderly and quite spritely and she was directly opposite the gate, watering with a hand-held hose. As Kirby stepped through the gate the magpie attacked from somewhere near its mistress. It half flew and half ran directly at his ankles, its beak rattling like the sound of automatic small arms fire.

Clack, clack, clack, clack, clack, clack.

Kirby was an unwanted intruder and the pain in his ankle had him emphatically on the side of the injured girl next door. He immediately knew all he needed to know about the offence and began to feel confident about his task, though the bird was causing him considerable discomfort. He kicked free and raised his trouser leg for an inspection.

The magpie came in for another attack. Kirby's right ankle was bruised and bleeding already, and the pain was excruciating. *Peck.* It got him on the left shin.

'Jeez! Damn bl–ow!' Kirby hopped around for a minute before he re-gained his composure.

'Georgina, don't do that,' Dorothy called. 'You naughty girl.' She stopped watering her sweet peas and hurried over and picked up the magpie. It was perfectly at ease with her. Being bodily handled did not worry it one bit. The bird's mistress cradled her pet in her arms like a doll – its legs poking up in the air.

I wonder what would happen if I did that? Kirby thought. *Perhaps that's what the little girl did – perhaps she put her head and face in the firing line.*

'Hello, I'm Kirby Wellington. I'm a wildlife officer and I'm here because the department had a complaint about a magpie attacking children. I think I've found the culprit and I reckon there may be some justification for the complaint.'

Kirby, still looking at the blood streaming down his shin, immediately recognised his error. *Bum. Dorothy would know about the problems next door and I've just told her who complained.*

'I know it was the bitch next door who complained,' Dorothy said, as if reading Kirby's mind. 'I know Georgina pecked her daughter, but that's because the kids tease her. It's not the bird's fault if the kids tease her, is it?'

'But,' Kirby interrupted, 'I didn't tease it and it attacked me too. Besides, magpies are protected and you're not allowed keep them. This one actually attacks people and that just makes things worse.'

As they talked Kirby looked around the yard and saw an extra dimension to the protected bird case he was there to solve. The yard contained two cages, one housed a pair of Eastern Rosellas and the other some cockatiels and two Red-rumped Parrots. Without asking, Kirby knew he had stumbled onto additional offences and he did not want to know.

'Where did the magpie come from?' he asked.

'We found it up on the farm,' Dorothy said. 'It was a baby that fell out of the nest. If I hadn't rescued it, and hand raised it, it would be dead now. It's a Black-backed Magpie. The ones around Melbourne are all White-backed Magpies.'

'How long have you had it?' Kirby continued without acknowledging the bird's identification.

'About four years. We thought it was a boy but it's a girl. Clarrie, my husband, called it George, but we had to change its name to Georgina when it built a nest on my dressing table and laid an egg. You can't call a girl George, can you? Come on I'll show you.'

Dorothy led the way inside, still carrying her pet. As they stood at the end of her bed the old lady pointed out an untidy nest on the top of her dressing table.

'It took her weeks to make it,' Dorothy explained. 'She carted every stick and blade of grass all by herself. We did get some straw and bark and put it in the yard so she had plenty of stuff to choose from, but we didn't help her carry it. Clarrie went to hospital before she finished the nest and he never saw the egg. I told him all about it though.'

Murray's stupid manual hasn't got the answer to this one, Kirby thought.

'She never sat on the egg you know,' Dorothy continued. 'Do you think it would have hatched? Georgina did have a boy magpie visit her in the yard. Would it matter that Georgina is a black-back while the boy was a white-back?'

'I've no idea,' Kirby confessed feeling like a snowball in a warm oven. He did have some ideas though. They related to what Murray Stephens would say if he knew one of his officers was spending time, on duty, with a woman in her bedroom. He used the rosellas and parrots as an excuse to get back in the yard.

'Where did they come from?' he asked.

'We brought them with us when we shifted down from the farm,' Dorothy explained. 'We've had them since the kids were teenagers. When we retired our son took over the farm and he didn't want them so we brought them with us. They were more the daughter's pets than his anyway.'

'Back to the magpie,' Kirby said. 'You can't keep it. It's too dangerous.' The last three words were an after-thought, an excuse for doing his job.

'You're not going to take her away are you?' Dorothy Sampson looked at Kirby in absolute dismay when she realised what he meant.

'I have to,' Kirby said. 'It's against the law for you to keep it and the department received an official complaint involving an injury to a child. I simply can't leave it here. What happens if we get another complaint? What happens if it attacks someone else, like it did me?'

'But you can't.'

'But I must.'

'Georgina would be OK if the kids didn't tease, I'm sure.'

'I don't think she would. It's far more likely that Georgina attacks because she is trying to protect her nest. Perhaps she even thinks you are her baby. Willy-wag-tails chase hawks away from their nests and the larger birds always leave in a hurry. I reckon Georgina's kamikaze attacks are simply natural aggression against intruders in her territory.'

Suddenly, Kirby found himself grabbed by the arm.

'I know what will happen,' Dorothy cried. 'It will be just like always. All my life I've tried to do the right thing and now you're going to take away the only thing left that matters to me. On the farm we had a hard life, but we were happy. The kids were good then but now the daughter's turned against me. I've always been good to them. John Lucas that husband of hers has poisoned her mind against me. That's why Val dobbed me in.'

'Hang on. I didn't say it was your daughter who complained.'

'You didn't have to,' Dorothy sobbed. 'I know it was her, she has turned into a bitch and you are no better. Since Clarrie died, Val and that mongrel son-in-law of mine want me dead too so they can get my money. Now you want the only thing left in the world that loves me. You're going to take the only bit of happiness left in my life.'

Dorothy now had her arm around Kirby's neck and her thoughts jerked into words as she blubbered into his uniform shirt. Kirby was desperate. For the second time in a few weeks he had visions of getting the sack from the job he had thought was the best in the world.

It's not bloody fair. I haven't been trained for this. Kirby had absolutely no idea how to handle Dorothy Sampson, her daughter or the bird. He knew he could not go back to the office and say there was no one home, or that there was no magpie. No doubt Valarie Lucas would be keeping a bit of an ear open over the fence and would be aware of his visit. Kirby felt nauseous.

How can I take the old lady's pet? But what about the little girl who nearly lost her eye? The bird is ferocious – I can vouch for that. It's all bloody right for Murray Stephens. He says to keep the situation under control. What the hell would he do now if he were me? He's always on about his stupid manual but mother and daughter hatred isn't in it.

'Look,' Kirby eventually negotiated, 'you'd have to agree. Georgina can't stay locked up for the rest of her life can she?'

'Oh no, I couldn't bear that,' Dorothy conceded shaking her head, firstly one way then the other.

'And if Georgina stayed here she would get over the fence again wouldn't she?'

'Yes, probably.'

'And you won't be able to stop her attacking everyone who comes into your yard?'

'No I wouldn't.'

'Look I'll tell you what we'll do. I'll forget I saw the rosellas and parrots. I'll let you keep those if there is no more fuss about me taking Georgina.' Kirby prayed silently his bribery would work and that no one would find out.

'And if I don't agree? What then?' Dorothy Sampson had obviously driven a hard bargain or two in her time.

'I have no choice,' said Kirby. 'I'll will seize the parrots, the rosellas and the magpie. I will also include in my report that you were uncooperative. Wouldn't it be better all-round if you just donated Georgina to the department? She can then go to the zoo or the Healesville Sanctuary where she'll have a good home. That'd be best in the long run. How'd you feel if Georgina actually pecked someone's eye right out?'

'You make it all sound so bad. I really don't know.' Dorothy's words were interspersed with loud sobs and sniffles.

'Look, this way you still have the rosellas and parrots,' Kirby reasoned. 'I'm putting my job on the line over them and I can't be any fairer.'

Kirby did not wait for an answer. He went to the car for the cage and when he returned neither he or Dorothy spoke. With a loving kiss from her owner, Georgina found herself a true captive – for the first time in her life.

Just as well I didn't have to catch it, thought Kirby. *I don't think I would've been up to a second volley of shots from that clacking beak.*

For years afterwards Kirby had nightmares about what he did to the only thing left in the world that loved Dorothy Sampson. Sometimes he dreamed he was a soldier struggling to cope with murder, legalised through war. He tried to comfort himself in the knowledge that an illegally kept bird that attacked a child was unacceptable.

After all. I'm simply a servant of government. Soldiers don't start wars and wars are always over money.

Kirby knew that war was hell and wished he had not been involved in the one between Valarie Lucas and her mother.

Chapter 3

TRAPPED

'Neil Lyons needs help nabbing some duck trappers up at Kerrisdale. You'll be leaving this arvo,' Murray told Kirby when he arrived for work a few Mondays later. 'You'd better go home and pack your gear now.' Murray handed him the papers, then added, 'and keep your eyes and ears open, son, he's a good officer, he'll teach you plenty. Expect to be away on the weekend – the whole week. If you haven't got 'em by Friday there's nothing surer than you'll get 'em on Sat'day or Sundy. They'll drop their guard a bit then, probably after a few beers on Sat'day arvo.'

Kirby nodded, already concerned about being away from home, or more to the point away from Nicky, his wife. He turned and began to leave.

'And take the red sedan – it doesn't look so much like one of ours,' Murray called as an afterthought. 'Neil thinks a couple of the local rascals are responsible and if it is them they'll be real hard to catch. They listen to our radio calls on a scanner and keep tabs on Neil's car. When you get to Kerrisdale don't use the radio for anything, not even if you break down. Don't go to the office and don't wear your uniform. Neil's expecting you at his house by five this arvo.'

'I'll be home in about an hour,' Kirby told Nicky by phone the moment he arrived back at his desk. 'I've got to pack because I'm going to Kerrisdale for a couple of days.'

This would be the first time they had been apart since their marriage and Kirby was anxious about being away for so long. Zac was twenty months old now and Nicky was nearly seven months pregnant again. When he arrived home Nicky helped him pack.

'I'll need enough clothes to last until Sunday,' Kirby announced.

'Why didn't you tell me that on the phone?' Nicky demanded, bursting into tears. 'Why do you need a whole week?' Her usually perfect smile vanished. She bit her lip in an attempt to stop it quivering.

Kirby saw this and hurt. He cursed himself silently for making her cry. In the three years of their marriage he had hardly stopped gazing at her beauty. He loved her smile and her long golden hair that turned up at the shoulder.

'They're real pro duck poachers,' Kirby explained. 'Tough, local hoodlums. Once we start we've got to stick it out till we nab 'em.'

'A week,' she brooded. 'Well don't you get killed. I'll shoot you if you do.'

'Sorry,' was all Kirby could say as he put his arms around her. 'I knew you'd be upset and I didn't want you worrying. It'll be good training for me and it's only for a few days really.'

Kirby did not say that he desperately wanted to go. Nicky knew anyway.

'I don't think Monday to Sunday is a few days,' she sobbed. 'And you've just told me they're tough hoodlums. How can you say you don't want me to worry?'

The trip north to Kerrisdale was uneventful. It was January and hot. When Neil Lyons answered Kirby's knock he ushered the young officer inside the moment Kirby said his name. There was no handshake or proper introduction. Neil appeared paranoid – as though standing at the door put the two men in some sort of physical danger. Once inside introductions seemed unnecessary and the older officer never did tell Kirby his name.

Neil Lyons was a big man with a big voice. He looked the type to just sit in a recliner all weekend watching cricket, or footy, and having a beer or two. In real life though, Neil was a very active and energetic person. Kirby knew this and knew he had a well-earned reputation for turning up at unexpected times and in unexpected places to catch a good number of poachers. Over coffee Kirby heard Neil's plan.

'A couple a weeks ago I got a tip off that Bill and Jim Pappas had a duck trap on their family farm,' Neil explained. 'Last Friday night I found the trap. Trouble is, it's set between a vineyard, a market garden, some irrigated pasture and the main driveway. There's people crawling all over the property at the moment with extra staff on, helping pick the fruit and vegies. Both brothers and their parents live on the place and the houses aren't far away either. It's only possible to get to a decent surveillance position at night – and the only place I can find to hide is beside a small dam. There's a willow tree at one end and that tall cumbungi reed growing all round. We'll be able to keep in the shade for most of the day so that's good. I've arranged for one of the research blokes to drop us off an hour before daylight in the morning. If we don't catch 'em he'll pick us up after dark. I'll leave my work car at the office so it looks like I'm there. But if someone comes in and asks for me, the office staff will tell 'em I'm in Melbourne for the week. We need to use your car 'cause no one will recognise it. We also need an early night 'cause if we don't catch 'em for a few days this'll get bloody hard. We can't use the radio till we nab 'em so when we're in there, we've got no backup. We've got to rely on our wits and the tucker we take with us.'

Kirby was enthusiastic. It would be good to help catch these poachers. Next morning, as planned, the two officers were hiding beside the dam before daylight. Just before the sun rose the Pappas brothers drove down to the area in a beaten up farm utility. The trap was empty and after a cursory inspection of the area they drove away. Kirby and Neil then had to sit, waiting for darkness, still fourteen hours away.

'They tell me you've caught your share of poachers,' Kirby prompted, remembering Murray's advice about learning from Neil's experiences.

'I suppose I've pinched a few,' admitted Neil. 'But you don't always win you know.'

'What do you mean?' asked the younger officer.

'Well I remember one time,' Neil reminisced. 'It was full moon, a favourite time for illegal duck shooting at night. I answered a complaint about shootin' on the moon at Pyamble Swamp, not far out of Kerrisdale. They put out decoys and shoot at the splash the ducks make when they land on the water near the decoys. The splash is easy to see in the moonlight and it's a very effective way of getting a feed because if you hit the splash you hit the duck. Anyway, I was out there this night and hadn't been there long. I was sitting, waiting and listening when I heard a single shot. You know some of our blokes do this sort of job with the windows up and the car radio on. You can't hear shots with the radio on. You remember that. Anyway, after the first shot I drove closer with me lights out. I stopped and listened again. Not long after I heard another single shot. I decided I'd be risking everything if I went any further by car so I walked from there.

I was sneaking along this irrigation channel towards the shooting and reckoned there was only one poacher because every time I heard a shot there was only one. I figured he had an old single-shot 12 gauge gun in case he got caught and had the gun seized. That was all an assumption and assumptions can be dangerous in our work. What was another explanation do you reckon?'

'That he was a real good shot,' suggested Kirby.

'Could have been I suppose,' said Neil. 'But that's not the reason – it was a gas scare gun and not a shooter at all.'

'You're a mongrel,' Kirby laughed. 'What about someone you did catch?'

'Well I remember Joe Zanos and Jim Kalari. That was at Guildford's Waterholes, out near Pyamble Swamp too.' Neil was off again. 'I suppose you know Joe is the Australian name for Guiseppie and Jim is the equivalent of Dimitrios?'

'You mean English,' corrected Kirby. 'No I didn't know.'

'I caught 'em a couple of times,' said Neil without acknowledging Kirby's redress. 'The first time they had a wonderful duck opening – got about twenty legal ducks, a dozen bigga blacka ducks and thirty odd coots. You know what bigga blacka ducks are?'

'Swans?' Kirby guessed correctly.

'The second time I booked 'em was a year later, out at Pyamble Swamp again,' continued Neil. 'It took two trips to court to educate those two but they've been coming up here every year since and they're no trouble at all now. I guess when they first migrated to Australia they didn't understand our hunting laws. When I first booked 'em they'd only been in Australia about a year and they hardly understood a word of English. We did nothing to educate hunters back then – or fishermen, or any of our clients for that matter. We took their licence fee and said they could go huntin' or fishin'. Then we booked 'em, fined 'em and sent 'em on their way again. They came from a country where the open season meant you could take anything, not just a few species. Back in their home country it was common practice to bribe officials. They'd 'ave thought the fine in Australia was a bribe and we didn't even hand out pictures of the ducks they could legally 'ave. Not very professional when you think about it. You know those two are model hunters now – despite what we did to 'em. They love their sport and wouldn't ever do the wrong thing. I've actually seen 'em picking up rubbish left by others. What do you reckon about that?'

'What happened when you got them the second time?' Kirby asked without answering Neil's question.

'The red fin were biting and I was checking anglers on the irrigation channels,' Neil responded. 'I could hear a lot of shooting coming from Pyamble Swamp. The duck season was open and at first I didn't take much notice. Then I got a bit uneasy because part way through the open season, and in the middle of the afternoon, there were just too many shots to be legit. I drove round and found a car parked in some long grass off the side of the track. Through me binoculars I could see one person in the vehicle and another bloke in a duck hide down near the swamp. I was watching pretty close 'cause I was awful suspicious. You know I could hardly believe it when I realised the bloke in the hide was takin' aim. Next thing he fired directly into a mob a coots that were grazing round the water's edges. He got seven or eight in two shots. I didn't know who it was till I got down there to him. It was Joe Zanos. In the hide I found eleven more coots. Anyway, I booked him up and took him over to the car. Sure enough, Jim Kalari was the second bloke. No, he hadn't been shootin'. I searched the boot and found a second gun, but no other birds. I was absolutely positive I was on to something by then. One person wouldn't have done all that shooting, and I reckoned if the number of shots I heard were any indication, they'd have got fifty, not eighteen or twenty. Anyway I had a proper look round after that and under the car were two chaff bags. They had sixty-eight coots altogether. One of them, I forget which one, asked me what I was going to do with 'em. I told him I was going to bury 'em. Do you know what he said?'

Kirby obviously did not.

'He said "That's a disgusting waste of good food. You should be ashamed of yourself." He was probably right and I reckon that put it all in perspective. Their shooting hadn't been wanton killing. It was an excursion to gather meat in the tradition of their old society.'

The next morning the duck trap was still empty and the Pappas brothers still did not get out of their car. Kirby again prompted Neil for stories as they began their long, hot wait for nightfall.

'The job isn't just about booking people you know. We've got a big education role too. If I'd understood that a bit better when I first booked Joe Zanos and Jim Kalari they mightn't 'ave got into trouble that second year.'

'Murray Stephens told me you shouldn't enter extraneous conversation when you're booking someone,' Kirby remembered, expressing his thoughts out loud – almost as a challenge to his senior partner.

'I totally agree,' said Neil. 'But what I said still stands. Remember yesterday when I told you we didn't even hand out pictures of the ducks that you could legally shoot? Now the department runs waterfowl identification tests and there are mountains of good pamphlets and booklets we hand out. Education can never be extraneous conversation.'

'Yeah, I see what you mean,' said Kirby. 'But isn't that a bit dull compared to catching crooks?'

'I don't think so,' said Neil. 'I've had one or two good times that had nothing to do with law enforcement. You know that Prince Phillip the Duke of Edinburgh has been the patron of the World Wildlife Foundation for many years?'

'Yes, I think I knew,' Kirby lied.

'Well, in 1973 I think it was, on one of his visits to Australia, he came to Phillip Island where we were catching koalas. There was nothing put on about this; it was just part of the normal work program – an official koala re-location exercise. Anyway, the department acted as host for most of the day and when we were catching the koalas the Prince joined us in the bush. There was no red carpet out there – he was really just one of us. You know he even joined in searching the bush for koalas to catch. At the time I didn't go much on his leggings but now I suppose they were OK. In places the scrub was pretty thick. He even pitched in and helped carry the crates of koala back to vehicles. They can be pretty heavy too, but you'd know that if you'd carried one.'

Kirby did not know.

'When we were out in the bush there were press and photographers everywhere. I got the idea they were as impressed as I was with the way the Prince got involved. He really was one of the boys. Are you impressed?'

Kirby did not know if he was or wasn't.

'At lunch time we all went from the bush to Sir Charles McGrath's home for a barbecue. The luncheon party included the Prince, heaps of VIPs and hangers-on, the McGraths and about half a dozen of us officers. The barbecue was strictly out-of-bounds to the press and they hung round the front gate waiting for another picture. The paparazzi had a bit of respect then – not like for Princess Diana.

Anyway, at the rear of the house was this massive outdoor living area that included a huge barbecue. Us officers had the job of the actual cooking and we drew straws to see who'd wear the apron and wield the irons. As usual I drew the short straw. At the time I was a bit crooked on having to be cook but it's sure given me heaps to skite about ever since. How many people do you know who can say they've cooked for royalty?'

'Not too many I suppose,' agreed Kirby giving Neil the answer he wanted.

'The barbecue burnt wood, not gas, and it smoked — awfully — all day.' Neil continued to boast. 'I conjured up all me culinary skills and cooked steak, lamb chops, sausages and onions. This was a bit 'ard 'cause me eyes were smarting and streaming tears. The smoke was acrid and 'orrid. When it was time to eat the Duke still had to be one of the boys. The rules were the same for everyone, if you wanted food you had to help yourself. When he came over Phil asked me what there was to eat. I told him and he said, "I would very much like a couple of the chops, thank you". I picked out the ones I reckoned looked best and, as I put 'em on his plate, tried to be real upper class and intellectual. That was a bit hard but I made a special effort to speak proper despite crying me eyes out from the smoke. If I remember right, me best gibberish was something like "I hope I have cooked them to your liking". Anyway, he came back for more when he finished that plate full. I thought that was pretty good – the Duke of Edinburgh asking me for more of my cooking. You know what he said this time?'

Kirby did not know the answer to this either.

'He said, "I think I'll try some steak this time. I must say, I have changed my opinion of Australian Lamb". The bludger didn't say whether it was for better or worse though.'

Kirby laughed again, realising Neil was enjoying his captive audience. The young officer didn't ask any more questions for the whole, long day.

'Best get on down to the trap to see if they've got anything yet,' Neil said when they arrived in position on the third morning. 'And while you're there, see if there's any grain in the thing. I can't understand why they 'aven't caught a duck by now. Don't dawdle though; it won't be that long before they get here.' Neil was obviously getting impatient.

Kirby walked down to the trap trying not to leave footprints in the sand. There were no ducks but there was plenty of wheat, carefully placed to lead the victims through a funnel device and into the cage section of the trap. From there the ducks would have no hope of escape. Kirby returned to Neil in a few minutes and reported what he saw. The utility arrived not long afterwards and the occupants did exactly the same as they had on the previous mornings.

'Why don't we just nab 'em?' Kirby asked as the vehicle turned and began to drive away. 'It's obvious they're guilty.'

'There are several reasons why not,' the senior officer began to lecture. 'Firstly we only think it's the Pappas brothers. It's not possible to identify them in the half-light through the closed windows of the car. Secondly, you should never try to stop a vehicle unless you can actually stop it. If we tried to stop them on foot we would probably both get run over and killed. More importantly, we don't know who set the trap. These two haven't even got out of the car so far. The offence is to take wild ducks in a trap and we know they haven't done that in the last three days, don't we? We need 'em to actually catch a duck, and we need to nab 'em when they're out of the car. Their intent may be obvious but the obvious ain't evidence. If you want to be any good at this job you've got to know the law. More importantly, you've got to know how to make the law work in the field and in all sorts of situations.'

'That's what Murray Stephens told me,' said Kirby, remembering the gist of one of Murray's lessons.

That afternoon, during the hottest part of the day, Kirby's schooling continued.

'Leave it to me,' Neil announced out of the blue. 'We'll get 'em in the morning.'

Kirby somehow knew he was listening to a statement of fact.

As the day wore on Kirby thought about his need to know the law. He realised that officers would have to apply the law consistently across the state, but he could see that Murray and Neil were different. Despite their idiosyncrasies though, it was obvious both officers took notice of the manual.

'How much do you rely on the manual when you're working out how to do a job?' Kirby asked.

'Well the manual isn't much good without the law,' Neil explained. 'But I suppose it's the basis of just about everything. A bit of common sense doesn't go astray though. You've got to ask yourself what you're trying to achieve. Is the situation one where enforcement is more important than education or visa versa? If you've decided that the best thing is for the crook to have a trip to court, then you've got to get all the evidence to make the charges stick. That's where you've got to use common sense and knowledge of the law together. Don't forget too, a good court case usually generates a bit of publicity, a few headlines in the local rag, and that's bloody excellent extension value for the rest of the community.'

'What about education qualifications?' Kirby asked. 'I've been doing a course, part time, for years. It's the one the department recommends, with a major in Natural Resource Management. Do you reckon that'll help?'

'Bloody academics,' Neil snorted. 'All the boffins in head office are academics. That's the way of the world I suppose. If you want to be a boss in head office you'll need a degree but personally I reckon it's a lot a bull. The manual was mostly written by us ordinary blokes from the bush and it's a bloody good document, even if I say so myself. A whole heap of officers were asked to draft various chapters and when we finished they were edited, then included. I suppose I shouldn't be too critical – that just shows the department still recognises the importance of practical experience. Won't be long though and the academics will take over everything. You mark my word.'

'What chapters did you write?'

'I did the one on the seizure of wildlife and the one on occupation health and safety. I reckon it's quite an honour to be asked to contribute to the manual.' Neil's smile was one of pride.

Next morning as the two officers walked into the dam together Neil carried a hessian bag. Instead of going directly to their usual hiding place they walked to the duck trap. Out of the bag Neil lifted two Pacific Black Ducks and into the trap they went.

'But, but,' Kirby spluttered. 'What? Where? How? Eh. Where did you get them?'

He thought he now understood the statement of fact from the night before, but he didn't have the guts to come out and say, "You can't do that, or, I'm not having anything to do with this". After all, Kirby was very junior in the job and Neil Lyons was something of a legend, both within the department and the community.

'I've got a mate who owns a private zoo,' Neil explained. 'He lent me the ducks for the morning.'

'But, but, but what about entrapment?' Kirby gasped, feeling some relief that he finally managed to ask a legitimate question. He hoped it demonstrated he was rather uneasy about the whole affair and did know something about the law.

'Entrapment?' The senior officer was indignant. 'You've been watching too much American TV. There is no such thing as entrapment in Victoria. I'm simply oilin' the wheels of justice me boy, oilin' the wheels of justice.'

Kirby thought he knew what Neil meant but he wasn't sure. It was actually a number of years before he understood the subtle difference, in law, between entrapment and the inadmissibility of evidence obtained illegally, improperly or unfairly.

The officers settled down and waited. Right on cue the utility arrived and two men jumped out.

'Don't go too soon,' Neil instructed in a whisper. 'It's still too dark to identify them properly. Our timing has to be right. We don't want 'em to be able to hop back into the car and drive away. And of course we have to get the evidence to show what they're going to do with the ducks. We don't want 'em to be able to argue they were just going to let 'em go. Not yet, not yet. Now!'

Like Batman and Robin the two officers exploded from the reeds and caught Bill and Jim red handed – covered in duck blood. The timing was perfect for the pinch but fatal for the ducks – they both had their necks wrung. It was not until the following March, when he returned to Kerrisdale for the court case, that Kirby realised the delayed interception may have been part of Neil's master plan.

That night Kirby did not ring home. He surprised Nicky by walking in a little after four o'clock with a bunch of red roses.

Chapter 4

THE WALLABY AND THE EMU

If the home gardener ever complained about his lettuces, Kirby never found out. The case involving MT and the wood duck and Stubble Quail came on for hearing at court in the first week of April. Kirby, Murray Stephens and Martin Hamilton were standing in the foyer of the court when MT arrived with sticking plaster across the bridge of his nose. He wore a relatively clean jumper but his trousers and shoes were something else. They looked like the ones he had on when he rolled around the garage floor with Murray. They also looked as though they had not been washed, or even taken off, in all that time.

After the close of the prosecution case, MT who defended himself, entered his defence with gusto.

'Yer Honour,' he began. 'I intend to prove me innocence by showin' the court two things. The prosecution's left 'alf the story out. To start with. Them ducks weren't mine. They hit the power-lines, just like I told the inspectors on the day. If the ducks weren't mine I shouldn't be charged with bein' in possession of 'em. Yer left with no alternative but ta dismiss that charge. Then on the second charge, I didn't assault Mr Stephens. He just barged into me shed where I was feedin' me birds. Without warnin' he attacked me an' wrestled me to the ground. Then, when he fought me in the shed, he deliberately bust me nose. Look, it's still in plaster. I wan' you to fine Mr Stephens for assaultin' me.'

'Now Mr Morrison,' Murray began the cross-examination. 'When did you first go to see the doctor about your nose?'

'The day after you deliberately bust it,' MT replied.

'Are you saying you went to the doctor the day after we seized the ducks and quail from you?'

'Yeah. Course I am.'

'And do you agree that was in early December last year?'

'I dunno. I suppose it was before Christmas. You oughta know. I seen yer makin' notes when yer was there.'

'Now could I see the doctor's certificate please?'

'I don't need one. Every-one can tell me nose is bust. Look at the stickin' plaster.' MT was indignant.

'Could you tell the court the name of the doctor you went to see?'

'I can't remember. What does that matter. I told yer me nose is bust.'

'Now, if your nose was broken in the circumstances you describe, you would have reported that to the police wouldn't you?'

'No. I don't dob like youse blokes do. I look after me own problems.'

'Now then Mr Morrison, your broken nose story is false and the sticking plaster is a cheap attempt to give credence to a lie. What do you say to that?'

MT did not answer.

'Mr Morrison I think you said you were feeding your birds in the garage. Is that correct?'

'Yeah.'

'Well if they were your birds, how do you say you were not in possession of the quail?'

'That ain't fair. You're just tryin' to trick me.'

'And the real story behind the ducks is your unlawful acquisition of them,' Murray continued. 'They didn't hit the power lines. Some died after you acquired them and you deliberately attempted to incinerate those. That's the truth isn't it?'

'That's only what you say. I say they hit the power lines because that's the only way they coulda ended up in me backyard, with singed feathers an' everythin'.'

'Could you please explain how electricity could arc, and singe the duck's feathers, when there was no possibility of it earthing way up in the air where the ducks hit the power lines?'

'The electricity was in the wires when the ducks hit 'em o' course,' MT explained sincerely.

'And how long do you say the ducks had been in your yard, Mr Morrison?'

'Just a few days. I went out one mornin' an' there they was. I was gunna ring yer up but I'd only just moved to Melbourne from Costerfield. With all the unpackin' an' everythin' I just never got 'round to it.'

'Now to conclude Mr Morrison, are you asking the court to believe ten ducks flew into the power line and all fell into your yard on the one night?'

'Musta been a big mob o' ducks,' MT replied with a shrug of his shoulders.

Someone once said a solicitor who defends himself in court has a fool for a client. MT was not a solicitor.

Less than a week later Murray called Kirby and Martin into his office again.

'I've just had an anonymous phone call,' the boss explained. 'MT is supposed to have a full grown emu in the paddock out the back of his house. I've got an appointment with the Director in a few minutes so you two will have to go out there and catch it. See if MT will admit he's been feeding it. Find out how long it's been there. Talk to the neighbours – someone must know how it got there and who's responsible. Any questions?' Murray was obviously in a hurry.

'How are we going to catch and handle a full grown emu?' Kirby asked, bewildered. He could not even handle three small quail and he knew the size of an adult emu. Kirby's promotion from mere mortal to wildlife officer had not involved any training in emu catching. 'That paddock's about half a hectare. It will take a miracle for just two of us to catch a full grown emu in there.'

'Get one of those big wooden crates out of the store,' Murray directed. 'Get a bit of that heavy blue netting, twenty or thirty metres long. Use the net to herd the emu into a corner of the fence. You'll be able to catch it if you go out there with a positive attitude. Don't get in front of it though. Emus can kick like nothin' else. They've caused some terrible injuries by kicking people that got too close in front of them. Their feet and legs are strong and horny. Don't forget – keep behind it! Emus aren't like a horse or cow. They can't kick backwards, only forwards. Get behind and stay behind. Grab the wings, like the handlebars on a motor bike and you'll find you can walk along steering it. You'll be right. Off you go. If you're not sure there's a bit in the manual – in the chapter on seizure. Look for the bit about large animals.' Murray was gone.

Kirby and Martin, with the netting and cage loaded on a trailer, set off in pursuit of MT and the emu.

'What are you talkin' about?' MT said when Kirby knocked on the front door and explained why they were there. 'There ain't no emu in the paddock, or if there is, it ain't got nothin' to do with me. I only rent the house, not the paddock.'

'Let's have a look shall we?' Kirby suggested.

Over MT's back fence the emu was walking continually around the fence line.

'Well I'll be,' said MT. 'Fair dinkum I didn't know it was there. Yer ain't stitchin' me up with that like yer did with them ducks though. No bloody way!'

Kirby began to think MT was telling the truth.

'He's full of bull,' Martin whispered. 'Don't listen to him. Unfortunately though, I don't think we've got a thing on him. Come on, let's get this over with.'

The paddock still contained the goose, ducks and dam. On the far side of the dam the distance between the fence and the water was less than a metre.

'Hey Martin,' Kirby suggested. 'What do you think? The emu has been in here for weeks.' Kirby pointed to hundreds of footprints and mountains of droppings on the bare earth between the fence and the dam.

The two officers discussed their plans with MT interjecting from his yard. His head sticking over the top of the fence like a puppet. The officers decided to ambush the emu between the fence and the dam. They expected to be able to slowly walk the bird into that area then carefully approach, one from each side. Whoever was behind the bird at the appropriate moment would grab it, then steer it back to the crate they had waiting in the corner of the paddock.

When the moment of truth arrived Kirby somehow managed to grab the emu by its wings. As he did he realised the funny little noises Martin had been making were a ruse designed to make the emu turn and look towards the sound. Naturally the bird's behind was closest to Kirby when it really mattered.

After the initial trauma, Kirby found the plan appeared to be working. He began to steer the unhappy creature towards the crate. As they walked though, Kirby became aware the path between the dam and the fence was slippery. He soon realised it was very slippery. Before long he knew it was too slippery! As the gravity of his situation dawned, Kirby had visions of him and the emu in an even more compromising position – with the two of them embracing on the ground. He then imagined the emu's kicking feet ripping out his intestines. He hung on as tightly as he could and soon discovered emus can't, or don't, kick either forward or backwards when standing in water up to the top of their backs.

The mud in the bottom of the dam was not too sticky and as the ducks, geese, Martin and MT looked on, Kirby continued to steer his captive as Murray had instructed. They walked to a corner of the dam, up the bank, across the paddock and into the crate.

'What did you find out from the neighbours?' Murray asked when the young officers reported they had caught the bird and transported it to the Healesville Sanctuary. 'Where did it come from? It was MT's wasn't it?'

'Well we think so. But we really don't know. I ended up in the dam with the mongrel thing when we were catching it. We couldn't do a door knock of the neighbourhood with me soaking wet and muddy so we didn't ask anybody. I had to go home and change my clothes. MT swore black and blue he didn't know anything about it though. He claimed he didn't rent the paddock.'

'You should've made your enquires before you caught it. You may have been out of order just assuming MT was responsible and therefore the bird was illegal. Assumptions can be dangerous in this job. What happens if the emu was on agistment from a licensed emu farm or something?'

'But,' Martin protested. 'It wouldn't have mattered what anybody said – MT was never going to admit it. It's obvious who was responsible. Anyway, emu farms have specified premises on their licences and it wouldn't be legal for someone to have an emu in town like that. If an emu farmer comes along now and claims it's his I'll book him up for failing to comply with the conditions on his licence. That emu was MT's and that's that. Unfortunately we are never going to pin it on him.'

'I think you better re-read the section in the manual about positive attitudes. In fact there's another bit too. It's about the obvious not being evidence. You should have found a neighbour who knew what was what, as far as MT and the emu were concerned. You could have taken a witness statement from the neighbour and got a case that way.'

I've heard all that before, thought Kirby.

After a few minutes more discussion Murray agreed there was now little point trying to take the matter any further. Kirby and Martin were left with no doubt the boss was unhappy they approached the investigation with preconceived ideas about the outcome. Kirby knew he had predicted that the emu would be hard to catch and as he walked back to his desk wondered if his little romp in the dam was a result of his negative attitude. He refused to accept that it was. He knew Murray was seldom wrong but this was not the first time Kirby had found that practical application of the law, his boss's instruction and the manual lacked a degree of harmony.

'There is a kangaroo on the Nepean Highway,' an excited caller explained when Kirby answered the duty office phone the following Friday.

'This'll be a good chance for you to practice your newly acquired wildlife catching skills,' Murray said with a wink when Kirby presented him with a copy of the telephone log. The boss dispatched Kirby and Martin to the rescue.

As the officers approached the reported address a large group of people on the footpath indicated they were on the right trail.

'It's in there,' someone advised as they pulled up. 'We shut the gate so it couldn't get back on the road. It nearly got hit by a car, hopping like crazy everywhere.'

The gate comprised part of the front boundary of a house yard along the busy highway. The fence was higher than normal, designed to keep out some of the traffic noise. Kirby soon learned it was also a good height for keeping the leaping marsupial in. After giving strict instructions that the gate remain closed, Kirby and Martin entered the yard and knocked on the door. There was no one at home. An inspection of the yard revealed no kangaroo, but on the north side of the house was one of those little doorways giving access to the sub-floor area. It was open and Kirby crawled in. There was no kangaroo under there either – it was a full grown Black-tailed Wallaby.

Using the back of his head, Kirby tested several of the floor joists for rigidity. Once satisfied the house was not going to fall on top of them, and realising he needed help, he called Martin in too. Kirby knew it was not going to be possible to get the wallaby out from under the house with someone standing at the only exit point. He also knew that in the cramped space under the house the wallaby had an enormous advantage. The muster the two officers then performed on their hands and knees in the restricted, cobweb infested, dusty hole did nothing to improve the appearance of their uniforms.

Once the wallaby was out, Kirby closed the door and the animal was locked in the yard with nowhere to hide. There was no garden, just two or three bushes and lawn in the front and back yards. The wallaby careered around the fence line and stopped in a narrow passageway between the garage and side fence. When Kirby and Martin approached it accelerated away again and madly did another lap of its prison yard.

'Hey,' Kirby called Martin. 'This should be pretty easy. The wallaby's got nowhere to hide. It's terrified. We don't want to stir the poor thing up too much but I reckon that area beside the garage gives us a real advantage.'

'Yeah,' jibed Martin. 'An advantage like between a dam and a fence – nowhere to go.'

'Shuddup. If we just sneak in slowly when it stops between the fence and the shed we must be able to grab it. Those palings are pretty high and on the other side is the solid wall of the garage. You go that way and I'll go this way. Get it by the tail if you can.'

The officers closed in and the wallaby had no chance. No chance that is, until it demonstrated how well it could jump. The height and the length of its leap took it easily over Kirby's head when he ducked out of the way.

'Wow! Blimey! Did you see that? Let's try it again, we'll get it next time.' Kirby crouched in readiness.

The second time the wallaby went through the narrow passageway it made its escape just as impressively. Again it simply bounded straight at Kirby's head and instinctively he ducked and turned his face away from the supersonic marsupial.

When Martin and Kirby swapped places the wallaby leapt straight for Martin's face too. His survival instincts were the same as Kirby's. He too ducked out of the way making no attempt to grab the animal.

'More brains required,' Kirby said thoughtfully. 'Why didn't we bring some of that mesh from the store?'

He looked around the sterile yard for inspiration. There was a galvanised rubbish bin, nothing else. Kirby emptied the contents of the bin onto the paving near the back door.

'OK. Chase it through again will you. Slowly now.'

As Kirby peeked around the corner and watched, the wallaby bounded away from Martin. Kirby held the rubbish bin poised.

Kirby's little throw of the bin was perfect and the wallaby went straight in – crash! A head shaped dent appeared in the bottom of the bin, but they had the wallaby. Kirby grabbed it by the tail and dragged it out. The animal fought wildly and seemed to have the strength of an animal three times its size. It was nimble and agile and it jumped, twisted and turned in frantic efforts to escape. Kirby held on desperately. Martin eventually managed to get a hessian bag over the frightened animal's head. From there it was not difficult for the two officers to get it completely into the bag. Once the darkness of the material surrounded the terrified creature it quietened down. Kirby replaced the garbage in the bin and the officers carried the wallaby out to the car.

Chapter 5

POMP AND CIRCUMSTANCE

During the next week, Japan's Crown Prince Naruhito and Princess Masako, visited Victoria on a State Tour. The Premier's Department arranged the itinerary that included a special display of native animals and a sheep shearing demonstration at the historic homestead, Emu Plains. Kirby and Murray attended a special protocol meeting where strict instructions about behaviour were explained and emphasised again and again. Nothing less than exemplary conduct would be acceptable and the royal visitors were to be offered every courtesy. The staff from the Premier's Department stressed the Government's wish that the international guests leave with a good image of Victoria, Australia and Australians.

Early on the morning of the big day Murray and Kirby travelled to the animal nursery at the zoo and there collected some specially chosen native wildlife. They had a koala, a joey Red Kangaroo and a young Agile Wallaby. In addition there were two or three Fairy Penguins, a variety of parrots and a Pink Cockatoo that talked. They took these to Emu Plains where a makeshift zoo was ready and waiting. It contained an enormous, freshly cut branch from a eucalyptus tree, dug into the ground for the koala.

The day progressed with an official welcoming ceremony and a guided tour of the historic homestead. The native birds and animals were an enormous success. The international entourage all wanted individual photos taken with the koala. The banquet luncheon was magnificent and uniformed waiters treated everyone as though they were the royal couple. Kirby had never seen such a spread. During lunch the lure of free alcohol saw everyone drink about three glasses of good Australian wine more than they needed. At the completion of the feast, the Master of Ceremonies announced the sheep shearing demonstration and invited the multitude to move to the shearing shed.

Three or four musicians played Click Go the Shears, Once a Jolly Swagman and Waltzing Matilda from the sheep pens at the back of the shed. Two expert shearers went through their paces and absolutely pinked the crossbred weaners. Blow for blow the shearers scorched the wool off three or four sheep each. Roustabouts picked up and demonstrated how to throw the fleece.

At the conclusion of the shearing demonstration the local Member of Parliament made a speech. It was about the importance of the wool industry to Australia, her early settlers and the current balance of trade figures. He made reference to the important market Japan had become for Australian wool.

'None of this would have been possible without the pioneers in our wool industry having a go in difficult circumstances,' he said. 'This historic property is now an icon to the Australian Spirit. I know the shearing demonstration we have just witnessed made it all look easy but I assure you, sheep shearing is very hard work – and hard work is part of that Australian Spirit. Now before we move on, would anybody like to have a go at sheep shearing?'

'Yes, I'll do one,' Kirby volunteered pushing his way into the pen with no regard for the protocol meeting.

Apart from a few nervous giggles, the whole shed fell silent. Kirby had shorn a few as a youth on his father's farm and was about to show the crowded shed he was no city slicker. He flipped the nearest sheep over and saw it was a wether. He dragged it out onto the board and pulled the handset into gear.

As he was about to take the first blow down the belly the handset stopped. The shed supervisor stood tall above him, glaring down and muttering.

'The Member of Parliament was only joking. What the hell do you think you're doing?'

'I'm going to shear the sheep,' Kirby answered, re-engaging the handset.

'Don't you cut its pizzle,' the supervisor warned.

'I won't.'

What do you think I am? I wouldn't cut the poor things dick off. Not with

Royalty and all these other people watching anyway. Kirby took his first blow down the right-hand side of the animal's belly.

When he finished Kirby had sheep manure on his uniform shirt and first-hand knowledge of the problems associated with wearing a neck tie whilst sheep shearing. He nearly cut the tie in half, several times, before one of the real shearers saw the dilemma and leant over and tucked the tie into a shirt pocket. Kirby's sheep went down the chute to thunderous applause, far louder than that received by the experts. The poor sheep though, looked like someone had tried to pluck it by hand but when that didn't work had taken to it with a chainsaw.

Kirby looked up and smiled across to Murray. Murray did not smile back. The senior officer's consumption of wine had been insufficient to obliterate the protocol lesson and he knew what sort of reaction Kirby's behaviour would get from the Premier's Department. The uniform would tell them precisely where to send the official complaint.

The applause died down and the Member of Parliament stepped up beside Kirby.

'Thank you, and well done,' he said shaking Kirby's hand enthusiastically. 'I don't know when I have seen such a brilliant, impromptu demonstration of the dinkum Aussie Spirit.' The member turned and looked directly at the royal couple. 'We Australians love an under-dog, especially when he comes through. It's an old Australian tradition to back any individual prepared to have a go. The applause you just heard for this man was a demonstration of that.'

On the way back to Melbourne Murray did not say one word.

Chapter 6

THE HIDDEN AGENDA

'Have you seen the roster?' Martin asked Kirby the next morning. 'You're down to go to Phillip Island on Monday for a couple of days, then you're going straight to Kerrisdale for court on Thursday. You're never home.'

Kirby did not want to go to Kerrisdale. He had been to court a few times and knew all too well that evidence was on oath. He knew this meant telling the truth and he dreaded giving sworn testimony against the Pappas brothers.

If only they would plead guilty, he wished. *Neil Lyons could then give a summary and I wouldn't even have to go to Kerrisdale.*

Kirby racked his brain for an excuse to get out of the trip. That afternoon he went to speak to Murray.

'Could I talk to you about the roster?'

'Sure, what's the problem? Murray asked, motioning Kirby to take a seat.

'Nicky is due any day now and I'm down to go to Phillip Island and Kerrisdale next week. I was wondering if I could stay home a bit more till the baby is born. I was wondering if I have to go to Kerrisdale. I don't mind going to Phillip Island. That's not as far and if anything happens I could be home in a bit over an hour.'

'The Pappas Brothers are pleading not guilty. The case is booked in for a contested hearing at court and I'm afraid there's no option; you'll have to go. The Phillip Island trip's just as important. The Minister's Office has been getting complaints from the local tourism committee about mutton-bird poaching. What with Phillip Island being an international tourist attraction, this trip's been given a top departmental priority. Sometime in the next few weeks the young mutton-birds will leave and in the meantime we have to get some scalps for the Minister. We just have to keep up a strong enforcement presence, whether we want to or not. I've already got officers in from all over the state and I simply can't spare you. Sorry. I've arranged for you to work with Neil Lyons and he'll pick you up here on Monday on the way down to the island. You can then go to Kerrisdale with him on Wednesday ready for court. After court you come back to Melbourne on the train. See Lola. She'll organise the ticket.'

'OK, it was just a thought.' Kirby realised argument or further discussion was pointless. He stood to leave.

'Make sure you give Nicky the gateway number for the trunking radio so she can ring you at any time if she has to. If she does go to hospital you can come straight home,' Murray called after Kirby.

The young officer kept his mouth shut even though he realised the offer to return home was very shallow. If he was in Kerrisdale when Nicky went to hospital it may take him a day, or more, to get home – depending on the train timetable. That would be the good scenario. If the call came after the court case had started he would not get it until hours later because the radio would have to be switched off whilst the court was in session.

On the following Monday, Neil and Kirby drove to Phillip Island together.

'You know much about mutton-birds?' Neil asked.

'They're really Short-tailed Shearwaters.'

'Yes, but do you know anything about them?'

'No, not really. They must be a rare species are they?'

'No, there's millions of 'em. There are several species of shearwaters but Tasmania has an open season for these ones on a couple of the Bass Strait Islands. You can legally buy them to eat at the fish market but personally I wouldn't give you tuppence for one. They taste like sardines gone off in the sun. They're bloody awful if you ask me, and to make it worse, they repeat on me dreadfully.'

'Then what's all the fuss about? What's all this bull about a departmental priority?'

'Well the timing of our enforcement effort is related to a relatively short poaching season. These mutton-birds are an international migratory bird. They nest on the islands off South Eastern Australia and come back to make their nesting burrows at exactly the same time each year. The breeding colony has a cycle that is as regular as clockwork. They lay their eggs at the same time, the young hatch at the same time and they migrate to sea at the same time. Near the end of the time on land the mutton-bird chicks are so fat they can't fly. These are the only birds the poachers want and that's why we're on this job now – and because the Minister wants a bit of good publicity to counter the complaints. The parent birds are out of the way, gone back to their life at sea and the chicks are in the burrows. They're easy to get, left to fend for themselves like that. They've been living off their fat reserves and will go to sea sometime in the next week or two – when the strong winds arrive before the March equinox. The equinoctial gales actually teach 'em to fly. At night they stand on the highest ground and face the wind. They hold out fluttering wings and before you know it, they're up in the air and away.'

'This departmental enforcement effort is a bit of a stunt then – to stop the Minister getting letters of complaint.'

'That's about it,' the senior officer agreed.

'Well I reckon it's over the top,' Kirby mused. 'It must be costing the tax-payer a fortune to bring officers from all over the state on a political whim. It's a pity the Minister isn't as concerned for the mutton-birds as he is about his bloody votes. Besides, Nicky is due any day now. I would've much preferred to be home till after the baby is born.'

Kirby said nothing about his real problem – the prospect of giving evidence at Kerrisdale.

The Monday night on Phillip Island was uneventful. The Tuesday night was cold, wet and windy. Kirby and Neil sat for hours in the marram grass, keeping watch over a remote rookery. In no time they were cold and wet. The howl of the wind and the ghostly calls of the mutton-birds keep the officers awake – despite their hypothermia, boredom and weariness. Neil tried to keep alert by reminiscing about past experiences but this only made Kirby more disgruntled.

'This job's a joke,' Kirby said. 'Sitting here catching pneumonia because the Minister wants a few votes. Surely we could be doing better things with our time, and the taxpayer's dollar. Neil, you've been round a while, seen some pretty important environmental jobs pulled off. Surely politics doesn't just buy votes at the expense of real conservation needs?'

'Oftentimes I'm afraid it does,' Neil confided.

As the night wore on the boredom increased. Before midnight both men held their current task in total disdain.

'This is bull-dust,' Kirby repeated several times as he and Neil half dozed as they waited for morning.

'Don't worry about it mate. Put it down to experience.'

But Kirby did worry – about the Kerrisdale court case. Even though he had little experience in these things he knew that witnesses were often ordered out of court during the evidence of other witnesses. If that happened Neil would be first in the witness-box. Kirby was worried what Neil would say if cross-examination pointed to the real origin of the ducks. More importantly, the young officer worried about what he would say. He knew that it was going to be virtually impossible to omit one or two small details under the guise of a summary. Murray Stephens had told him several times that the oath was fundamental to the court system and he knew the oath included the words, "the truth, the whole truth and nothing but the truth". Kirby was even more worried about the words, "I swear by Almighty God."

'How's my new baby?' Kirby asked when he rang Nicky from Kerrisdale the next night.

'Just fine,' Nicky assured him. 'I had a little chat with bubs earlier and I've been promised that nothing's going to happen till Daddy's home. You're still coming home tomorrow aren't you?'

'Not even the Minister could stop me. I can't believe how politics can stick its ugly head into everything.'

'What do you mean?'

'Well that Phillip Island trip was nothing but a political stunt. All those public dollars spent making us officers spend a couple of nights sitting in the cold and wet so the Minister could get a bit of political mileage. We didn't catch anybody – there was nobody there to catch. The money would have been better off spent on some habit restoration work or something. I didn't have much fun, and now I'm up at Kerrisdale and it's no fun here either.'

'It's not half obvious you're grumpy. Never mind, when you're boss you can change the way things are done.'

'When I'm boss I'll write a chapter for Murray Stephen's stupid manual.' Kirby continued the banter. 'I'll give it some real teeth – a chapter titled "How to Make Politics Work for Conservation". Hey, guess what I bought Zac when I was at Phillip Island?'

'You tell me.'

'I got him a pencil and ruler set. You know the sort. The pencil's got a little plastic koala stuck on top and there's transfers of seals, koalas and penguins on the ruler.'

'And what did you get me?'

'Oh, you'll have to wait and see.'

'Aw, com'on. You're supposed to be nice to me. I'm nine months pregnant don't forget.'

'It would be nice, but I suppose a chockie frog might be a better idea.'

It was good to talk to Nicky but even she could not keep Kirby's mind off the evidence he had to give the next day. That night Kirby managed less than two hours sleep and he was not in the mood for any tom-foolery next morning when Neil picked him up to go to court.

'I reckon I can talk the solicitor into getting the Pappas boys to plead guilty,' Neil announced. 'I know him pretty well and they really haven't got a leg to stand on.'

Kirby marvelled at Neil's cool attitude to the whole affair. The younger officer had not said a word to anyone since they detected the brothers with the ducks in the duck trap. He did not want to put Neil's weights up over the origin of the birds but he knew he had to speak up before the case started – and he was quickly running out of time.

When they arrived at court Neil announced his appearance at the clerk's counter then spent a few minutes talking to the solicitor representing the defendants. The senior officer was smiling when he walked back to Kirby.

'They're going to plead guilty,' he remarked nonchalantly. 'You won't have to give evidence. I'll just give a summary.'

'Thank goodness for that,' Kirby answered. 'By the way, would you have said how the ducks got into the trap?'

'What for?' Neil asked. 'That's irrelevant. They're charged because they took the ducks out of the trap and killed them. Nothing more, nothing less.'

When the case started Kirby sat at the back of the court and listened to Neil's summary. It seemed so remote and impersonal – he was as irrelevant as the origin of the ducks.

'Upon receipt of a complaint I discovered an illegal duck trap concealed on the Pappas family farm. The position of the trap, amongst the houses and the day to day farm activity, made it impossible to keep under surveillance without superhuman effort. A second officer was needed to assist with the surveillance.'

Neil seemed to take delight in explaining the difficulties associated with long days of observation in trying conditions. Perhaps he reasoned this would add substance to the seriousness of the offence – or perhaps he was on stage, putting on an act. In reality the important evidence involved what the offenders did, not how the officers detected them – unless the evidence was unfairly, improperly or illegally obtained. In a summary for the court the officer's hardships were certainly not relevant but Neil was on a roll.

'On the day in question the two defendants arrived as usual. There were now two ducks in the trap and when they saw the trapped birds the defendants promptly killed them.'

The only hiccup was a question from the court.

'What happened to the ducks, Mr Inspector?'

'Naturally we seized them Your Honour. The Act gives the power for this in section …'

'Yes, yes I know that,' interrupted the Magistrate. 'I want to know what happened to them after that.'

'They were donated to charity Your Honour.' Neil paused. 'And charity begins at home.'

Chapter 7

WE ALL NEED A ROLE MODEL

Kylie Anne Wellington was born at seven minutes past midnight the following Sunday. Kirby took paternity leave until Nicky had been home from hospital for three days.

A couple of Saturdays later Kirby and Murray Stephens paid MT another visit. They went to his home early expecting to catch him before he went to the trash and treasure market. As the officers stepped off the footpath and through the front gate, Mrs Morrison came out the front door.

'Maxwell is not in residence at the moment. I would be most obliged if you would come back when he is,' she announced. Her speech and grammar belied her appearance and surroundings.

'Now that we're here we must inspect the birds,' Murray said quietly. 'Mr Morrison doesn't have to be at home. You'd be more than welcome to accompany us.'

Murray changed course from the front door and moved towards the driveway and rear yard. Mrs Morrison protested loudly. Her first verbal volley fell on deaf ears and Murray continued to advance. Kirby followed like an obedient puppy.

When Mrs Morrison realised the invasion was almost complete she jumped down from the veranda and engaged the officers at close range – toe to toe with Murray. Her use of the Queen's English suddenly disappeared and she used some choice expletives to vent her feelings and to describe what she thought of the officers. Murray was confident of his legal power of entry and he encouraged Kirby to keep close. Murray walked around Mrs Morrison's left-hand-side and Kirby around her right.

In one of the cages in the yard were fifteen Diamond Firetail Finches and eight Red-browed Finches, housed with some introduced species. Kirby was familiar with the red brows but had only seen pictures of the firetails. Their appearance was striking. Red beaks and fire tails stood out. Snow-white abdomens and throats, separated by a black band across the breast and along the flanks held Kirby's gaze for some time. Diamond spots, regularly spaced, contrasted vividly with the black flanks.

They are the most exquisite birds I have ever seen, Kirby thought.

The aviary had a padlock on the door and Mrs Morrison refused to give the officers any information about the birds.

'They're nothing to do with me. You'll have to talk to Maxwell. You'll have to come back when he's home.'

'Oh, we'll talk to Mr Morrison all right,' Murray said. 'We'll talk to him today, I promise.'

Murray fully intended to keep that promise, as soon as he found MT at the trash and treasure market but, in the meantime, he was taking the protected birds with him.

'Could I have the key for this cage, please?'

'Like hell!' Mrs Morrison exploded. 'I know wot yer wan' it for. Maxwell's right. Yer can't trust youse blokes. Yer just gunner seize 'em and yer didn't 'ave the decency to say so. I ain't getting' yer no key and yer aint takin' them birds.'

'Well, if you don't get the key we'll have to break in. This will no doubt result in some damage to the cage and we might not be able to prevent other, legal, birds escaping when we've finished.' Murray's advice was calm and succinct.

After a defiant protest that he could not do that, and a threat or two that legal action would follow if he did, Mrs Morrison really went off.

'Get me the gun, get me the gun,' she shrieked as she headed for the back door. 'Get me the gun, I'll shoot the bastards. Get me the gun, get me the gun!'

Her ploy worked like fast acting laxative. Murray and Kirby could hear her ranting and raging about inside the house, continuing to threaten them with untold violence when she got her hands on the fouling piece. Neither officer waited around to find out the calibre, make or model.

The local police were very helpful and Murray and Kirby soon returned under the cover of two patrol cars, a divisional van and six armed officers. Kirby felt quite brave once the police had been into the house and reported there was no firearm. An officer handed Murray the key to the aviary and after that the seizure of the finches precisely followed the manual. Murray wrote up Florence May Morrison for obstruction and threatening officers in the execution of their duties.

When the officers had finished with Mrs Morrison they left the seized birds at the zoo and went in search of MT. He was selling ornaments for canaries and budgies at the trash and treasure market. He had some small cages, a few motley looking canaries, some budgies and three Californian Quail. Murray and Kirby could find nothing illegal. MT's dog was tied to the back of his ute by a chain and although it snarled it did not prevent Kirby searching the cabin.

'Mr Morrison we have just been to your house,' Murray explained. 'There we found fifteen Diamond Firetail Finches and eight Red-browed Finches. Your good wife tells us they're yours.'

'Bull-dust. Absolute bull,' insisted MT. 'They aren't mine and she wouldn't 'ave said they were. She knows full well that they belong to that German bloke. You're just tryin' to set me up again.'

Kirby tried to remember Mrs Morrison's actual words.

She did say the birds were nothing to do with her, Kirby remembered clearly. As he racked his brains he recalled that both Murray and Neil Lyons had warned about the dangers of making assumptions. He then recollected, again, that Neil and Murray had also said 'the obvious is not evidence'.

'I think MT might be right,' Kirby whispered to Murray. 'She only said we would have to talk to MT. She didn't say the birds were his in as many words.'

'Whose side are you on?'

'Yours,' Kirby continued in a voice MT could not hear. 'You told me I had to always tell the truth.'

Murray knew his young apprentice was correct.

'If the birds aren't yours, whose are they?' Murray now directed the question to MT.

'A German bloke called Hofrich or somethin'. I was only lookin' after 'em for 'im. I met 'im 'ere at the market th'other day. You bastards would do anythin' to stitch me up again wouldn' ya?'

'How long have you been looking after the finches?' Murray continued, ignoring MT's question.

'Since Thursd'y,' MT admitted. 'You can't do a man for keepin' someone else's birds alive. I've been feedin' and waterin' 'em. It'd be different if I killed 'em or neglected 'em or somethin' like that. I could understand you wantin' to charge me if I did that or I were cruel to 'em. I'm lookin' after 'em good. Anyway, I've got a padlock on the cage and yer won't be able to get 'em. You can't do nuthin' 'til yer talk to the owner.'

MT had just given Murray the evidence he needed.

'You're in control of the birds when you feed and water them in a locked cage,' Murray advised. 'Ownership is irrelevant and I will be submitting a report about this matter. Is there anything more you wish to say about it?'

'Yeah. You're a dead shit,' MT muttered.

'I think it is just as well I did not hear that,' Murray said. 'If I had, you'd be facing an additional charge of using insulting words to an officer.'

Kirby and Murray left without telling MT about his wife's little adventure, or what had already happened to the finches.

'Who is this Hofrich bloke?' Kirby asked Murray as they walked back to the car.

'It will be Gottfried Wilhelm Hoffrichter. He's got a pet shop and I think we might pop round to see him. I bet you a dollar he doesn't know anything about MT's finches though.' Murray was smiling.

The Hoffrichter pet shop was towards one end of a long terrace in the heart of an inner suburban shopping centre. Like every Saturday, parking spots were hard to find just on lunchtime.

'That's the place,' Murray said as he drove past looking for a park. 'There's a residence upstairs and that always gives us a bit of a headache. You know we've got the legal power to search the shop but we can't go up the stairs without an invitation or a warrant.'

'Yeah, I do. I've read the bit on powers of entry and inspection in the manual. I read the Wildlife Act too and I bet you don't get too many invitations upstairs. Why don't we just get a search warrant? The Act allows us to get a warrant doesn't it?'

Kirby felt his reference to the manual, the legislation and his suggestion about the warrant would please his boss – demonstrate he understood what he had been reading and show an aptitude for the practical side of the job.

'You can't get a warrant unless you've got good reason to believe there's something illegal hidden there,' Murray replied. 'Most times we don't have any information and we just do routine inspections. Despite the odds being against us though, you should always approach this type of job with a positive attitude. I've written Gottfried Wilhelm Hoffrichter up so many times I even learnt how to spell his name.'

Murray found a park and when the two officers entered the shop he introduced Kirby.

'Good morning Mr Hoffrichter. I'd like you to meet Officer Kirby Wellington.'

'Goot mornink,' the grey haired, elderly man behind the counter replied.

He glanced for a moment at the two uniforms trespassing in his space, but he did not stop work. These men were likely to be a nuisance – they were certainly not customers.

Like many similar businesses this one sold raw meat as dog and cat food. Mr Hoffrichter had been busy cutting up second grade meat with an evil looking knife. A pile of diced flesh and smelly offal grabbed Kirby's attention. It sat on a battered, rusty old tray near the cash register. The shopkeeper picked up the tray and carried it to a walk-in freezer, situated near the foot of the stairs. He placed the tray on a bench and crashed both heels of his hands upward at the bar bolting the door closed. He did this a second time before the bolt gave and the door opened.

'Mr Hoffrichter, I wonder if you could spare me a few moments,' Murray said after the shopkeeper deposited the tray in the freezer and re-entered the shop. The door closed behind him with a loud bang.

'We've just been to Maxwell Morrison's place and we found some Diamond Firetail Finches and some Red-browed Finches there. Mr Morrison tells us the finches belong to you.'

'Dis ez a lie,' Hoffrichter said slowly and deliberately through clenched teeth.

'Mr Morrison was pretty emphatic they belonged to you,' Murray continued.

'Lies, lies!' The shopkeeper screamed as he grabbed the knife from the counter and lunged at Murray. Murray half tripped as he stepped back. Hoffrichter continued to scream. He advanced further. In an instant Murray had his arm forced up his back and Hoffrichter had the knife at his throat.

'Zer freezer weel help you decide whose birds,' he hissed in Murray's left ear.

In the few seconds after Murray broached the subject of MT's finches, Kirby had stood silently by, dumbfounded. He suddenly realised the action was for real and he was about to witness his boss being locked in a freezer, perhaps with the handle of a knife sticking out from between his shoulder blades. Kirby also knew it would be stupid to try to grab the weapon. Hoffrichter was irrational and such a move would escalate the danger.

Kirby began to talk. He surprised himself when his voice was calm.

'Steady down Sir. We only want to talk to you. It was Max Morrison who said the birds were yours. Officer Stephens didn't believe him – he told me that. He even wanted to bet me the birds weren't yours.'

Kirby expected his little lie about the exact nature of the bet wouldn't matter in the circumstances. He kept talking.

'I know you will understand why he had to ask you about them though. We didn't want Max Morrison getting off the hook by being untruthful. Look, if the birds are nothing to do with you, just say so.'

'In zee freezer mit you. No trouble for Wilhelm. Not my birds. Not my problems. Lies, lies!'

The shopkeeper appeared not to hear Kirby and Murray now had his head against the freezer door. Hoffrichter's hands were both fully occupied and the door was bolted shut. Murray only had one hand free and he was doubled up awkwardly, bent forward from his waist down. Kirby saw this as an opportunity.

'Mr Hoffrichter,' he continued gently. 'The freezer door is very hard to open. You can't do it and Officer Stephens can't do it. Let's talk about this a bit more. You've told us the finches are not yours and we believe you. What about you give me the knife and let Officer Stephens go.'

Kirby held out his hand. Hoffrichter looked at Kirby then glanced back at Murray and the bolted freezer door. He looked back at Kirby. Their eyes met and Kirby tried to hold the gaze of steel grey eyes. As Kirby watched he saw the old man's eyes change. They lost their gleam and became sunken and tired. The shopkeeper's gaze left Kirby's face and moved to his outstretched hand. Murray felt the pressure come off his arm. Kirby slowly took the knife.

'It's OK now,' Kirby said quietly.

Murray thought Kirby was speaking to him.

Hoffrichter thought Kirby was speaking to him.

'Vot 'ave I doon?' The shopkeeper spoke slowly, asking himself the question.

'Take it easy. It's OK,' Kirby answered. 'It might be best if you sit down for a while.'

Kirby reached behind the counter and dragged out a stool. Hoffrichter slumped down on it.

'Do you think you could handle the interview?' Murray whispered to Kirby. 'It needs to be done now.'

'I'll give it a go.'

Murray was shaking visibly and sat silently whilst Kirby cautioned the shopkeeper, asked a series of questions and carefully wrote down the answers. There was no more trouble but two things worried Kirby. The first one came when he tried to spell Gottfried Wilhelm Hoffrichter. He solved that by putting "G.W.H." in his notebook and leaving a blank line. He knew the manual emphatically prohibited leaving blank lines when taking notes but Kirby figured it was his best option in the circumstances. Murray obviously knew how to spell the name and Kirby worried that asking the shopkeeper to spell it out for him may cause another melee.

Kirby's second problem — why a seventy-five year old man flew off the handle so far and so fast — defied logic.

'Thanks for that back there,' Murray said as he and Kirby walked from the shop to their car. 'You're pretty cool when it matters. I'm not sure what the Conflict Avoidance and Defensive Tactics section in the manual says we should've done. Hell there was no time to do anything. What would you have done if he hadn't handed over the knife?'

'Called the cops, I suppose.'

'I'm glad you didn't leave. I wasn't too sure what to do. I think I would have used it, if I'd had my pistol.'

'I'm glad you didn't. Have it, I mean. I think it's best we don't think about what might have been.'

'You did a good job with the interview too. You can be proud of how much you've developed and learned since you started with us. I'd be sad to see you go, but the other day a little bird told me the second in command job at Mafeking Bay might be coming up. It's all hush-hush at the moment but if Darren Wossfold does quit it'll leave his position vacant. You wouldn't normally be in the running because you haven't passed the grade two exams but, well, who knows? If you want to have a go for it I'd be prepared to have a word where it matters.'

'Would you really? Thanks. I haven't given a shift much thought at the moment.'

'Well keep it in mind,' Murray continued. 'Why don't you talk to Nicky about it. It would be a smart career move. Greg Bayliss, the other officer at Mafeking Bay, isn't the worst officer in the world. He'd be your boss. You could do worse than go and work with him.'

That night Nicky became excited at the prospect of living by the sea.

'Don't get too carried away,' Kirby told her. 'Darren Wossfold hasn't even officially said he's leaving. Besides, I haven't got enough experience yet. But Murray Stephens said he would put in a good word for me if I wanted to try for the job.'

'Would it be a promotion?'

'The job is a band one position so it wouldn't be a promotion as such. It sounds good though. Second in Command at Mafeking Bay.'

'How many officers are there?'

'Just two.'

For the next couple of weeks Kirby was busy in the office. He had his usual share of days manning the phone and radio and between calls was busy with three statements of evidence he had to write. Rather than learn how to spell Gottfried Wilhelm Hoffrichter, Kirby put the name into a template on the computer and simply inserted it wherever needed.

The weeks passed and during May Kirby attended his first fisheries and wildlife officer's conference. These annual events gave the bosses an opportunity to preach the gospel of the day, mostly in relation to new legislation and enforcement policy. Keynote speakers kept the officers up to date on other matters related to conservation, natural resource management and the environment. Loose-leaf amendments to the manual were handed out and discussed.

The conference emphasised, in a dozen different ways, that the work of a fisheries and wildlife officer involved much more than offence management and animal welfare. Extension activities were part of the package and good officers needed competent public speaking skills. Every conference agenda included an oration given by one of the officers and this year Trevor Squires from Glenlofty was the speaker.

It was common knowledge that after these conference talks the senior officers would invite the speaker's peers to ask questions. The number and depth of the questions measured the level of audience attention and, in turn, audience participation established the standard of the talk. This aspect of conference life was designed not only to develop the eloquence of the presenter but also to educate the other attendees.

During his talk Trevor used a computer program to project a series of colour slides on a large screen at the front of the auditorium. His presentation covered many aspects of his work and the country he travelled. There were several post-card shots of Lake Konica; one on a misty winter morning and another with the tree-lined bank reflected perfectly in the water during a still, summer evening. The lake-wall in the background shone brilliant in golden sunlight. There were several spectacular shots of the spillway in full flood. There was a series on the work at the local fish hatchery, including the life cycle of the trout, graphically illustrated and explained in detail by Trevor.

The officer showed magnified pictures of trout eggs and the methods used in stripping and fertilisation. He showed the tiny fry with grotesque egg sacs as they hatched and developed through various stages of growth to maturity. There were photos of feeding frenzies of trout in the hatchery and individual fish showing changes in colour evident during spawning. A couple of comparative pictures demonstrated the differences between the hook jawed males and the finer lines of the hen fish. One or two shots of proud anglers holding trophy size trout caught in Watsons Creek interspersed pie charts and graphs. Trevor explained the importance of angling to the economy, especially through the sale of tackle, boats, motors, fuel and tourist accommodation.

The presentation moved to the hills around Glenlofty. There were contrasting scenes of magnificent snow covered peaks during winter and beautiful sun drenched wattle and wildflowers in spring. The speaker described in detail various vegetation types associated with wildlife distribution in the region, pointing out that some areas around his home were similar to those found in the Dandenong Ranges.

'The margins of Watsons Creek,' he said, 'are very similar to those along Sheep Station Creek at Yellingbo in the Dandenong Ranges. For the benefit of the younger officers here, the vegetation along Sheep Station Creek is the stronghold of the Helmeted Honeyeater. I'm sure you've all heard of this very rare bird, and the Yellingbo State Nature Reserve that was established especially for its survival. You'll all know, I'm sure, that Victoria's floral emblem is common heath, Epacris impressa. Our animal emblem is Leadbeater's Possum and the bird emblem is the Helmeted Honeyeater.'

Trevor was now near the end of his allotted time and the prolonged period of dimmed lights had caused some in the room to lose concentration. Kirby was sure Neil Lyons and a couple of the other older officers had been snoring. The mention of the famous Helmeted Honeyeater though, had Kirby and most in the room, wide awake.

'The habitat along the margins of Watsons Creek must be the same as at Yellingbo – the Helmeted Honeyeater has been seen.' Trevor paused. 'In fact, I have been lucky enough to get a photo.'

Trevor pushed the button to reveal his last slide.

Geoff, Trevor's young son, had on a plastic bike helmet and a wide grin as he sat with a large spoon poised above an open tin marked 'HONEY'. Trevor sat down. The applause was deafening.

After the conference Kirby had difficulty settling back into the constant struggle with paperwork and phone calls. Relief from the boredom of the duty office came with a week away catching koalas as part of the departmental relocation program. The Coromby Island koala colony was cut off from the mainland and on the island the number of animals had increased to the point they were eating themselves, and their food trees, towards extinction. Kirby helped catch animals from the island and transport them to the mainland for release in other areas of suitable habit. All the while the prospect of a shift to Mafeking Bay distracted him but the worry associated with three pending court cases prevented him day-dreaming too much.

The Morrison court cases were heard before the Hoffrichter case. Outside the court MT looked as reprehensible as ever but Mrs Morrison had undergone a remarkable transfiguration. At first Kirby did not recognise her.

'Have a gander at Mrs Morrison,' Kirby whispered to Murray when he realised MT was with his wife. 'Some gifted physician must have performed a personality transplant.'

'I doubt it,' said Murray. 'Probably just reversed the charisma by-pass operation she obviously had before our last visit.'

Both officers remembered how her presentation matched her temperament on the day she threatened to shoot them. At court she wore a pretty little green Robin Hood number, complete with a feather in a cute green cap. In court she was not too severe on the eyes, her voice was soft and sweet and she once again used her perfect grammar and English. The court found all the charges proven and proceeded to convict and fine MT and Mrs Morrison. By the time the officers had gathered the file and other papers, and walked out of the court, the Morrisons were already driving away in a huff.

When the Hoffrichter case came on at the beginning of July the defendant appeared, unrepresented. He pleaded guilty. Kirby sat at the back of the court whilst Murray gave a summary of the events that had given rise to the charges. The incident involved a serious assault and Kirby expected Hoffrichter to receive appropriate punishment.

The bird dealer had an old prior conviction for smuggling native birds out of Australia and this and his other previous fines for possession of illegal birds should ensure he got what he deserved.

The court announced it found the charges proven and asked Mr Hoffrichter to stand.

'Now what do you want to tell the court about all this?' the Magistrate asked.

'Neffer did I vant to leave vrom d' schop like dis. I am 78 years olt and av retired now and d' schop vas solt. Ven Mr Stephens vas komming hier to d' schop an' say d' finches mine der vas a terrible accident – nearly. Py golly what happened vas not d' schmartest thing I dun. Vy it happened I tink dey vant me in trouble vor birds I neffer had. Den I vas not goot. Now I am sorry.'

The court, in summing up, said it was fortunate to know a little about the defendant. It went on to explain some specific aspects of that knowledge.

'Last month Mr Hoffrichter was a witness for the police in this same court,' the Magistrate clarified. 'During that matter the court learned of Mr Hoffrichter's bravery, and how he had served in tanks for the German Army during World War Two.

'No doubt this experience gave Mr Hoffrichter certain personal qualities. One of these is the physical and mental courage he showed a few months ago when he caught an armed hooligan who had thrown a brick through the window of a neighbouring shop. After exercising his citizens' arrest, Mr Hoffrichter handed the vandal over to the police at about three o'clock in the morning.

'This society needs more people of Mr Hoffrichter's calibre. He is really a hero as vandalism is a big problem for our community. Without model citizens there is insufficient deterrent against the misfits in our society; the police cannot be everywhere, all of the time.

'In all the circumstances the court considers punishment to be inappropriate. This incident only arose because of a little misunderstanding over a few silly birds. Birds, incidentally, that were not even on the defendant's premises.'

After this glowing eulogy the court placed the defendant on a good behaviour bond for two months. Murray and Kirby both felt they had been personally reprimanded, as if they had been the ones breaking the law.

PART 2

SECOND IN COMMAND AT MAFEKING BAY

Chapter 8

ELEPHANT SEALS

Three weeks after the Hoffrichter Court Case Darren Wossfold left Mafeking Bay to work on a prawn trawler in the Gulf of Carpentaria. His vacant position was advertised two weeks later and Kirby and four other junior officers applied. In early October a very happy Officer Wellington took Nicky, Zac and Kylie to live in Mafeking Bay.

Greg Bayliss was delighted. He was quite open about coming from the old school and he spoke as if this gave him an absolute right not to learn to use a computer. He hated them and called the office network terminal FRED – that Friggen Ridiculous Electronic Device. Kirby soon learned Greg was generally not the best at office work. In the months since Darren Wossfold left Greg had been there by himself and in that time a mountain of log sheets, journals, reports, requisitions, accounts and summaries had piled up. Greg had deliberately left them for his new junior on the basis that it would be a good way for him to begin a relationship with FRED. Greg also reasoned that the new chum needed this experience so that he could learn what the real job was all about – working at a country station. Kirby spent his first week at Mafeking Bay keying data into the computer – and of course, answering the phone.

On the Thursday of Kirby's second week out of head office a bull Elephant Seal came ashore on Sheoak's Beach right in Mafeking Bay. The animal was an absolute monster and it became a celebrated tourist attraction. Unfortunately an occasional person became too friendly and this added to the seal's distress. Elephant Seals only occasionally visit Victorian shores and when they do they sometimes moult. Over a period of about forty days their skin actually peels off and they look incredibly dilapidated – like an old sofa coming apart at the seams. It is a trying time for the animals as they do not feed and the itch of their peeling skin causes considerable torment.

Whenever anyone ventured too close to the Elephant Seal at Sheoaks Beach it would rear up its head and forequarters. In that position, with its mouth wide open, the seal exposed an impressive set of yellow teeth, a large red tongue and a gullet big enough to swallow a football. Some idiot threw a lit cigar butt into the gaping mouth and the seal suffered a nasty burn to its tongue. Greg arranged for a vet to attend. All the vet could do was run in and jab the unfortunate creature in the tail with an antibiotic injection then run back out of harm's way when the seal shuffled around to face its antagonist.

Greg and Kirby erected a barrier and cordoned off the area. They had a sign specifically made giving information about the seal and details of its normal home – the Antarctic waters around Macquarie Island. The sign requested the public keep behind the barrier and away from the moulting visitor. In addition Greg gave a talk on the local FM radio station. At the end of this he announced a twenty-four hour, seven days a week guard for the seal. Mafeking Bay's entire departmental staff would, from then on, ensure that no further harm came to the visitor.

The senior officer drew up a roster and on paper things looked OK. Greg had the shift from eight AM to four PM and Kirby had from four PM to eight AM. It didn't take too many nights for Kirby to realise the allocated times demonstrated a certain inequality. The young officer resolved to talk to his new boss about it.

During its stay the seal became restless and it left the security of the cordoned off area and moved a few hundred metres to the north and a different beach. This happened during the day shift and Kirby missed the fun of relocating the barriers. A couple of nights later, at about midnight, the seal went walk-about. It left the sand and lolloped up the grassy slope toward The Esplanade. Kirby watched helplessly. He had visions of a fatal car accident and newspaper headlines, 'Killer Seal—Wildlife Officer Witness.'

The seal turned near the top of the hill and galloped back down to the beach. Well almost to the beach, it reached a bitumen access track running between the sand and lawns around the foreshore. Kirby had the departmental car parked near the vehicle barrier at the beginning of the track. After its sojourn up the hill the seal came under the barricade directly towards Kirby's location. As it neared the front of the car Kirby switched on the headlights and sounded the horn. That startled the seal, but instead of turning in fright, it stood up to fight. The seal reared up its forequarters and the height of this and the gape of its mouth, breathing all over the windshield caused Kirby considerable consternation. The prospect of explaining, on an accident report form, just how a seal flattened a near new Holden flashed before his eyes.

How am I going to show all this in the little box diagram? How does one depict the point of impact between a seal and a car, with the car stationary and the seal moving at about fifteen kilometres per hour downwards?

There was no impact. In reality the car appeared to the seal to be a competing bull in a display of strength when it stood its ground and bellowed. When the seal's rival failed to move, the car actually bluffed the real animal into submission. There was a lesson here, but at that time Kirby did not recognise it. Eventually the seal backed away and, as Kirby sat there shaking, he resolved to talk to Greg about it.

A few nights later Kirby was almost in the land of nod in the early hours of the morning when a couple of big game hunters arrived with a ·303 rifle. Their inebriated and raucous voices had Kirby fully awake the moment they got out of their car. They had no idea Kirby was nearby and their conversation was loud and revealing. They intended to bag a trophy from Macquarie Island.

These fellows were a real credit to the human race. Their intoxication prevented them recognising Kirby sitting less than 100 metres away in the departmental car. However, they did see the significance of a blue flashing light and siren and immediately aborted their plans. Kirby laughed as he watched as they tried to hide the firearm and sober up when the police divisional van arrived.

After the cigar in the mouth incident, Greg had taken the precaution of discussing his seal protection plan with the local police. They lent the department one of their portable radios and Kirby had immediately used this when he realised the visitors had an unhealthy interest in the seal. The van had arrived almost instantly and the boys in blue held all the aces.

The police arrested the big game hunters and carted them off to the station for questioning. Kirby later heard the charge sheet included a hamburger with the lot – possession of a loaded firearm in a public place; unregistered firearm; no licence to possess a firearm; drink driving; drunk in charge of a firearm; breach of the peace and drunk and disorderly.

A week or so later when Kirby reported for duty, Greg made an announcement.

'This is getting a bit too much. Head office are unrealistic expecting just two of us to guard the seal twenty-four hours each day with no back-up or relief.'

'I agree. I'm starting to feel the pinch and sure could use a good night's sleep.' Kirby could find no fault in his senior officer's logic.

'I'll be back tonight at midnight.'

Greg arrived at about eleven thirty.

'Come on. Let's get it over with.'

The boss encouraged Kirby to walk with him to the seal. He did a full circle of the sleeping animal examining it closely.

'Anybody about?' he inquired.

There wasn't. Greg drew his issue pistol. Kirby started to protest.

'Greg, even though Elephant Seals aren't Victorian animals you can't ... '

Greg wasn't listening. He emptied the magazine, firing into the sand beside the seal. It woke with a fright and headed straight for the water. It disappeared with a splash into the blackness.

'Why don't you go home and get some sleep,' said Greg. 'You've been looking a bit tired lately.'

Kirby didn't argue and the seal did not return to shore in Mafeking Bay.

When a second Elephant Seal came ashore at exactly the same place a year later Greg Bayliss was on sick leave. Kirby rang head office and asked for assistance. Martin Hamilton arrived the next day to help. The second seal was also a large bull and it too created an enormous amount of public interest. The responsibility to guard the creature now fell to Kirby and he was confident he could manage things so that the task was not as onerous as it had been the year before. He had two additional staff to call on, Martin Hamilton and Angie Coyle the department's administration officer from Mafeking Bay. After a couple of hours work with a calculator Kirby managed to divide each 24 hour day into three equal shifts of eight hours. His brilliant maths became the basis of a new roster.

Kirby and Martin began erecting the old sign and barricades around the seal. They were about finished when one of the local animal welfare groups approached and volunteered to staff the entire 24 hour guard. That was fantastic, but it prevented Kirby pulling rank in relation to the best shift – there was no way he would have had the midnight stint again. Despite all the help with the roster it was still impossible to prevent the second seal causing considerable interference to everyday office functions. Kirby knew exactly what to do. He'd seen Greg Bayliss in action twelve months earlier.

After three or four days of disruption to normal office functions Kirby advised the police he intended to discharge a firearm at Sheoaks Beach to move the Elephant Seal to a less populated area. It would be in the best long term interests of the animal if it shifted away from the constant disturbance caused by the crowds.

That night, in company with two police officers and a member of the local animal welfare group, Kirby approached the seal with his ·38 Smith and Wesson fully loaded. The noise woke every person for a kilometre and it also woke the seal as Kirby fired into the sand beside it. Instead of disappearing into the water in fright, it charged at Kirby and chased him up the beach. For the second time Kirby found himself shaking because of a close encounter with an Elephant Seal. This time was a good deal worse than the first because Kirby came perilously close to actual physical harm – he nearly shot himself in the foot six times!

Kirby had now learned the lesson he should have when the first seal moulted at Sheoaks Beach. When an Elephant Seal comes ashore to moult, it comes ashore to moult and that takes a certain amount of time. Kirby now realised he needed to be the submissive one. It was useless trying to make an adult bull Elephant Seal on a beach do anything if it did not want to do it. Kirby now knew that when the moult was finished a clap of the hands would probably send the largest seal racing for the water. It was all a matter of timing.

Chapter 9

PRIVATE PETS

Kirby's work at Mafeking Bay proved stimulating but it was not always planned or expected, thanks mostly to his new boss. Kirby and Nicky found their private life rather hectic with two young children, new friends and dozens of picturesque and exciting places to visit along the coast and around the bay. Their favourite restaurant overlooked the harbour but Kirby's unpredictable work hours and the ages of Zac and Kylie prevented them spending too many evenings there. The Mafeking Bay lifestyle meant there was no time left for Kirby's part time studies. He was now twenty-six and although he had completed all the core subjects of the course, his degree was an eternity away and in a different direction to where his life now appeared headed.

Dropping out of study meant Kirby's aim of becoming officer in charge at a station was also on the back burner. This abandonment of his career goal was beginning to worry Kirby when a lucky academic break came out of the blue. The Government Gazette contained an advertisement for a legal systems course. The units were compatible with Kirby's Natural Resource Management Degree and recognised by the Board of University Studies. Students were required to live-in and the time table was intensive. Greg Bayliss supported Kirby's application for paid study leave and when his letter of acceptance arrived Kirby remembered Neil Lyons thoughts about 'bloody academics' taking over. Ever since his trip to Kerrisdale in the first few weeks of his career Kirby knew he wanted to be an officer with both practical experience and qualifications. He now began to imagine that perhaps one-day he may replace Murray Stephens as the department's most senior fisheries and wildlife officer.

The course was Melbourne based and ran from the beginning of November to just before Christmas. It involved lectures, case studies and scenarios presented as practical exercises. Student assessment was on written exams and other criterion judged during class time. Student appraisal was the joint responsibility of the course convenor, senior departmental officers, lecturers and an external examination panel. Species identification, officer mannerisms, operational planning, ability to recall detail, reaction under pressure, detection and interviewing techniques, gathering evidence, conflict avoidance, defensive tactics, report writing, court work and legal studies were all covered.

Kirby's major course assignment was the planning and implementation of a raid on a couple of the largest bird dealers in Melbourne. A total of four fisheries and wildlife officers were on the course and this assignment was specific to their assessment. Kirby divided the officers into teams and allocated premises from a prepared list supplied by Murray Stephens. Kirby handed in his operational plan and, on the morning of the raid, held a briefing for the teams. He emphasised the importance of synchronised inspections to negate the effect of the bird dealer grape-vine. He gave advice on how officers should watch for body language and the need for them to be vigilant. Kirby was sure his plan and briefing would impress the senior officers and lecturers. For good measure he concluded with; 'Remember the obvious is not evidence. Good luck.'

Murray and the course lecturers added the obligatory departmental and course overview and then, without warning, made a major change to Kirby's plan and briefing. Kirby was now to team up with Conrad Holmes, a brand new recruit, and the XLCR Bird Supply became their target.

XLCR had not been on the original list of premises and had been in business only a few weeks. Murray, who was to accompany Kirby as an assessor, knew MT Morrison had some involvement with the new business but Kirby had never heard of it. He did not give MT a single thought. Kirby's ability to handle the unknown, and especially his approach to MT, were to be key areas in Murray's assessment.

The owner of XLCR Bird Supply, Howard Koren, employed MT to look after the day to day running of the business. In his inimitable style MT told anyone who would listen that he owned XLCR. The real owner was frequently away and MT's charade remained undiscovered until Kirby's visit.

At precisely eleven o'clock Kirby led Conrad and Murray down the driveway at the given address. The small, old wooden cottage had a new sign advertising the 'XLCR Bird Supply'. Another sign indicated that the cottage was now the 'Office'. Paintings of birds covered the galvanised iron on the side fence. The only species Kirby recognised in the paintings was a very second-rate imitation of a Sulphur Crested Cockatoo.

The place had once been a plant nursery and the relatively large rear yard was full of cages and enclosures. These were very haphazard in design – built from frames that were once fern and shade houses. Kirby soon realised a thorough inspection would take over half an hour, even if they found nothing illegal. The moment MT appeared Kirby knew his estimate of half an hour was hopelessly inadequate.

As they entered the enclosed section of the yard Kirby saw some Plumed Tree Ducks locked in a pen. He gave Conrad a lesson in writing up an offender and then, for security reasons, requested the caged birds be locked in the vehicle. Conrad was eager to leave and could not understand why Kirby insisted he return to the yard at the completion of the errand. After the formal introductions when they arrived Conrad had followed Kirby as he whisked around all the cages on a cursory survey. The purpose had not been to inspect and identify all the birds, but rather to gauge MT's body language. During that initial tour Kirby became acutely aware of another hot spot in the yard and he wanted to know what was going on.

Murray understood Kirby's actions but Conrad had no idea the inspection had only just begun. What he did understand was that MT was already annoyed at being booked and he was becoming vocal and uncouth. The new officer suspected his return to the yard would only make matters worse. He thought the duck case was enough but Kirby knew MT and suspected the crime rate was higher than the current statistics revealed.

Back at the hot spot Kirby was gazing intently into a large enclosure containing a number of Indian Ring-neck Parrots. He could not see any protected species or anything out of the ordinary, but something did not ring true. He could not put his finger on it. The back and one side of the suspect cage formed part of the external boundary of the yard. The other side abutted another enclosure and that too, contained no species of interest. Kirby stood looking through the mesh comprising the top section of the front of the Indian Ring-neck aviary. Corrugated iron, up to a height of over a metre, made up the lower portion of the cage in front of him. The only human access was via the adjacent aviary and Kirby was contemplating a physical inspection inside the enclosure. As he stood looking he realised the parrot noises he could hear were not coming from the Indian Ring-necks. He listened carefully.

Kussick, kussick.

Kirby could hear rosellas but stood looking at Indian Ring-neck Parrots. He started to open the door of the adjacent aviary, intending to find the rosellas.

'Yer can't go in there,' MT insisted, 'them birds 'ave a infectious disease and I don't wan' yer spreadin' it all 'round the place. It's 'ighly contagious even to hoomans. Yer might get crook yerself. Yer could even kark it – it's toxic yer know and there ain't no cure. Yer wouldn't wan' that would yer?'

Kirby's heart skipped a beat then began to race. He had heard of the systemic illness psittacosis and knew humans could contract it from infected birds.

Is it psittacosis or coccidiosis? Either way I think it can be fatal. Hang on a minute, MT's not for real. He's just trying to divert my attention again.

Kirby took a deep breath and walked through to the corner cage. There, within a few centimetres of where he had been, he found a tea chest. This had been very carefully positioned – the corrugated iron on the front of the enclosure completely hid it from the outside. The chest had a wire netting top and contained eucalyptus leaves as well as birds. Kirby carried the tea chest out of the aviary and had another little chat with MT.

The birds were ready for transport and the timing of the raid had been lucky because the crowded conditions in the chest would have quickly led to deterioration in the bird's health. Ill birds were of little value and the vendors generally cared for their captives reasonably well.

'Has a supplier just delivered these?' Kirby asked, pointing to the birds he had just found. 'Or perhaps a purchaser is about to arrive?'

'Don't be bloody stupid,' MT replied. 'These are personal pets. They're owned by Mr Howard Koren an' just so yer don't make a fool a yer self, let me tell yer he's a very influential person. He's the owner of the XLCR Bird Supply an' he's got friends in high places. Very high places.'

The three officers watched and listened as MT undid the corner of the wire netting top of the tea chest. This had unspoken approval as an accidental escape could not have occurred where they were standing, within the completely enclosed section of the yard.

MT reached into the chest and lifted out a king parrot. Up until that moment none of the officers realised exactly what the tea chest contained and the appearance of the king parrot surprised Kirby. He had heard rosellas and when he looked into the chest he saw exactly what he expected, not what was there. MT held the king parrot gently to his chest and began to lovingly stroke the top of its head and nape.

'I've been asked t' look after these birds for their owner. See they're tame. They've come from Queensland where they're legally held under licence. They're personal pets an' nothin' t' do with the business. Besides, them rosellas aren't even from Victoria. If yer look proper yer can see they're Golden Mantles, not Eastern Rosellas.' MT pointed to the colour on the back of one of the rosellas still in the chest.

'Don't yer know nothin'? Everyone knows the Golden Mantle's got gold coloured edges on its back feathers an' Eastern Rosellas 'ave a yellowish-green colour. Are yer blind or somethin'? Can't yer see this golden colour? Them birds is from up the coast an' Golden Mantles ain't even on yer protected schedule.'

'Eastern Rosellas are Eastern Rosellas,' Kirby said. 'It doesn't matter what you call them. Under the Act it doesn't matter if they are tame or wild or from Victoria or Queensland or wherever. You know as well as I do that Golden Mantles are really Eastern Rosellas and you can't have them, or the king parrots.'

Kirby knew the edge colour of a few feathers did not alter certain biological facts – these were all protected birds and he intended to seize the whole box full. MT continued to stroke the king parrot as Kirby persisted with his questions.

The parrot was unhappy about the attention it was getting and it eventually twisted its head far enough around to get its beak into the fleshy web between the thumb and first finger on MT's right hand. A piece of flesh came right out. Blood gushed.

By the time Kirby finished the interview MT's light coloured shirt was scarlet, all the way down the front. As MT told his touching story about the beloved pets and very influential boss, the tone and the octave of his voice did not alter. He did not miss one syllable or bat an eyelid even though the pain must have been intense. MT continued to demonstrate his devotion to the pet king parrot until it was time for the officers to leave – with it and the other eleven birds from the chest.

During the exercise debrief Kirby said nothing about his surprise at finding the king parrots or MT. The marks Murray awarded indicated the senior officer did not suspect the truth and at the end of the course Kirby had successfully completed his degree.

Chapter 10

THE ONE ARMED
BANDIT

Kirby had six weeks leave after Christmas. Zac was nearly four and Kylie was under two. Despite the children's young ages, Kirby and Nicky decided they would chance a houseboat holiday on Lake Hume. They hired a six-berth boat and spent ten glorious days relaxing, sunbaking, swimming and fishing. Zac caught his first fish and Kylie decided she wanted to try fishing too. Kirby rigged up a rod for her but the lack of action was too much and the little girl soon toddled off to play with her dolls. When Kirby later caught a carp he put it on Kylie's fishing line and threw it back in the water.

'Kylie, come quick,' Kirby called. 'You've got a bite.'

Kylie came excitedly onto the back deck followed closely by Nicky with the camera. Proud parents watched as Kylie's little face beamed absolute ecstasy when she wound in a very tired, half-dead fish. Nicky took a series of snaps as the carp was unceremoniously winched over the rail and dumped on the deck. Nicky and Kirby hugged and kissed her and Zac even left his rod and sauntered over for a look.

'It's only an old calf,' Kylie said nonchalantly after looking at the carp for a few moments. She dropped the rod and went back to her dolls.

That evening Kirby took Nicky and the children for a run in the punt. They motored towards a backwater in the Victorian section of the lake intending to watch the water birds, and hopefully get some wildlife photos as the sun set. About twenty-five metres out from the bank the outboard motor became tangled in a net.

'What is it Dad?' Zac asked as Kirby tilted the motor and began to untangle the mesh from around the propeller.

'It's a net, son,' Kirby explained. 'It's illegal. Someone is trying to catch lots of fish instead of being a sport, like we were this afternoon. Good sports use lines, not nets.'

'Come on Dad,' said Kylie. 'I want to go fast again.'

'What are you going to do?' asked Nicky.

'Try to contact the local office I suppose. Sorry kids the trip's off. Daddy's got some work to do. We'll have to go back to the houseboat.'

Back on board Kirby made contact with the houseboat hire agent via the CB radio. In turn the agent relayed the message about the net, via the telephone, to the local departmental after-hours number. Eventually the CB on the houseboat crackled and Kirby learned that no officers were available because of a major operation involving deer poachers. He decided he would try to catch the netters himself.

'You're on leave,' Nicky protested. 'Forget about the net. We could have another nice quiet evening together – just the two of us with no telephone. The kids have been so active these last few days they'll be asleep as soon as it's dark.'

'I can't just forget about the net,' Kirby reasoned. 'People who set illegal nets are selfish and ignorant – and I've got no time for them. Every officer in the state needs a bit of help with illegal netters and if I could I'd stitch up every one of them.'

'You'll never catch them all. This one case won't make any difference in the long run. You know that – be honest.'

'I am being honest. I'm being honest with myself. I'm going to do this because I'm an angler, not because I'm a fisheries inspector. We're always asking anglers to help by passing on information. It just happens that I can do a bit more than pass the info on this time.'

'Well I'm not happy about it. Can't you ever forget about your job and think about me for a change?' Nicky was sombre and wanted Kirby to know how she felt.

'That's not quite fair. Anyway, it might only take an hour and I'll probably have to come back for court. You could come too – that way we'd make a long weekend of it. Wouldn't another trip up here, staying in a motel at Wodonga or Wangaratta at the department's expense, be worth it?'

'That depends if you catch them and all your other plans work out. If they pleaded guilty, or court was on a Wednesday, then what? I think you've just thrown a night of our holidays away. Oh, what's the use? I know you're going no matter what I say or promise.'

Kirby drove the punt back towards the net, hugging the bank in the hope it offered some cover. He stopped and waited, listening carefully for any indication the netters were there. He heard the beat of the ibis wings as they made their way to roost and he heard the squabble of the coots as they positioned themselves for the night. Occasionally a Musk Duck called eerily to its mate from somewhere in the reeds to Kirby's left. The only human noise he heard was the drone of a distant truck as it travelled the road towards Tallangatta. When it was completely dark Kirby motored slowly into the open water and found the net exactly where, and exactly how he did before. He untangled the propeller again and, leaving the motor tilted, pulled his boat along the length of the net. It was long, and as best the he could see, contained numerous trout and other fish. One end of the offending equipment was tied to reeds near the lagoon entrance and the other was tied to a small plough anchor out in the lake.

There was nowhere to hide the punt and Kirby decided there was only one thing to do. He used his pocket-knife and cut a pathway into the reeds right beside the end of the net. He then backed the boat into the passageway, keeping the cut off vegetation to use as camouflage over the bow. He poured a cup of hot black coffee and began the wait. As he sat waiting Kirby was haunted by thoughts of what the evening may have been. Eventually, despite the hard metal seat and cramped legs, he dozed off about three in the morning.

Kirby woke with a start at the sound of a man coughing. Initially he thought someone was in the punt with him, but that was a trick of his tired mind. As he sat listening and hardly daring to breathe, Kirby heard it again, a good distance off towards Tallangatta. The officer's adrenalin pumped hard as he sat listening and still waiting. Feelings of expectation gave way to trepidation.

Who am I about to encounter? It's a very dark night and whilst Nicky knows where I am, no-one officially does. This may not be too compatible with the OH&S rules in the manual.

As Kirby worried about the occupation health and safety issue he had brought upon himself, the coughing became louder. After a while he could hear the sound of oars in squeaky rowlocks. The sounds were coming steadily towards the net, and Kirby's end of it! He resolved not to make a move until the netters had begun to lift the gear. With part of the net in the boat and part in the water the culprits would be in real trouble for two reasons. Firstly it would be hard for them to abscond and, secondly, their intentions would be blatantly obvious. Kirby glanced at his watch – it was still well before four o'clock. He prayed the camouflage would stand the test.

The silhouette of two people in a car-top dinghy came into view. Kirby suppressed an almost irresistible desire to immediately break cover and pounce, but he remembered how some predators use camouflage as they wait for their prey to come into range. He reasoned his best chance was to remain undetected until the right moment.

'It's just about here,' one of the men said out loud enough for Kirby to hear.

The net, being so easily found, meant the suspects did not have to search at all and perhaps Kirby's camouflage was not even tested. He sat like a statue and watched.

Dione and Mick Harvey then set to, working their boat along the net as they lifted it on board. Kirby waited until he saw a couple of fish glisten as they cleared the water tangled in the net. He reached for his spotlight, stood up quietly and switched it on. He deliberately aimed the beam right in the suspect's eyes.

'Kirby Wellington,' he yelled. 'Fisheries Inspector! Don't move.'

Dione, who had been rowing obeyed, but Mick didn't – he fell in a heap in the bottom of the boat.

With one pull on the starter rope Kirby's motor burst into life and he was beside the offenders within a couple of seconds of the light going on. Mick, still in the bottom of the boat, was wheezing very badly.

'He's got a bad ticker you know,' Dione explained.

In the spotlight Kirby could see Mick was not acting. The wheezing was bad enough, but when he also began a bout of coughing he stopped breathing. Had it been daylight, Kirby knew Mick would have been blue.

Perhaps it's best it is dark. What happens if he has a heart attack and dies? What can I do? What will I do? He is going to die – I just know he is. Kirby realised he was frightening himself.

As Kirby's thoughts raced from ambulance to Coroners' Court, he noticed that Mick was very old and that he only had one arm! Kirby's face dropped when he saw it.

'Lost it in the war you know,' Dione said. 'Lucky to be alive. A mortar shell landed in a foxhole with him. Mum always says it was a miracle he came home. I'm never quite sure though if she means the war nearly killed him or he knew if he came home it would be a hell of a life on the farm with all us kids to feed. In the circumstances she would not have blamed him if he had stayed away.'

'What can we do about his attack?' Has he ever done this before?'

'He smokes too much. The doctor told him to give up the fags or they'd kill him.' Dione spoke with no apparent concerns for his father.

I got in before the lung cancer had time to kill him, Kirby thought to himself.

'He'll be OK in a minute,' Dione eventually volunteered. 'Just leave him lie quietly for a while.'

Kirby did not like the inactivity but gradually the old man began to recover. Kirby gave him a cup of coffee. Mick managed to drink a little, but he spilled just as much as he sat there shaking, coughing and yet still smoking.

'I needed that,' he said.

Kirby was sure his reference was not to the coffee, but to the cigarette he was dragging heavily on. Mick convinced Kirby he was OK and after they retrieved the net, Kirby towed the offender's dinghy back to their car. There he searched their panel van and wrote them up with Mick sitting in the car all the while. As he conducted the interviews Kirby began to think about the difficulties he would have if he seized their dingy – what was he going to do with it on the houseboat?

'I've decided not to seize your boat,' Kirby announced when he neared the end of his questions. 'I must be getting soft in my old age. Dione, help me get it onto the roof-racks on your panel van before I change my mind.'

It was not long before dawn when Kirby set off for the houseboat. He was chilled to the bone when he arrived and decided to shower to warm up. Afterwards he crawled into bed and Nicky listened to the story with her back to him.

'That's one of the worst excuses I've heard,' Nicky said when Kirby told her Mick only had one arm. She turned over and put her arm around his neck. 'We had a date and you've been out all night. You've got some cheek standing me up for a one armed bandit.'

Chapter 11

WHAT BIRD IS THAT?

Not long after Kirby returned to work after his holidays Greg Bayliss began making arrangements for the coming duck season. There was a rush of applicants wanting to do Waterfowl Identification Tests and Kirby took over running these in between the compulsory waterfowl counts and wetland assessments. Predictions about the condition of each wetland and likely duck numbers for the opening weekend were discussed with Greg before Kirby keyed the data into FRED. Management in Melbourne collated the information from each station and prepared a state wide operational plan. An associated roster finally came out a few days before the opening and Kirby learned he would be working with Greg at Natte Yallock Swamp, about forty-five minutes' drive from Mafeking Bay.

On the morning of the duck-opening hunter behaviour was very good. When Greg made the scheduled radio call to head office at nine o'clock he happily reported they had found no breaches of the law. By this time the intensity of the pursuit was over and many hunters were already off the swamp. The officers continued working their way around the shoreline speaking to hunters and inspecting bags and licences. As they worked they came across a car and unoccupied tent a few metres from the water's edge. They surveyed the general area.

'Looks like they got one mountainy,' said Greg pointing to a recently killed, unplucked mountain duck lying under the vehicle in the shade. 'If that's all they got they haven't done too good. Most hunters don't bother to shoot at mountain duck because they reckon they're too tough. Come on let's go. We're wasting our time here.'

With not another thought they drove off, up the relatively steep bank and back to the track. All morning the officers had taken turns doing the introductions and the inevitable paperwork. Like every officer in the state they were participating in a hunter survey that involved asking questions about the species that had been taken, the number of people in the party, the number of shots fired and a host of other data. After a few hours the number of sheets of paper had begun to pile up and back at the office the data would need to be checked and collated before transmission to Head Office.

Along the track a little the officers came across four hunters walking towards the camp where the duck lay under the car. Greg introduced Kirby to Ron Wilson, Daryl Stacey, Roy Briggs and Graeme Coats who were members of the Mafeking Bay Beer, Wine and Cheese Club. Greg was also a club member and it was obvious he was pleased to see his mates.

'Well, fancy meeting you blokes here,' Greg said. 'How'd you go?'

'No bloody good. Only got one mountainy between the lot of us,' Ron Wilson volunteered.

'What! Weren't you blokes trying,' joked Greg. 'Or did you all have too much of the dooin's last night? We saw the duck under your car back at the camp. I didn't think you blokes were that desperate you'd start shootin' mountain duck. Never mind, you don't have to pluck 'em if you don't shoot 'em do you?'

The group of hunters did not respond to Greg's witticism and Kirby could feel the tension in the air. He did not understand. He knew his boss and the men were best mates and concluded there must have been some problem at the club.

'Best have a look at your shooting and duck hunting licences please,' continued Greg. 'For the damn statistics you know. We have to send all sorts of crap to the bean counters in head office.'

The four hunters began to silently rummage around in pockets and wallets but each was unsuccessful in his efforts to find the appropriate papers.

'Kirby'll go back to your camp with you,' Greg suggested. 'It's only routine I know, but we have to show the young bloke how to do things properly don't we? I'll just go on down here and have a look at these other hunters. You catch me up when you're finished Kirby.'

Greg pointed to some more people coming out of the swamp a couple of hundred metres ahead. It was his turn to complete the hunter survey with his mates but he had an additional reason for getting the 'young bloke' to do the paperwork. Greg planned his action carefully. He too had felt the tension and thought one of his club-mates had left his licence at home. He intended for Kirby to do the survey and the follow-up checks regarding the licence. Besides, if a licence happened to be out-of-date it would be up to Kirby to decide what should happen. Kirby had worked with Greg long enough to know what his boss was thinking. The junior officer was positive he was being forced to do Greg's dirty work because one of the hunters had a licence that was out of order.

Kirby drove back to the camp with Roy Briggs and Graeme Coats in the cabin with him. Daryl Stacey and Ron Wilson rode on the bonnet, holding onto the bull bar for support. Back at the tent Kirby inspected their licences and, just as Greg expressed, everything was in order. Kirby was relieved nothing was wrong but still a little annoyed that he had to take Greg's turn at completing the hunter survey. There was twice as much work when there were multiple members in one hunting party.

'Thanks fellas,' Kirby said when he finished. 'I hope you do a bit better this evening or tomorrow morning. Think about me still working when you start on the beer, wine and cheese won't you?'

Kirby drove back up the hill in the same place he and Greg travelled earlier. As he did, the officer glanced in the mirror. In his reflected view he saw feathers blowing in the wind. Bells rang wildly.

What's going on here? These blokes only have one duck and it's got all its feathers on.

Kirby concluded he knew four people who had been hunting the night before, in the closed season. He was sure he now knew the reason for the cold response to Greg's introductions and he figured the claim to have only one duck between four was an attempt to divert attention from the truth. He wheeled the Toyota around and visited the camp for the third time. He was now conscious of a considerable pile of feathers that had been there the whole while. He remembered the king parrots in the chest and realised this was the second time in a few weeks that he had looked and not seen. Heaps of feathers were commonplace on duck opening mornings and he wondered how often he missed the obvious and therefore the truth.

'OK, who wants to tell me about it?' Kirby said addressing the still assembled group of hunters.

'What are you talking about?' Graeme Coats responded.

'You blokes have a bit of a shoot last night did you?' Kirby challenged.

'Come off it,' Daryl objected. 'We only left town after work and by the time we set up the tent it was dark.'

'Yeah,' agreed Ron. 'It was too dark to do anything after that.'

'Yeah,' Roy chipped in. 'We always have an early night before the opening—have to be early to get the best hunting—and we're planning a big night tonight.'

Kirby began to search the tent. No one objected, but no one accompanied him. Once inside the canvas Kirby saw the typical assortment of stretchers and blow up beds, unmade and unruly with pillows, blankets, dirty clothes and sleeping bags strewn around the floor. There were dirty dishes and empty drink bottles scattered amongst sleeping gear, dirty underwear and smelly socks. A dozen bottles of red wine, still in the carton, were stacked near five Eskies in the far corner.

The first Esky Kirby inspected contained ice, beer and white wine. A probe into the second and third revealed the same essential items of sustenance. The fourth held cheese and other foodstuffs, crammed in. The one remaining had another actually placed on top of it. Kirby lifted that down and opened the last lid.

What bird is that? I'm sure glad I didn't have to identify that for my exams.

Kirby gazed at the open Esky that contained several wild ducks and a huge bird, about the size of a turkey. They were all plucked and with no feathers to give him a clue, Kirby simply failed to recognise what the large bird was. He was glad he had gone back to investigate the feathers but for a moment thought it may have been a turkey, brought from home for the beer, wine and cheese feast. In a second after this consideration he knew the bird was not a turkey or other domestic species.

Is it a swan? No, it's too plump for a swan.

Kirby knew that his statement, "OK, who wants to tell me about it" meant he now had to identify "it". Neil Lyons, and the gas scare gun he assumed to be an illegal shooter, flashed before his eyes.

Conscious of the need to be more specific in his allegation when he went back out to the hunters, Kirby continued to gaze at the bird. He noticed a little green colour on its legs, at the severed knee joints. Gradually the identification began to take shape and suddenly he knew. He walked out of the tent full of confidence.

'OK. Who shot the Cape Barren Goose?'

'Hell, Kirby, it was me,' Ron Wilson admitted.

'We best have a little chat about this,' Kirby said quietly.

He walked with his customer, away from the group, and the two sat together on the grass. Kirby wrote down Ron Wilson's personal details but during the questioning found he could not concentrate on the job.

His mind wandered. There had been considerable publicity about the departmental crackdown on the killing of protected species but the most amazing thing was how close they came to missing the whole episode. Very few officers in the state had detected a person shooting a Cape Barren Goose and Kirby had caught one of his boss's mates! Perhaps Ron Wilson knew Greg would be working at Natte Yallock Swamp and had therefore assumed he would be OK no matter what he shot.

'Why did you shoot it?' Kirby asked. 'You must have known it was protected and you must have known what it was. They fly like B52 Bombers and are one of the most unmistakable species on our wetlands.'

'I just couldn't help myself,' Ron answered.

Kirby accepted this was the truth and the deed had only taken one shot. He knew Ron Wilson was now extremely sorry for a decision he knew was wrong even before he squeezed the trigger – but why did he do it? Kirby would never find out but he did know it would soon become common knowledge in the beer, wine and cheese club – Ron Wilson shot a Cape Barren Goose and got caught. Perhaps his embarrassment would cause him to resign from the club because Greg Bayliss was a fellow member.

'You know the score,' Kirby said. 'I have to seize your gun. Grab it for me, will you?'

Ron Wilson stood up to obey and Kirby reached for the seizure receipt book. He had left the only one they had with Greg because this was just routine. Kirby took possession of the firearm and goose. He then apologised for not being able to complete the paperwork. He drove off in search of his partner and the official seizure receipt book.

'What kept you?' Greg inquired as Kirby pulled up.

'Oh, I just booked one of your mates for shooting a Cape Barren Goose. I need the receipt book for his gun.'

Greg thought the receipt book was window dressing on a bad-taste joke, until Kirby pulled back the tonneau cover on the punt and showed his boss the proof. Kirby filled the receipt out there and handed the book back to Greg.

'You best get a wriggle on,' Kirby joked. 'It won't look too good if the junior officer gets the only case for the day.'

When Kirby drove back to the camp again he noticed the feathers were visible from at least one hundred metres. Ron Wilson was still sitting on the grass, separate from his mates. As Kirby walked up to hand him the receipt the hunter was crying. Loud sobs and real tears interspersed his next statement and question.

'My wife gave me the gun as a present for my birthday yesterday. Now you've got it. What am I going to tell her?'

'I'm not sure,' Kirby replied. 'I figure you and I are in the same boat though. It appears we will both have to report this incident. My advantage is that I already know what I'm going to say – I'm going to tell the truth.'

Chapter 12

DOLPHINS

In the weeks after the opening of the duck season Kirby and Greg received several reports about two dolphins in Mafeking Bay. The animals were in past the natural barrier formed by the sand spit between Rocklyn's Point and Point Alistree.

'No worries,' said Greg when he discussed the problem with Kirby. 'Big fishing boats come and go through the channel every day. The dolphins are OK. They can navigate back into Bass Strait anytime they like.'

'One of the callers I spoke to yesterday said they were porpoises,' said Kirby. 'What's the difference between a dolphin and a porpoise?'

'You look it up and tell me tomorrow,' Greg replied. 'I'll give you a hint. These are dolphins for sure. It's not the first time I've seen 'em in Mafeking Bay. In fact the bay's the only place I've actually seen one caught in a net.

'A few years ago, just on daylight, Darren Wossfold and me set off on a boat patrol and about half way to Rocklyn's Point we came across Luka Poljak. You know Luka – he's a local professional fisherman. Anyway, as we passed I gave Luka a wave but his reaction wasn't quite right. You need a sixth sense in this job sometimes and me sixth sense told me somethin' was wrong. I thought perhaps that he was using a net that had too small a mesh or somethin'. Anyway I pulled alongside and Luka was haulin' a mesh net. I asked him what was going on and he said he'd caught a porpoise. You'd a thought a pro fisher would know the difference between a dolphin and a porpoise wouldn't you?'

'I don't know. Should he?'

'Sure enough,' Greg continued as though Kirby had not answered. 'Tangled in his net was a three-quarter grown dolphin. Drowned, dead as a nit. 'Til then I reckoned they were too clever to get caught in a mesh net. They're really intelligent you know, and they've got real sophisticated sonar that I thought'd stop 'em getting' caught – except perhaps in a great big seine net shot round dolphins feeding on a school of bait that was the target of the seine shot.

'Anyway the museum always wants specimens of whales and dolphins and this one wasn't rottin' in the sun on a beach somewhere. I got on Luka's boat to help recover the body but we couldn't. Part of the bloody net got 'round the boat's prop and we had to cut the thing to get it off. When we did the dolphin just rolled, and it rolled right out of the net. It sunk and we couldn't do a darn thing about it.'

'Well what's the difference between a porpoise and a dolphin?' Greg asked the next morning.

'The name porpoise is commonly, but incorrectly used in reference to dolphins in Australia. Both porpoises and dolphins are cetaceans – the same as a Killer Whale – but the porpoise only occurs in the Northern Hemisphere. The two best known species of dolphin are the Common Dolphin and the Bottlenose Dolphin. Both these occur in Australian Waters and both have a worldwide distribution.'

'Right on.' Greg was obviously pleased with his protégé.

All through March and April Kirby and Greg continued to receive reports about the dolphins in the bay and even though they were there for weeks, right inside Mafeking Bay, the officers were still not concerned. Just on dusk on the first Thursday in May, Kirby received a call that a dolphin was on the beach between the refinery pier and Warranooke Lagoon. Kirby rang Greg's number to tell him about the stranding.

'He's out at a beer, wine and cheese night,' Bonny, Greg's partner, said.

Unaccompanied, Kirby went to investigate and when he arrived discovered the dolphin had beached in an area of shoreline covered by rocks, ranging in size up to about thirty-five centimetres across the widest part. Some were irregular and rugged in shape. The animal was still alive and its mate was swimming back and forth, out in deeper water. A small group of people standing on the shore watched the distressed animal.

'Somebody like to give me a hand?' Kirby asked. 'We've got to get it off the rocks and it's too heavy for me to lift by myself. If I try to drag it I'll only hurt it. If we can get it into water deep enough we can hold it in a swimming position for a while. If we do that it might be OK. With luck it'll swim off to its mate.'

With the help of three onlookers Kirby managed to lift the dolphin off the rocks. They moved it to deeper water and held it, floating on the surface so it could breathe. The touch of its skin was beautiful, not rough and scaly like a fish, but soft and smooth – like silky velvet.

The wind was cold and brisk, blowing directly from the south. It was difficult to hold the animal, not because it struggled, but because the waves were directly onshore at that spot. Kirby and the volunteers were up to their groins in the water and the waves were making them wet up to their armpits as they bent to cradle the dolphin. Kirby's chest waders filled with water and became dangerous so he discarded them. In a short time the cold was intense.

Angry marks and abrasions on the animal's flanks were conspicuous and during their rescue attempt the waves continued to buffet it cruelly against the rocks. Several additional nasty lacerations resulted. In his heart Kirby knew the dolphin was in a critical way but he pushed the reality of this into the back of his mind and refused to accept what it meant. After half an hour or so the dolphin began to struggle and this encouraged the rescuers.

'I think it's trying to swim back to its mate,' Kirby said. 'Everyone let go on the count of three. One, two, three.'

The animal swam off in a circle but immediately returned to the shore and the jagged edges of the rocks. The consequences were devastating.

With darkness completely set in Kirby and his helpers now had real difficulties. They were fighting hypothermia and working blind. It was difficult to find a decent footing between the rocks. They strained to get the animal floating for the second time and eventually their efforts seemed to be paying dividends. They began to move towards the deeper water again. Then, without warning, the dolphin trembled all over and died in their arms.

Kirby backed the Toyota Land Cruiser as far as he could towards the water and, with a lot of help, managed to load the dolphin into the back with the seat down. He drove home and left it there overnight. Next morning, after contacting the museum about the dead mammal, he rang his senior officer. Greg didn't want to know – he'd had a good night on the beer, wine and cheese. Kirby made the decision to take the dead dolphin to Melbourne. He left immediately and was back by eight PM.

On the Friday of the following week the museum rang Kirby. The dolphin had not been one of the common species. It was a Fraser's Dolphin and this was the first specimen recorded in Victoria.

'As far as we know,' the curator of mammals explained. 'The Fraser's Dolphin is more of a tropical species. Perhaps this one, and its mate, headed north through the entrance to Mafeking Bay trying to go home. Once in the bay they did not leave as that would mean travelling south – the opposite direction to where their instincts told them they would find warmer water. As the summer faded and the autumn nights grew colder the urge to travel north would have become stronger and stronger. Have you had any more reports about the second one?'

'Not a whisper,' said Kirby. 'If we do, do you want a call.'

'Yes please,' the curator almost implored. 'It's not a bad bet that the second one was a Fraser's too but unless someone identifies it we can't record it as a sighting. Many dolphins are gregarious and different species are known to frequent the same pods. If it's still about, the museum would send a field team down.'

Not one additional call was received about the second dolphin and nobody discovered its fate. A month or so later the official museum receipt for the dolphin arrived together with a precis of the known science related to the Fraser's Dolphin.

"Habitat:	Little known
Locomotion:	Little known
Distribution:	Tropical waters of Pacific and Indian oceans. Stranding in NSW and one in Vic.
Status:	Little known
Food:	Nothing recorded
Voice:	Nothing known
Habits:	One school of c. 400 recorded".

A hand written note on a sticky pad read: 'The Victorian stranding is yours!'

Chapter 13

THE RIGHT WHALES

The rest of May flew by. The first of the whales made intermittent appearances along the coast in the middle of June. By the end of July there were half a dozen cows, with calves, along the cliffs to the west of the entrance to Mafeking Bay.

In the days of whale harvesting, when men chased the giants of the sea in open rowing boats, they preferred to hunt the Right Whale. It was the right one because of its high oil content, large size and buoyancy. A floating carcass was easier to handle after death from harpoons and hand lances and during transport back to shore. In the heyday of whaling in Victoria, lookouts on the cliffs sent smoke signals back to the whaling stations to indicate the presence of whales. As a result of the signal the whalers left port in search of their quarry.

Kirby and Greg felt like whale lookouts. There were hundreds of identical calls to the office from tourists.

'Are the whales in?'

'How many are there?'

'When's the best time to see them?'

'Can you guarantee they'll be there if we come down Sunday afternoon?'

'How long will they stay?'

David and Barbara Browning contacted head office and sought permission to film the whales for a wildlife documentary they were making. Greg supported the application when he was asked and in

89

less than a week copies of the necessary permits arrived at Mafeking Bay with a memorandum requesting the local officer's involvement. The communication read, in part:

> 'It is requested that you cooperate fully with Mr and Mrs Browning between now and the end of July. An undertaking has been given to the permit holders that the fisheries patrol boat and rubber dinghy from Mafeking Bay will be made available. Please note that it is imperative that at least one officer accompany the film crew at all times whilst they are at sea.'

When David and Barbara arrived, Greg and Kirby joined them and together they formulated an operational plan.

'It'll be best to take both the Shark Cat and the inflatable to sea on each trip,' Greg concluded. 'We'll all go the first few times then take turns.'

Next day the officers used the larger boat, loaded with cameras and gear, to tow the inflatable from the main boat ramp in Mafeking Bay, out through the entrance then west to where the whales seemed to congregate most frequently. Here they anchored the Shark Cat to act as mother ship and the filming began.

David, dressed in a wet suit and accompanied by Kirby, approached the whales in the dinghy. This involved rowing to the windward side of the animal and then drifting, and hoping they ended up on the path a whale was travelling. Sometimes it worked – mostly it didn't.

Over the next two and a half weeks Kirby's experience filming the whales was unforgettable. These animals were giants and their tremendous dimensions constantly overwhelmed him. He knew they were big but could not come to grips with how big – he found it impossible to visualise their proportions. When close to a whale it seemed he could only concentrate on a single part. It was just a flipper, an eye or a callosity that was in focus, not the whole animal.

After they had filmed the whales for several days, everyone involved began to recognise some individuals. One of the mothers had a large piece missing from a tail fluke. It became obvious some females did not mind the approach of the dinghy as much as others did. All mothers though, appeared to know they should be between their calves and the boat.

On one occasion Kirby was rowing David in the dinghy. A mother and calf were between them and the shore, very close to the small boat. David slipped over the side with his camera and, as usual, the men felt excitement at the prospect of some good underwater footage. There was also trepidation about David being in the water right next to a whale. Suddenly the mother came up under the dinghy and lifted it clear of the water on its back. Kirby's heart nearly stopped and he prepared himself for disaster. The dinghy did a gentle three hundred and sixty degree turn then settled quietly back on the water. The whale and calf moved off, David climbed back on board and it was all over.

On many occasions the dinghy would quietly follow tantalising close to a mother and calf for hours, just to have the animals move off without any filming at all. As the crew became familiar with individuals they tried to target the more tolerant ones. The males were always most difficult to get close to, but as time passed the whales seemed to accept the people would not harm them.

Zac turned five on the twenty-seventh of July.

'Now remember Zac's party tonight,' Nicky reminded Kirby as he left for work that morning. 'You won't be late will you?'

'No, I promise.'

All day as he rowed the dingy after uncooperative whales, Kirby was conscious of the time. As the sun moved towards the west he calculated how long it would take to get home. Towing the dinghy back to the boat-ramp was always slow and then the gear had to be unloaded and the boats retrieved and washed down. The Shark Cat had to be re-fuelled and only after all this, with the boat securely locked in the depot, could Kirby go home.

'We're going to have to call it quits in ten minutes,' Kirby eventually told David. 'I promised I wouldn't be late for Zac's party.'

Filming wildlife is always painstaking, or at least being in the right place at the right time can be a frustrating and time consuming business. It takes a great deal of dedication and a special sixth sense. David possessed a generous portion of dedication, patience, ability and the required sixth sense.

'I've a feeling something's about to happen,' he said excitedly. 'The male's been hanging around the female all afternoon and they seem too preoccupied to worry too much about us getting close. We've just got to stay a bit longer.'

David was ecstatic at the prospect of being in the water and filming the whales as they mated. Kirby reluctantly agreed to an additional thirty minutes. Nothing happened and after more pleading from David, Kirby begrudgingly agreed to more time. Still nothing happened. Kirby knew by now that he would already be a bit late for the party.

'We're going!' Kirby was finally adamant.

David miserably unloaded the photographic equipment from the dinghy onto the Shark Cat then climbed aboard. The sun was partly set as Kirby fired the motors and pushed the throttles forward to begin the slow haul back to the boat-ramp. As they moved ahead the two whales, which had been the focus of attention all afternoon, were almost directly in front about a hundred and fifty metres away.

'Look!' David exclaimed. 'Quick!'

Kirby had never heard such excitement in just two words. He looked to see a whale breach – the ultimate dream of all whale watchers. It was an amazing sight. A leviathan, hurling itself upward into another world, propelled by some unseen force. The whale completely cleared the water, leaving Kirby breathless. His mind was heavy with guilt. It was his impatience that had taken David away from the position to capture that wonderful moment on film.

'Quick! Quick!' David urged again as he prepared his camera. 'Get closer, quick, quick!'

Frustration was understandable with all the equipment previously packed and stowed for the trip home. Kirby ignored the dinghy and gave the throttles a fair handful, trying to appease David but thinking all the while he was on about nothing – they had already missed the action. By now the Shark Cat had reached the place where the breach occurred. White water showed an area of considerable turbulence.

As Kirby continued to motor along the whale was not visible but its position was. The whale, moving fast under water, made a pressure wave on the surface and, in that relatively shallow water, the powerful tail disturbed the sand leaving an easy trail to follow. Kirby became conscious they were travelling too fast for the dinghy. The typical Shark Cat rooster tail was sending a spout of water directly into the open boat behind.

Too bad, he thought, *there's real action out front.*

The whale breached a second time – again before David had the camera ready.

Rats, Kirby thought, *it's my fault this chance in a lifetime's gone begging.*

The bow wave and disturbed water clearly indicated the action was not over and by now the camera was rolling. David was standing right behind Kirby, propped against the back of the seat for support.

The whale breached again. Out in front of the pressure wave in undisturbed water, the black monstrous head emerged, shooting upwards at about seventy degrees. It appeared out of nothing and continued to climb as if propelled by a rocket. At first all was silent. Then, as the hulk emerged, water began to cascade back to the sea. The water lifted and pushed up with the whale's flight, glistened white in contrast to the black body.

As the whale reached the peak of its flight it's body curved forward and it half rolled as its tail became visible above the waves. For a split second it appeared motionless, the noise of the waterfall audible above the sound of the motors. Then came a thunderous crash as fifteen metres of blubber hit the water. The whale disappeared in a mighty splash that reached the boat.

Did I really see that? Kirby asked himself.

The cold seawater on his face helped re-assure him he was not dreaming. On several occasions in the previous two weeks Kirby had been close enough to hear, smell and feel the fine spray from whales as they spouted for breath, but this was different! Kirby was mesmerised. David was thinking. The magic of that moment did not overawe the photographer or distract him from his task – to capture that incredible whale on film.

'Quick, quick!' David exclaimed. ''Round the other side, get on the other side!'

David's professionalism told him that from where he was filming the shoreline was in the background. Excellent wildlife footage simply does not include man's scars on nature, not even the silhouette of buildings or rows of Norfolk Island Pine trees on the horizon. The next breach was imminent.

This time the Shark Cat was between the shore and the animal. The last remaining rays of the sun streamed over David's shoulder and eventually everything was perfect. The camera rolled for a number of additional breaches that followed in relatively quick succession.

Disappointingly, the whale soon fatigued visibly. The herculean effort required to launch those tonnes of blubber out of the water was not sustainable. With each breach the amount of whale's body that actually cleared the water became noticeably less. In all there were nineteen or twenty leaps, with only the first two or three completely clearing the water.

David was ecstatic. His footage would thrill thousands, perhaps millions of viewers as they watched the unthinkable. Kirby loved to watch wildlife and the miracles of nature depicted in TV documentaries. Being there was utopia.

The magic of the short time Kirby spent with the whale soon disappeared. His guilt flooded back at the missed potential of that first spectacular breach. David's footage justified all the hours they had previously spent, but it should have been better.

Kirby was nearly two hours late for Zac's party and next morning there was no filming because of bad weather. Kirby went to the office and was back in the world of the public service where the reality of civilisation and its computers, machines and timetables replaced the guilt and ecstasy of the previous evening. Here there was no time for utopia or the world of whales. The phone rang – again!

'I want to speak to the Officer in Charge,' the caller advised. 'I have a complaint about people harassing the whales.'

This was serious – information about an indictable offence.

'He's not here at the moment,' Kirby said. 'I'm second in charge. You can tell me about it. When did it happen?'

'Last night just about sunset. I was at the viewing platform and there were some whales way down to the right. There was this big white boat with red writing on the side and it was really giving one whale a hard time, chasing it and all. In the end the whale got so mad it jumped right out of the water at the boat, about a dozen or more times. They were lucky it didn't get 'em. Just between you and me I wish it had.'

'Do you know who they were?' Kirby inquired.

'No, I'm sorry.'

'Did you see the registered number of the boat, or read the writing on the side?'

'No, it was too far away and by the time they went past the viewing platform it was dark. But it looked like they came into the bay. Someone else must have seen them.'

Kirby knew instantly the red writing on the boat read 'FISHERIES PATROL' and he was listening to a complaint about himself. From the viewing platform the perspective of direction and distance between boat and whale would have been impossible to judge.

'I'm sorry,' he said. 'There's probably little we can do to investigate this unless you can tell us who was responsible. I appreciate your concern and I'll pass it on to the boss.'

Kirby tried to make his apology sound genuine. He thanked the caller again for her trouble and got back to the accumulated mountain of papers and files on the desk. The weather and sea conditions remained dreadful until the end of July. There were no additional trips in the boat and David and Barbara only managed to get a little additional footage from the cliffs.

A few weeks later, during August, Kirby realised it had been three years since Darren Wossfold left creating the vacancy he had filled. Everything seemed dull after the whale filming and Kirby had become restless. He felt a need for change and a couple of weeks later Martin Stein, the officer from Costerfield, announced his retirement. Kirby discussed the vacancy and the prospect of a shift with Nicky.

'I guess if we've got to shift,' she mused, 'it would be best to get it over with. Couldn't we leave it till the end of the year though? That way Zac'll be finished kinder. It would be best for him if we shifted during the holidays, before he starts school.'

'You're doing it again,' laughed Kirby. 'Martin's retired but the job isn't even advertised yet. When it is there'll be no guarantees about who'll get it.'

'You've got the qualifications now,' said Nicky. 'You've got a fair bit of experience too. I reckon you'll get it. I'll go on the interview panel.'

'I love you. You're always so positive. I reckon we'll buy a house instead of renting this time.'

'You're worse than me. If I know you, you'll have the house picked out already. I want one with white roses in the front garden and Waterfall Pansies in hanging baskets near the door.'

The Public Service Notices in early September contained the advertisement for the position of Officer In Charge at Costerfield. Conrad Holmes was the junior officer there and he, Kirby and seven others applied. Kirby's application was placed on a short list and he travelled to Melbourne for a third interview. At the end of an hour the interview panel gave him the news he so desperately wanted.

The Wellingtons purchased their first home in December and they shifted to live at Costerfield during the last week in January. There were no roses in the garden and Nicky had to wait till July before the nurseries had any in stock. She purchased six standard Icebergs and planted them along the driveway.

PART 3

OFFICER IN CHARGE AT COSTERFIELD

Chapter 14

TOO DRUNK TO WALK

'It's the bartender from the Star Of The West on the phone and he says there's a koala on the bar,' Nicky called out.

'Pull the other one! I suppose it's refusing to pay for its drinks,' Kirby responded.

During his first week as a fisheries and wildlife officer Kirby had answered a call from a member of the public who rang about an echidna she found lost in the bush. That call began Kirby's education with respect to the origins of wildlife welfare calls and now, five years later, he was the senior officer at Costerfield with sole responsibility for the department's after-hours telephone calls. He had no choice – the phone was diverted to the lounge-room of his home. On this Saturday afternoon it was obvious from the background noise that the caller was ringing from a pub.

The bartender eventually convinced Kirby the call was genuine and he changed into his uniform and drove to the hotel, entering the saloon to loud cheers. In a moment he realised many of the patrons had consumed enough truth serum to give his task an interesting perspective. The koala, a large male, was sitting on one end of the bar with its back against the wall. Kirby's arrival delighted the customers. The staff, who were trying to clean up at the end of their shift, watched Kirby expectantly. The koala sat with his chin on his chest and eyes nearly closed, almost oblivious to his surroundings. He may have been sitting in the fork of a gum tree out along the river.

'Waddaya gunna do?' Kirby heard one voice above the other rabble.

It did not take Einstein to work out that this koala had not just wandered in from the bush and climbed up on the bar by himself. There had to have been a certain amount of human intervention and Kirby thought it had to be a set-up.

'Where did it come from?' he demanded of the bartender.

'A bloke just brought it in,' the bartender responded amid merriment and boisterous laughter from the patrons.

'You don't just bring koalas into pubs!' Kirby spat out the words hoping the noise and jovial atmosphere in the place would not disguise his annoyance. He trusted his next question would make his attitude abundantly clear and buy him some time in which to devise a plan to discover who was responsible, without making himself the butt of a joke.

If I show enough authority over this situation, and it does turn out to be a set-up, those responsible may think twice before playing their punch line.

'Well who is he? Where is he? I want to talk to him, and I want to talk to him now!'

'I didn't see who it was but I think you need to talk to Bluey Davis. That's his beer. I think he's just gone to the men's room.' The bartender pointed to a half-empty pot on the bar.

Kirby noticed the drink was closer to the koala than any other.

'How did he get it in here?'

'They said he just carried it in and plonked it on the bar. Do you want a beer?'

'No thanks.'

'He's on duty,' was one of the wise cracks from the drinking audience.

'Can't drink when he's got the uniform on,' was another. 'Come on, we won't tell.'

That's just what I need. My wits dulled when I have to handle this little monster in front of a dozen well primed drinkers and a bartender who's already rostered off-duty.

Kirby knew about catching koalas, having been involved on several occasions with the official koala relocation program from Coromby Island. Koalas, especially grumpy old bulls like this one, are about seventy centimetres long and their claws are longer, sharper and more powerful than most imagine. Whilst the koala itself is not fast, it can swipe a paw at you with amazing speed and accuracy. During one of Kirby's koala catching trips he saw a small koala swat a colleague's hand whilst the officers were attempting to secure the animal in a crate. The contact left a torn uniform and a gash requiring a trip to the doctor for stitches and an antibiotic injection. Ever since the Coromby

Island experience Kirby had been particularly careful when handling wild koalas. Their cute cuddly appearance is not indicative of their true nature. They can be obnoxious, smelly, biting, scratching bundles of fur and, once grabbed, very likely to urinate. Kirby shifted his gaze from the koala to the bartender.

'Just carried it in and plonked it on the bar did he?' Kirby was surer than ever he was being set-up.

The bartender simply raised an eyebrow and handed Kirby a glass of lemon squash.

'Thanks,' he said, but there was no gratitude in the word.

Kirby had a carry-cage, Koala-noose and hessian bag in the car and his mind raced through what he should do. All the while he could sense the tension mounting. The patrons wanted him to do something. Kirby suspected this was because they were in on the joke. The staff wanted Kirby to do something – half of them should have been off duty by now but they could not finish their chores until the koala was off the bar.

He's in a bad spot with his back against the wall like that. I will never be able to simultaneously grab him by the seat of the pants and scruff of the neck unless I shift him first.

Kirby knew there was a chance the koala, if disturbed, would climb up the shelf and destroy all the glasses. Worse still, it may jump to the floor and climb up someone's leg. He reasoned that the best thing to do was to try slipping the noose over the koala's head whilst it sat where it was. He figured that he could get a couple of people to hold the bag and that he should be able to just drop the koala in – if only he could manage to get the noose on without the koala shifting.

Heck I hope this works. This crowd will be critical of my performance and I'll have to get it right first go.

'Hey, Blue! The Fisheries and Games are here. He wants to talk to you, and he wants to talk to you now.'

Kirby glanced at the patron who had announced Blue's return from the men's room. The officer immediately, and most unfairly, labelled the messenger as ignorant. His English tweed jacket and hat indicated he was reasonably well to do, and he was not drunk. It was his reference to the Department of Fisheries and Game that got Kirby offside. That name was thirty years out of date and it was only the old-timers who knew and still used it. Kirby assumed this fellow had seen the words written on a summons he once received.

Kirby's operational planning was over and he turned to face the prime suspect. A Geelong football beanie covered his hair but, from his complexion and freckled face and forearms, Kirby had no doubt about the source of his name.

'G'day,' said Blue. 'How d'yer like me teddy?'

'I'd like him better if he wasn't in the pub. And he is a koala, a wild animal, not a teddy to be treated like a toy. When I catch him, you and I best go somewhere and have a little chat about all this.'

'Yeah, sure. Wadda bout?'

'You just wait here. I'll be back in a minute.' Kirby left to get the hessian bag and Koala-noose.

The noose was simply a lasso with a toggle in the rope that prevented it becoming too tight around the animal's neck. Dog catchers use the same sort of equipment on a stick – the stick being a pretty important part of the kit for keeping the lassoed snarling dog at an appropriate distance from tender parts of the anatomy. The Koala-noose had no stick.

When Kirby re-entered the bar, and spotlight, he had all the equipment but was still not confident his plan would work – wild animals could be so unpredictable.

'Give me a hand,' Kirby almost demanded of the bartender. He was still worried about a set-up and figured if the bartender was on his side it would be better than if he were part of the prank.

'Yeah, no worries. What do you want me to do?'

'Can you and someone else hold the bag open? This brute will wriggle lots when I get the noose 'round his neck. He'll grab anything he can. If the neck of the bag isn't properly open he'll get a hold of the top going in. We'll be in real trouble then.'

A dozen hotel patrons volunteered to hold the other side of the bag. Kirby showed the bartender how he wanted the bag kept open. The bartender obliged and his hands confidently held the other side.

'Thanks,' said Kirby, firstly to the bartender then to the owner of a massive beer gut and a second pair of hands standing opposite, on the other side of the bag.

'It's OK if I get up here isn't it?' Kirby was already three-quarters of the way up a stool onto the bar. The answer didn't matter. Kirby was up there, standing amongst the beer.

The koala stirred but it didn't shift as Kirby approached. Backed against the wall like he was he must have felt relatively safe. He was, however, vulnerable from above. Kirby half-flicked and half-dropped the noose. To the enthusiastic cheers of the hotel patrons it fell perfectly over the koala's head. There was no time to hesitate. Kirby tightened the rope by yanking upwards and out on an angle to put the koala off balance. At the same time he stepped forward. As he moved, he swung the koala off his haunches and into mid-air, leaning out from the bar himself. As Kirby predicted, the koala tried desperately to free himself – his legs thrashed about wildly. He was heavy and difficult to hold steady with outstretched arms. The rope swayed back and slashing claws waved menacingly at Kirby's legs. He needed to hurry. Despite the violent struggle the men with the sack remained calm. With the chaff bag perfectly in position Kirby lowered the koala and they had him. Kirby dropped the noose into the bag with the koala and jumped down from the bar . The saloon again erupted into cheers. This time everyone seemed to speak at once.

'What about a beer now? You've finished work.'

'How are you gunner get the rope off?'

'What are you gunner to do with him?'

'Bloody public servant. The koala weren't hurting no one.'

'I suppose you're gettin' over-time for this?'

Kirby twisted the top of the bag closed and marched outside and secured his captive in the car. He had no intention of demonstrating how to get the rope off the animal's neck and any response to the jeers and questions would have been unprofessional.

The next task was to talk to Blue. He was up for another beer and wanted Kirby to join him. Kirby just wanted to go home, but he had to clear this up first.

'Yer can talk to me 'ere,' slurred Blue propped reasonably securely on a stool.

'It might be better if we went somewhere more private.'

Kirby soon realised Blue was going nowhere—till his next call of nature—or he fell unconscious to the floor. Kirby was not sure which would come first and decided not to press his luck. He simply asked his questions with the multitude listening to every word.

'Did you really just carry the koala in here?' Kirby calmly inquired over his lemon squash.

'Sure I did. Why?'

'Well, didn't it scratch or bite?'

'Nup. Why should it? I wasn't gunner hurt it.'

'Well the bar isn't really the place for a koala. You mightn't have intended hurting it, but it didn't know that. What were you going to do with it?'

'Just show it to the boys. Then I'd take it out the bush and let it go.'

'Where did you get it?'

'Found it beside the road at Ondit Flat, near the river.' Blue kicked at a flap of carpet that had come up. He would not meet Kirby's eyes.

'When was this?' the officer continued.

'Five or ten minutes before I got here, then you came down a bit after that.'

'You drove here then?' Kirby asked, raising an eyebrow.

'Sure I did. Too drunk to walk.' Blue was blatantly honest.

'I want you to understand something,' said Kirby. 'Koalas are protected. You can't just go 'round picking them up, carting them about in your car and parading them for your mates in the pub. It's illegal. You could be fined very heavily for this sort of thing and besides, they can be dangerous. You're lucky it didn't tear you to bits. What explanation can you give for having the koala in your possession?'

Blue sat up straight and tried to pull in his stomach.

'Well,' he began, then stopped.

Blue thought hard as he leaned towards Kirby and breathed beer and cigarettes into his interrogator's face. Their eyes met and time stood still for a moment. Just when it appeared Blue would topple off the stool he regained his balance and continued speaking. The time-delayed explanation unfolded as Blue fought to enunciate his words through blurred and sticky thought processes.

'If I'd left it beside the road it would'a got run over and kilt. It looked lost. I thought I was doin' the right thing.'

Blue's good posture soon disappeared. He slumped down and again nearly fell off the stool. Kirby had just heard a true confession and he put down his squash. Blue was so intoxicated he could never have made up the story and Kirby finished their little chat by recording the details from Blue's Driver Licence and giving a stern and solemn pronunciation: 'This matter will be reported.'

Kirby knew the consequence of the statement did not sink in.

By now the booze, the cricket and the horse racing on Sky Channel held the attention of the other patrons. Few, if any, were aware of Kirby's departure. Out at the car he made sure the lump in the bag was still breathing then drove out of town to the Mount Monea Forest. There, with no audience except Mother Nature herself, he untied the string he had used to secure the neck of the bag. From the time Kirby had dropped the noose in with the koala the rope had been loose. With no tension to hinder it, the koala had, as he expected, slipped its head free.

This had been a pretty slick operation. Kirby had never seen a koala in a pub before but his plan on how to get it out worked perfectly.

He felt proud that his training and experience had been so well applied – all it took was a little common sense. He'd done his bit for conservation and felt sure the koala would thank him, if it could talk.

Kirby knew the ordeal would have disoriented the animal so he selected the release site carefully. He lay the bag on the ground facing a large Manna Gum and stood quietly at the other end, leaning over to hold the neck open so the koala could see out. It took half a minute or so for it to register that it could simply walk free. Suddenly it lurched out of the bag and sprang up. It tightly clasped the tree trunk about fifteen centimetres above the ground. From there it scrambled quickly up to the first branch, about half a metre above Kirby's head. At that position the old bull stopped and turned around. In the bar he had been half asleep and indifferent to his human company. Now he was wide awake and his brown eyes pierced down at Kirby. He held the officer's gaze. Kirby blinked first. The koala immediately let out an awful pig like grunt, turned his dirty white rump and climbed away.

'And in yours too,' Kirby said out loud. 'I was only trying to help.'

Chapter 15

OUT OF THE MOUTHS OF BABES

The next four months proved uneventful. The duck season and the quail season came and went without incident and Kirby was beginning to think the role of officer in charge at Costerfield lacked challenge and excitement. He had expected the posting would involve more of a balance between fisheries and wildlife work, but so far he had been disappointed.

The telephone rang at first light one Sunday morning in July.

'Hello, Kirby,' a stranger's voice said cheerfully as though he and Kirby were old school buddies. 'It's Robin Alder speaking. Remember me? We met a couple of months ago.'

Kirby pretended to remember but it was some hours later that he recalled that Robin Alder sold used cars. They met when Kirby had a new muffler fitted to his old Holden at the yard where Robin worked. Whilst Kirby waited to pick up the car at the end of the job, Robin had unsuccessfully tried to interest Kirby in a second-hand Volvo 264 GLE.

'Look,' said Robin, 'I'm standing in my lounge-room and watching two blokes in a boat on Lake Bangerang. They're hauling an illegal mesh net.'

'Where exactly?' Kirby asked.

'Directly south of here,' Robin advised. 'About two hundred and seventy five metres from my boundary fence.'

Robin's directions were fantastic – had Kirby known the identity and address of his caller. He knew neither.

'How exactly do you suggest I get into the area without being spotted?' Kirby asked. He hoped he had contrived his question in a way that would remove the embarrassment about not recognising his caller.

After scribbling down the suggested directions Kirby hurriedly dressed then flew outside to catch the villains. In addition to the obvious fish protection issue, publicity about a good netting case was always helpful in building the department's image with the angling fraternity. These cases were an opportunity to re-enforce the need for public cooperation in giving precise, up-to-date information about illegal fishing.

Kirby knew he was running out of time. If these two were already hauling the net, their illegal activity would soon finish and they would disappear. The obvious problem this presented occupied the inspector's mind as he hurried to get into a position to make the pinch. His directions took him towards the lake through a gate and across a private paddock, through another gate and down towards the water. As he bumped his way across the field Kirby realised he would be able to approach quite close to the lake by driving behind a boxthorn hedge. This path took him in direct view of the farmer's house, but he would be invisible from the lake, provided he travelled slowly and made no disturbance.

After parking his car, Kirby peered around the end of the hedge and watched the offenders through binoculars. He made notes of what he saw and these included a description of the two suspects, their clothing and their actions. Kirby could see the net being hauled and fish being untangled. He was confident his observations were sufficient for a conviction except for some missing evidence – he had no idea who the men were, where they had launched their boat or how he could intercept them. There was no boat ramp for miles and he had to drive for five minutes just to get back to the road. Kirby was beginning to despair when he realised he was about to have a visitor.

He looked away from the lake at a utility approaching from the direction of the farmhouse. Its speed was a little more than casual and on the back was a young girl. Kirby guessed the driver to be the farmer – just a little annoyed.

'What the hell do you think you're doin' driving around in me paddock, without permission, at this hour on a Sund'y mornin'?' The farmer bellowed at Kirby through the open driver-side window.

'Kirby Wellington's the name.' The inspector held up his

identification card. 'I'm the local Fisheries Inspector. I had a complaint about netting in the lake and I'm more than a little interested in those two out there in the boat. I don't suppose you know who they are?'

Kirby hoped his question would prompt an answer giving the vital piece of information and allow him to get into position to intercept the offenders. Without some help Kirby knew it was unlikely he could accomplish his mission. Perhaps the farmer could tell him where the boat had been launched or give him directions on where he could wait to have the best chance of success.

'Wouldn't 'ave a clue,' the farmer replied.

'Yes you do Daddy.' Kirby heard the little girl's indignant voice from the back of the utility. 'It's Uncle Bill.'

Without another word the farmer put the utility into gear and the vehicle disappeared back towards the house in as much haste as it arrived. Then, within a minute of the betrayal, the hauling of the net was completed. Kirby sat waiting and still wondering where the reprobates would go and how he could get to them when they started their motor. To his surprise, instead of steaming off to the far side of the lake, the boat came directly to shore. As he watched, still from behind the boxthorn hedge, the boat beached and the suspects stepped out, less than a hundred metres away. What luck!

Uncle Bill and his mate left everything and began to walk towards the farmhouse where, Kirby later learned, they had parked their car. The officer made some mental calculations and when he estimated he could drive to the boat faster than they could run back, he emerged from the boxthorns travelling at the speed of the farmer's retreat.

The villains had seen the farmer drive across the paddock and in behind the hedge a few minutes before. This was of no concern – they knew that it was his paddock and they obviously knew him well. But what was this unknown car approaching from where the farmer had just been? They stopped walking and stood watching in surprise.

'Nice morning gentlemen,' Kirby said as he pulled up beside them. 'My name's Kirby Wellington and I'm a Fisheries Inspector. How about I give you a ride back to your boat?'

Kirby reached behind and opened the door. Two submissive offenders climbed in without speaking. The transport of two suspects in this way was clearly contrary to the Occupation Health and Safety section in the manual. It was very dangerous to have two offenders seated in rear seat and one officer in the front, driving and unable to watch or keep control of his suspects. Kirby remembered the manual as the door closed and he cursed himself silently. It was obvious that his half-smart introduction and laissez faire approach made him very vulnerable to attack – he certainly was not in control. In order to minimise his already compromised position Kirby kept half-turned in his seat while he drove the short distance to the boat.

William Neil Robertson and his mate had caught over one thousand mullet and with so many fish to untangle from the net they had taken far longer than expected to get off the water. To make matters worse for them, the fish weighed too much for them to carry back to the farmhouse. Uncle Bill and his mate were walking to get their car to transport the booty when Kirby intercepted them. Had it not been for their lucky catch the illegal activity would have finished before Kirby left home, perhaps even before Robin Alder saw them from his lounge-room window.

Chapter 16

THE ARMADILLO

'The Armadillo's just tied up,' Murray Stephens said excitedly when he rang Kirby in October. 'I want you to get down to the bay and get down there fast!'

This was red-hot information and Murray's instructions left no room for protest. It was already evening and Kirby did not want to go. It was his birthday and he and Conrad Holmes had only just arrived back in Costerfield after a long day on patrol. They were about to sit down to a roast dinner and celebratory drink. Murray's reaction to Kirby's protest demonstrated a total lack of humour or compassion – he didn't even say 'Happy birthday.'

Neither Kirby or Conrad had ever seen the Armadillo but they both knew of her infamous poaching exploits in several Australian states. The boat was larger than the run of the mill abalone boat and Alan Akers had connections down the bay. This was not the first time the boat had come into that port to unload the illegal catch.

On the previous occasion Martin Stein and several colleagues had acted on a tip off and raided the boat whilst it was berthed at the pier. On board they found huge numbers of frozen abalone and Alan Akers and Guy Dowling asleep. During the interrogation the suspects remained silent in response to most questions, especially questions about where the abalone had come from. They did however, adamantly insist their actions were legitimate.

'We're only in port seeking refuge and safety,' Alan claimed. 'We've come into the bay because of the terrible weather conditions in Bass

Strait. You'd know the Captain is responsible for all the lives on his boat.'

Martin seized the abalone and Murray Stephens issued legal proceedings against the two poachers. The charges included the unlicensed taking and possession of abalone. In court Murray relied on a reversed legal onus that required the suspects to prove where the abalone came from.

In court they did exactly that. During cross-examination of the prosecution witnesses the defence established the basis of their story. The boat had freezers on board and was capable of staying at sea for extended periods. It could even travel from the legal jurisdiction of New South Wales through Victoria and into Tasmania all in one day. In eastern Victoria the boundary with Tasmania is at thirty-nine degrees twelve minutes South Latitude, only a few nautical miles south of the Wilsons Promontory Lighthouse. The Hogan and Flinders Island groups in Bass Strait are excellent abalone habitat and close enough to Victoria for a day trip in a decent run-about. It was soon obvious the defence were going to argue that the origin of the abalone was in Tasmania, or perhaps New South Wales. Murray, Martin and the other prosecution witnesses began to sense the court would have to give the benefit of the doubt to the defendants.

The case for the defence included some intense drama with vivid descriptions of the high seas and near loss of the boat and the lives of the men who sailed on her. A pressing necessity existed for them being in Victoria. Everyone was exhausted after the brush with death and the crew had fallen to sleep soon after the boat tied up. The writing was on the wall and the court was left with no alternative – all charges were dismissed.

Murray did not want that to happen again and he was adamant about how Kirby and Conrad should handle this new case.

'Don't go near that boat 'til they start to unload,' he instructed. 'Then there'll be no arguments about what they're doing with the abs. Book everyone involved, including the truck driver. Seize the diving equipment. Oh, yes – someone said the boat's got a new name. It's called the White Wolf now I think. Keep me informed, we don't want to blow this one. All of Australia's watching the department's performance with these fellows.'

Nicky was ready to dish up the roast and pour the wine before Kirby got off the phone.

'Every time I cook a roast you get called to work,' she said when she realised Kirby and Conrad were leaving immediately. 'All that work for nothing . Look at the waste of food.'

'It'll keep. I'm not too proud to eat roast reheated in the microwave.'

'What about the wine? It's already open.'

'Don't get drunk,' Kirby teased. 'I'm not sure when we'll be back.'

'I'm never going to cook you a roast again. You'd better watch it. I just might drink the whole bottle myself.'

It was well after dark when the men arrived at the port. Kirby parked in the main street amongst the cars outside the hotel. The officers then made their way carefully through the parkland towards the jetty, hugging the shadows cast by the street lighting.

'This'll do,' Kirby suggested. 'There's not a better spot to watch from than here – not too far back to the car and a perfect view of the jetty.'

They stopped at the base of a large bushy tree. At the same time both officers began to scour the seascape with binoculars.

'There she is,' Kirby exclaimed. 'Tied up on the left-hand end. You can see a bit of the wheelhouse and some superstructure above the jetty outline.'

The boat had several lights burning but there was no movement on board. Kirby and Conrad waited, discussing the missed roast and Taylors 1995 Cabernet Sauvignon. A few minutes after ten, three shadowy figures walked from the hotel, down from the main street, along the jetty and directly on board.

'There'll be some action pretty soon,' Kirby observed expectantly.

There was – after another ten minutes the lights went out.

Nothing stirred during the next hour.

'I'm positive it'll be just before dawn before we need to do anything,' Kirby suggested. 'I'm going to ring Murray Stephens and see if he agrees to us getting some sleep.'

'Bloody oath,' Conrad agreed.

Kirby's call got Murray out of bed.

'Conrad and I should go back to Costerfield,' Kirby propositioned. 'We can get a few hours sleep and be bright-eyed and bushy-tailed when the action starts. If we're back here by four-thirty I guarantee we'll be in time.'

'OK,' Murray reluctantly agreed. 'But if you muck this up I'll kick your backsides 'til your noses bleed. On second thoughts, if you muck this up, don't bother reporting for work tomorrow.'

Kirby got to bed about midnight and set the alarm for four. The two officers were back at the bay thirty-five minutes after the alarm. Their car was pretty obvious now – it was the only one parked in the street. They left it there for want of a better place to hide it.

Back at the surveillance tree the officers were shattered – the Armadillo had disappeared! Kirby's stomach was instantly in a knot.

'Hell, what are we gunner do?' he asked not expecting Conrad to have an answer. 'Murray said if we mucked this up we needn't bother reporting for work this morning. Rats! I wish we'd stayed here all night. This job's got to be worth a hundred sleepless nights.'

'There she is!' Conrad suddenly exclaimed.

The design of the pier provided shelter for moored boats between the arms of the jetty but, on the outside of the seaward wall where the Armadillo had been lying there was no such protection. The outer position had some advantages though, should there be a need for a rapid departure. Tying up where she had been removed the potential navigation hazards caused by mooring lines and anchor ropes from other boats.

During the night a breeze had sprung up from the east and caused the boat to bump uncomfortably into the jetty. The crew had simply steamed off a hundred metres and dropped anchor. She was still in that position when Conrad saw her, her white riding light shining like a beacon for the whole world to see. Kirby was delighted he would not suffer a bloody nose or become responsible for increasing the length of the unemployment queues.

'The abs will still be on board, don't you reckon?' Kirby asked. He needed reassurance.

'Yeah, 'course they will,' Conrad replied. 'Why don't we shift the car down to the toilet block on The Esplanade? Whilst she's at anchor off the pier the car'll be more comfortable to sit in than on this wet grass. There'll be plenty of time to shift when the boat's lights come on, or the anchor's hauled or a suspicious looking vehicle arrives. We're not getting paid to be uncomfortable and the car'll be OK parked by the dunny. It'll be less suspicious there than where it is up in the street I reckon.'

'Not a bad idea,' Kirby agreed.

As senior officer he realised he would take the blame if the job was blown and his initial reaction to that possibility was one of shock. He simply was not thinking clearly and he realised Conrad had taken control for the moment. When they had parked down at The Esplanade he went for a walk to try to re-focus.

When Kirby got back into the car Conrad was in a deep relationship with his binoculars. The sky was just showing the first signs of light to herald the dawn.

'She's in a lot better condition than I thought she'd be,' mused Conrad as he adjusted his binocular lens to concentrate harder on the boat. 'Must've been up on the slip recently for a re-fit, probably when they changed the name from Armadillo to White Wolf. Must be money in abalone.'

Kirby used his binoculars too. The boat was sparkling and a deal larger than he expected. With a breeze still from the east she had her bow directly away from the officers but in the gentle air movement the boat swung quietly on the anchor revealing a better view of her port side. In that position, with daylight approaching, the registration number painted near the bow became increasingly visible.

'I'll be able to read the number soon,' Conrad said. His statement conveyed real progress in the investigation. 'Write down the time in your note book. It's er 'F', er, um, 'FWD 001'.'

'FWD 001,' Kirby exclaimed. 'That registration number belongs to a departmental boat.'

The Armadillo wasn't really the Armadillo – it was the Fisheries and Wildlife Department's brand new marine research vessel on sea trials.

Chapter 17

THE ORPHAN KOALA

The next Saturday, Kirby's day off, was ruined again. He was particularly annoyed when it happened as he had been in the shadehouse with his cymbidiums. The job and the children gave him very little time to spend on his hobbies and ever since the shift from Mafeking Bay Kirby's orchids had been neglected. Several had split their plastic pots. These and half a dozen others should have been re-potted before Christmas, not in the middle of the year. Kirby washed his hands and went in to answer another call about a koala.

'It's Karen Fitzgerald calling,' a pleasant voice advised. 'About half an hour ago, when I was driving towards Cornishtown, I found a baby koala in the pouch of its mother that had been killed on the road. Can you tell me how to look after it?'

'Where is it now?' Kirby asked.

'I've got it with me,' Karen said. 'Well, it's in my car, wrapped in a jumper on the front seat. I'm in a phone box, still in town. I've got to do the grocery shopping, then I'll be going home when I've finished. But don't worry, it's a beautiful sunny day and the car's nice and warm.'

'How big is it?'

'Not very big. It's pretty little really.'

'Has it got any fur?' Kirby continued, still trying to determine the extent of his problem. Karen's information about size, and therefore the age of the orphan, had not been at all helpful.

'No. It looks a bit like a baby mouse, pink, without a tail or fur.'

Kirby's heart dropped.

117

'It's tiny then,' Kirby said, conscious that his policy of honesty in relation to sick, injured and orphaned wildlife sometimes hurt. 'I don't think the poor thing will survive. It's way too young.'

I wish I didn't have to give bad news to people wanting to help. This is another hopeless case.

'If the poor thing's got any chance I'd like to give it a go – if you'll tell me what to do.'

Kirby gave what advice he could about an appropriate milk formula, the dangers of scours, the importance of warmth and the need for a surrogate mother.

'You know baby koalas in the pouch will not have bowel movements unless the mother gives the OK. They do this by licking the baby's bottom. I don't suggest you do that, but if you don't do something to make your koala go to the toilet it will die. A tissue soaked in warm water and wiped over its private parts will do the trick. That little tacker will need constant love, company and intensive care.'

Kirby gave Karen verbal permission to keep the protected animal whilst she cared for it. The officer believed the orphan would be dead within forty-eight hours and therefore the question about the letter of the law and his permission would never be a problem.

'It will be best if we officially put this in our volunteer wildlife shelter record,' he nevertheless suggested. 'I'd best have your name and address for the book. Oh, and your phone number please.'

'We don't have the phone on. I'm ringing from a phone box, remember?' Karen went on to explain that her home was on a remote farm at Diggora South. She explained how to get there but Kirby didn't even bother to write that down.

'I'll send you some written information on the care of sick injured and orphaned wildlife from the office on Monday,' Kirby promised when he finished the paperwork. 'Good luck with the koala, and thanks for your help.'

Back at his orchids Kirby worried about the baby koala. Thoughts of it dying took his mind to a kookaburra, with a badly broken wing, brought into the office the previous day. Smashed and splintered bone protruded through the flesh. Kirby had considered veterinary treatment but the cost and the on-going expense of rehabilitation were out of the question. Birds with such severe wing injuries never fly or fend for themselves again. With or without amputation the kookaburra would have been confined to life imprisonment. Such a life would then involve someone committed to daily care, expense and trouble.

Kirby's judgement to put the kookaburra down was only made

after reference to a comprehensive chapter in the manual. This looked objectively at general conservation values based on an analysis of costs and benefits. The kookaburra was not endangered, or even rare, and the value of an individual bird would not rate a mention in any economic rationalism debate. The baby koala was notable and unique, but that species was not endangered either. Kirby knew he could not have justified driving eighty odd kilometres out to Diggora South to collect an orphan that would die in his care anyway. On this basis he convinced himself he had done all he could for Karen Fitzgerald's baby koala – he then promptly forgot about it.

At the height of the next summer Kirby found himself on the grizzly task of collecting koalas burnt in bush-fires that ravaged the Diggora South area. Some were already dead and some he took for veterinary treatment and rehabilitation by the local Field Naturalist Club. Some had to be put down. This was a very distressing part of the job.

During the afternoon on the third day Kirby drove along a very stony, rough dirt track towards a farmhouse where he intended to request permission to drive over paddocks to inspect an isolated patch of bush where he knew there would be more causalities. Kirby parked where the track ended in a strip of bare earth between an old shed and a gateway.

The fires had been particularly bad and several brick homes had been destroyed. In the Diggora South area the loss of outbuildings, fencing and stock was enormous but the improvements on this farm seemed to be relatively intact. A walking path led through an arch, overgrown by a climbing rose. As he moved towards the house Kirby marvelled the whole place had not gone up. The garden was a jungle but the fire had simply by-passed it. A rough stringy-bark pole pergola held up a glory vine. The pergola and a nearby garden shed were covered and the vine had clawed its way up every plant it could reach. It stretched to the top of a monstrous cotoneaster bush and a silky oak. Amongst the shrubbery a camellia, reaching upwards for light, had grown tall and spindly. Despite the pergola's best efforts Kirby still had to duck under the vegetation as he walked. He rounded a curve in the path and found himself a few metres from the farmhouse door. Kirby knocked and as he waited realised the old fibro-cement house was like a lot of homes on farms – the door he approached was the back door.

When Karen Fitzgerald answered his knock Kirby did not recognise her.

'Good afternoon Madame. I'm Kirby Wellington, a Wildlife Officer and I'm looking for koalas burnt in the fires. I was wondering if … '

'Kirby,' she interrupted. 'How good to meet you. I'm Karen Fitzgerald. You might remember me. I rang you ages ago about a baby koala I found when its mother got killed by a car. You told me how to look after it and wrote my name in your book. Please come in.'

Karen's words were soft and gentle but somehow her request was a command. Kirby obeyed a lady who was about fifty-five years old and her face, like her voice, was very pleasant and amiable. Her hands though, told a different story – one of hard work on a farm. Kirby liked her immediately. In the large entrance foyer Karen took a woollen bag down from a peg where it hung between hats and coats on the wall. She reached inside and drew out the most adorable and friendly female koala imaginable. It was absolutely gorgeous.

'Meet Cuddles.' Karen said handing Kirby the soft, warm bundle of fur.

'Is this the koala?'

'It certainly is. Isn't she lovely?'

'How did you manage to raise the little mite? Did you take my advice and use an electric frypan to keep it warm?'

'No, we don't have the SEC on. The only electricity we have is from a 32 volt lighting plant that we cannot use for cooking. But I did what you said about being its mother. I carried it around with me the whole time. I even took it to bed. I made a special pouch that fitted between the cups on my bra, then when it grew I made a bigger pouch that fitted outside my clothes. Just as well baby koalas don't go to the toilet till you want them too, isn't it?'

'That's amazing,' Kirby said remembering the farm had no phone either.

The two continued to chat as Kirby nursed Cuddles and Karen percolated coffee in a pot on the wood stove. An urn boiled on the hob and the smell of the coffee mingled with the aroma of yeast from bread that was baking in the oven. Everywhere Kirby looked he saw Karen's special touches in what was otherwise a very basic home. He asked about the macramé, embroidery and knitting. They were all her work. She took a beautiful loaf of bread out of the oven and Kirby marvelled how she continued to work whilst she waited on him. The company and the incense and ambience of Karen's kitchen made the coffee and peanut cookies very pleasant indeed.

After that day Kirby called in and saw Karen whenever he was in the Diggora area. On his visits Karen relayed all the events in Cuddle's life. After the koala was released in the bush it never roamed far from the house and it never forgot its mother. When Karen called, Cuddles would come down from her tree and demand a cuddle. Even when she mated with a totally wild male, Cuddles did not leave the immediate area and the little orphan eventually became a mother. The next telephone call from Karen was a plea for help.

'About eight weeks ago we had a terrible storm out here,' Karen explained. 'I'm afraid there has been a disaster. The morning after the storm I found Cuddle's baby lying on the ground under her favourite tree. The baby was nearly dead and Cuddles would not take her back. The baby was very weak, too weak to cling to Cuddles and I had to take it in. It's OK now but Cuddles still won't have a bar of it. I've tried everything. Look I'm sorry but I just can't go through all that work looking after another baby koala 'til it is old enough for release. I would but Jack has a broken leg. We start shearing on Monday and I'm going to have to do all the mustering and all the cooking for the shearers by myself. I just won't be able to do a thing more for the next five or six weeks. Could you please come and get her?'

When Kirby picked up the baby it was about the size of a small kitten and just as cute as its mother had been when he first saw her. Kirby took the baby home and kept it overnight. Zac and Kylie were delighted. Nicky was not. Every three hours through the night Kirby got up and nursed and fed the koala so that it did not keep everyone else awake with its pitifully little cries. The next morning Kirby made arrangements for the Melbourne Zoo's Animal Nursery to raise the baby. That afternoon he drove to Melbourne with the koala sitting on his shoulder all the way. Nobody noticed until he stopped at traffic lights at the end of the freeway.

As he sat waiting a young lady in a red BMW stopped beside him in the next lane. She looked and saw the koala. That adorable baby visibly delighted the other driver and Kirby shared her pleasure as their eyes met for a moment. The lights changed and the BMW disappeared into the traffic, its driver pursuing some unknown destiny. Kirby slowly drove the last few kilometres and turned into the zoo's vehicle entrance.

After he delivered the orphan to the staff in the animal nursery Kirby drove home and on the way thought about the little koala. It had no choice about going to the city. In the circumstances it was the only place that offered a decent life, but what sort of a life was it going to be? It was alive but the koala would never know its real potential. Kirby's thoughts turned to Karen Fitzgerald.

Did such a capable person fulfil her potential on a farm? He thought she did, but realised that values differed between the city and the country.

The city seemed to offer everything at the expense of the country. The bureaucrats pushed economic rationalism to the point that nothing else mattered. Society seemed content that the best opportunities in education, employment and the arts and culture were in the city. Kirby suddenly felt like a traitor.

I'm no better. I took the easy option. I took the orphan away from the country because it stood no chance there – but what's its chance at the zoo?

The girl in the BMW had a moment of pleasure in a fleeting experience. Hundreds, perhaps thousands would also get some enjoyment seeing the baby koala in the animal nursery but nobody would know the truth about the koala or Karen Fitzgerald.

Does any of that matter anyway? Kirby wondered.

Chapter 18

BIRD'S EGGS

Murray Stephens rang Kirby on the following Monday and told him that Howard Koren had sacked MT Morrison from his job at the XLCR Bird Supply.

'Couldn't have happened to a nicer bloke.' Kirby was smiling.

'The only reason I have told you is because MT is supposed to have moved back to live in Costerfield,' Murray continued. 'You remember he used to live up that way don't you? His family had a farm out Diggora way I think.'

'It's August, not April Fool's Day.' Somehow he knew Murray was not joking.

'Check it out will you? Let me know what you find out.'

Kirby immediately rang Carl Goldick the local sergeant of police and gave him the run down on MT.

'Have the police heard anything about him shifting back to Costerfield?'

'Funny you should ring,' the sergeant said. 'I'm just organising a search warrant to do over the old house in Booroopki Road. A Max Morrison is supposed to have shifted in there and we've had a tip off that we might find a few chainsaws he can't account for. Do you want to come? I could get your name on the warrant because of all his prior convictions with your department.'

'I'd love to come.'

That night Kirby read through the chapter on search warrants in the manual and next morning arrived at the police station as arranged. He followed the police car out towards Booroopki and they pulled up outside a ramshackle old house on the outskirts of Costerfield.

Sure looks like the sort of place MT would live in, Kirby thought as Sergeant Goldick knocked on the door. MT eventually answered.

'Over the years,' MT began, 'I've learned a few things about youse blokes in authority. Yer reckon yer can walk all over us little people. I insist on checkin' the bona fides o' that there document before lettin' yers in me 'ouse. Anyway, the missus is in the bath. Yer can't come in.'

'We will not go in the bathroom,' Sergeant Goldick guaranteed him, 'Until your wife has finished and is dressed. In the meantime we will search the rest of the premises.'

He handed MT the execution copy of the warrant and pushed through the doorway, ignoring the protests.

'I understand you already know Kirby Wellington,' the sergeant said as Kirby entered next in line.

MT just stood looking, his mouth wide open. Kirby wasn't sure if it was his unexpected entry or the two burly police officers following close behind that destroyed MT's inclination for sustained objection.

'Good-morning Mr Morrison. It is nice to see you again.' Kirby knew he shouldn't lie.

The search failed to locate any chainsaws but the police who were present congratulated Kirby on his description of MT – an untrustworthy, consummate liar. The bath contained a substantial build-up of dirt and dust and it was obvious it had not been used since well before the Morrisons moved from Melbourne.

In the lounge-room was a large collection of bird's eggs housed in two cabinets beautifully crafted from Tasmanian Blackwood. The cabinets were a pair and each had two sides containing eight trays apiece. Each tray contained bird's eggs, graded for size and intricately catalogued by number. Kirby's previous tales, and MT's lie about the bath, left the police with an immediate and resolute suspicion that the cabinets were stolen, or unlawfully obtained. Kirby recognised some of the egg species and would have taken all bets that every egg was illegal because their origins were from protected Australian bird species.

'Mr Morrison,' Sergeant Goldick said. 'I believe these cabinets are stolen or unlawfully obtained. Where did you get them?'

'Bloody typical,' MT growled. 'A man can't win with youse blokes. What 'appened to the bit about a man bein' innocent 'til proved guilty? Eh? Youse reckon I'm guilty before yer start. I bet that bloody wildlife officer's filled yer head with crap 'bout me. Them cabinets is legit.'

'Can you produce a receipt for their purchase?' The sergeant was quietly confident.

'Course I bloody can't. Wot do yer reckon? I've just shifted from Melbourne and most of me stuff's still in boxes. 'Ave a look round the joint. I wouldn't know where t' start.'

'Well where did you purchase them?' Sergeant Goldick was now even more confident.

'Ask him,' MT said indignantly, pointing at Kirby. 'I used ta work at the trash and treasure markets in town. He knows I'm tellin' the truth. He knows I used t' work for a crowd what went round the clearin' sales up country and bought up this sort a thing. He knows I woulda got 'em legit. Ring me old boss. He'll remember.'

MT searched in his wallet and handed the sergeant a very dirty, very tatty old business card.

'What do you think Kirby?' Sergeant Goldick whispered so that MT could not hear.

'He certainly worked at the trash and treasure markets in Melbourne. I very much doubt MT purchased these though. More likely they fell off the back of the truck when he was supposed to be delivering them for someone if you ask me. Just in case though, why don't I seize them under the Wildlife Act? I can because of the eggs. You could then make some more inquiries.'

'Splendid idea. Go for it.'

Kirby seized the cabinets and eggs and questioned MT.

'I already told yer,' MT insisted. 'Them cabinets is legit and the eggs were in 'em when I got 'em. If yer really gunner seize 'em I'll be gettin' damages in court – against the police an' you personally.'

Sergeant Goldick made telephone contact with MT's old boss the next day.

'Yes,' he said. 'I remember those cabinets. Beautiful pieces. I got them for a song at an executor's auction up in the Mallee. Max wanted 'em and I let him have 'em in lieu of wages for a week. I did OK out of it and he was happy.'

The police decided to let Kirby run with the prosecution under the Wildlife Act and MT was in trouble again. Dr Groote, Curator of Birds at the Melbourne Museum, went to a great deal of painstaking research and effort to identify the eggs on the understanding that the collection would be donated to the Museum at the end of the court case, provided of course that the Crown won.

When Dr Groote finished there were over one hundred and fifty individual species named and a number of others identified, but only to the level of their genus. The collection contained many multiple specimens and when Kirby sent out the summons for service there was an absolute mountain of paper work. The first charge related to possession of eleven Welcome Swallow eggs, the next to seven Eastern Striated Pardalote eggs and so on through all the species. The last two charges were for five Wedge-tailed Eagle eggs and three Emu eggs.

When the court date arrived Kirby's parents were staying at Costerfield and Kirby invited them to come to court and watch their son the prosecutor in action – sort of like barracking at the footy.

The clerk called the case last and by this time the courtroom was nearly empty, except for Des and Flora Wellington, sitting at the back. Flora was knitting. Kirby began his opening address and the Magistrate stopped him. His attention was clearly on the clicking needles at the back of the room. He left no doubt such enterprise amounted to contempt for the hallowed institution of the legal system. Kirby already knew contempt of court was serious, but did not realise that knitting constituted one of the proofs. When the Magistrate started a lecture on just how serious it was, Kirby's parents began a sharp learning curve on courtroom etiquette.

The Magistrate was eventually benevolent and he let Flora off with a warning. The interruption had done little for Kirby's composure though, and his face was burning red. Members of the public in court are usually there to support the defendant and no one suspected any connection between the contemptuous knitter and the person in uniform standing at the bar table.

Kirby spluttered his way through the rest of his opening and the court's attention then turned to the defence. This helped relieve the prosecutor's discomfort – the Magistrate now had the lawyer in his sights.

The court file contained a copy of Dr Groote's witness summons addressed to 'The Curator of Birds, Melbourne Museum'. The Magistrate saw this and knew it meant a long, tedious case arguing about infinitesimal differences between some of the species of eggs. He also knew this did little for the prospects of an early finish for the day and a game of golf. MT had engaged Charles Ralph William-Peterson to defend him and the lawyer had a reputation for making cases drag on. The Magistrate knew Charles Ralph William-Peterson and what his appearance in a contested case meant for an easy day on the bench.

'Don't you realise Australia's leading authority on birds eggs has been issued with a subpoena?' the Magistrate asked. 'Dr Groote is appearing for the prosecution and it would appear the identity of the species will not be challenged. Is the defence on the basis that your client was not in actual physical possession of the eggs?'

'No on the basis that the prosecution cannot prove guilty knowledge,' the lawyer explained. 'My client had no mens rea, Your Honour. The collection of eggs was purchased from a deceased estate. I am sure the prosecution will agree those are the facts in the case.'

'Are you saying your client did not realise the eggs were in the estate?' the Magistrate challenged.

'He knew the eggs were there but he had no knowledge of the species,' the lawyer explained.

'You can't tell me he thought they were chook eggs, Mr Peterson. I don't have to tell you about wilful blindness. I suggest you think very carefully about the advice you give your client.'

Charles Ralph William-Peterson asked for a short adjournment then sought the court's permission to change the plea to guilty. Kirby gave a summary of the evidence, the charges were proven and MT was convicted and fined on the basis of $2 an egg. This amounted to a considerable fine but, even with all his prior convictions, the case was not serious enough to have MT imprisoned.

'Inspector Wellington,' the Magistrate interrupted as MT and Charles Ralph William-Peterson began to leave the room after the court adjourned for the day. 'I wonder could I see you in chambers?'

Kirby left the remainder of his references and the papers from the file on the bar table and followed the Magistrate through a door marked 'STRICTLY PRIVATE'.

'Don't ever do that to me again,' he instructed when the two men were alone.

Kirby's mind turned to the knitting and contempt of court. *Perhaps the Magistrate is aware of my close relationship with the offender. Perhaps he is going to charge me with being an accessory to the crime?*

'It is going to take me a couple of hours to make all the entries in the court register,' the Magistrate growled. 'You could have reduced the number of charges to ten or twenty, at most, by putting several species on each charge sheet.'

'But,' Kirby protested, 'if I did that and the defence raised sufficient doubt about the identity of one species in any one charge I would lose that whole charge, including all the other species on it.'

The Magistrate was not listening. He had a mountain of results to key into the computer, and was still optimistic about a few holes of golf.

Chapter 19

THE FERAL CAT

The Straw Necked Ibis rookery on Coromby Island in Lake Bangerang had been dwindling in size for years. Several species of cormorants, swans and Australian Pelicans also made the island home and constructed rookeries and nests there. With no predators on the island, and unlimited access to the larder of young birds in springtime, a feral cat population exploded. The department blamed both cats and foxes for poor breeding success and this triggered an official eradication campaign.

In reality, a rickets type ailment associated with residual poisoning was the problem. No one suspected this until Melbourne University published research results that revealed the truth associated with bygone farming practices when DDT (dichlor-diphenyl trichlorethane) was a commonly used insecticide in the rural war against Cockchafer Grubs in pasture. Unfortunately the ibis fed in the paddocks contaminated by the DDT and this resulted in an accumulating calcium deficiency in each subsequent generation of ibis. The parent bird's lack of calcium caused many eggs to break during incubation. The young that did hatch often had such acute calcium deficiency their body weight simply broke their legs when they tried to stand. Death was painful and slow – unless a feral cat or fox ended the suffering.

Like all wildlife officers Kirby and Conrad had an anti-cat disposition, based largely on an understanding of how feral cats threaten the very existence of some small species of native fauna. A considerable number of the general public fail to give the cat in the Australian bush the notoriety it deserves. John Williamson's song, 'Bill the Cat', helped promote the cause through the story of the well-fed family puss eating the budgie – even after the vet removed his man-hood. Cats also eat parrots, Fairy Wrens and young birds of any species.

Well before the CSIRO and John Williamson exposed the feral cat's antecedents, wildlife officers had pushed the anti-cat cause in a barbaric way, partly through their definition of a feral cat – 'any feline off the front veranda.' This was really meant as a joke but it became especially sordid when coupled with an in-house competition for the largest cat skin. Some argued these things simply demonstrated a dedication to duty – the protection of Australia's native fauna but others were not so magnanimous.

Over the years the cat skin competition became a favourite topic of conversation between officers, especially the disqualification of one entrant who resorted to foul play in his attempts to win. Lindsay Blackall, the officer from Costerfield before Martin Stein, knew of a cat large enough to eat two honeyeaters, four geckos and a Feather-tail Glider in one meal. He reasoned such a cat must have a skin large enough to take the prize. To be sure though, he decided to experiment with some genetic engineering. Lindsay's next step was to obtain a second cat skin with identical genes for hair length and colour. This presented no real difficulty. Cats come in litters and pure breeds always look the same. Collection of the genetic material did, however, present a challenge or two. The large framed Albert Charles Marigold the Seventh and the smaller Penelope Cleopatra Marigold the Fourth had a healthy attachment to their pedigrees, their owners and their skins. These attachments did not thwart Lindsay for too long and within a few weeks he had completed that part of his experiment.

An incision in the first piece of genetic material was simple – just cut the largest skin in half. The next procedure required the precision of delicate implant surgery and the operation produced spectacular results. The prize skin miraculously grew thirty centimetres body length when the competitor's spouse skilfully sewed in the torso section of skin from the second cat.

In reality this sort of behaviour was no solution to the crisis. Domestic cats entering the feral population are an enormous problem and to actually reduce cat numbers in the bush requires an exceptional level of public cooperation. The cat skin competition had considerable potential for the opposite effect.

When the department assigned Kirby and Conrad the task of implementing the official Cromby Island feral cat destruction program in July, the officers put everything into the task. Unaware of the DDT problem, Kirby and Conrad enthusiastically became fox and feral cat eradicators in an attempt to allow the birds to breed that spring. After a 1080 poisoning campaign they trapped, drove, dogged and shot foxes until they were confident these pests were under control. The cats however presented an additional challenge. There were more cats than foxes to begin, partly because they bred faster and also because they lived further into the labyrinth of honeycomb lava rock flows that made up the higher parts of the island. The officers knew that for most of the year the Cromby Island cats ate dead minnow that washed up on the shore. They expected the cats would relish a free feed of fish from a different source. They intended to offer toadfish for variety.

Toadfish cause rapid death through ingestion of a poison found in their livers and Kirby and Conrad were confident of the consequence of spreading toadies around the island. Kirby spoke to a couple of professional fishermen. They advised supply would exceed demand.

A couple of days later the phone rang. Gary Lucas, a professional fisherman, had the toadies. Kirby made arrangements to meet Gary at the port and, when Kirby and Conrad arrived, Gary was waiting with three fish bins full of toadies, probably two thousand or more. The officers expressed their genuine thanks and transported the booty back to Kirby's garage in Costerfield. As they carried the bins from the vehicle to the garage Kirby's next-door neighbour, Trevor Squires, came out of his house and walked over for a sticky-beak.

Trevor owned an orange cat with long hair and it was not Kirby's best friend. It was a pretty looking animal and Kirby had never seen it even stalking a bird but the cat liked to sleep on the Wellington's front door mat. When it did it left big clumps of long orange fur. It also liked to sleep in, and on, a dainty little pink flowered bush in the Wellington's front garden. These sleeping habits were bad enough but Kirby especially detested the way it evacuated its bowels in Kylie's sandpit. Kirby had no idea if the orange cat was responsible but he did not let facts spoil his abhorrence of it. Nicky and Kirby had become quite proficient at cleaning cat poo out from between little fingers and toes. Perhaps Trevor had heard one of Kirby's outburst about all cats and their Egyptian ancestors. He greeted Kirby and Conrad as they carried the last bin of toadies to the garage.

'I know what you want them for. If my cat dies I'll sue you.'

Kirby felt Trevor meant it and from that moment there was a

temporary cease-fire in his war with the orange peril next door. After Trevor's threat Kirby was hardly game to look at the cat sideways.

The three bins of toadies occupied Kirby and Conrad for the next thirty-six hours or so and the threat left Kirby's mind. The public gardens and river frontage in Costerfield had a healthy population of stray cats. On more than one occasion the officers had seen them being fed by an elderly person at about five in the morning. This Pied Piper of cats could actually call and bring dozens of her feral pets right up to her where she petted and fed them. Kirby and Conrad decided to feed them too – next morning at four.

Conrad's impersonation of the cat lover's call wasn't too good, but it did work on a few cats the officers generously fed fresh fish, complete with razor slits to expose the livers. To demonstrate their generosity they then left toadfish in as many catty places they could think of. This included every hay stack, shed and old barn between Costerfield and Lake Bangerang. They broadcast slit toadfish around the entire area of Coromby Island, at a rate of about ten to the suburban house block. When they finished they still had cat food to burn.

Kirby and Conrad travelled home the long way distributing toadies all the way. When they arrived there was not one left for the orange cat next door. Its fur continued to get onto the front door mat, the pink bush was still a favourite sleeping haunt and the sand pit received careful inspection before Kylie went out to play.

In November the cease-fire failed. Kirby dragged out the large artillery and sought assistance from Nicky.

'I need some cat bait. I'm going to set a possum trap to catch that mongrel orange moggie. Have you got anything you can let me have for bait?'

'There's a chicken thawing in the bottom of the fridge. But the only bits you can have are tip segments from its wings. Here, let me do it for you. You'll only hack it and it'll look awful.'

Nicky cut off the tips of the chicken's wings and Kirby took these and he set the trap between their house and Trevor's. The properties where divided by a galvanised iron fence, a little too high to see over and Kirby positioned the baited trap beside the base of the fence, just outside their master bedroom window. This was as safe a place as he could think of. In that position the trap could not be seen from next door and it was only accessible from the rear of the Wellington house because of a short security fence across the front.

That night Kirby caught nothing so next day he hid the trap, still baited, in the garage. The next night he reset the trap in the same place, but again caught nothing. By now the chicken wings were green and decayed and Kirby left the trap where it was, disappointed at the waste of time and not worried that anyone would discover his project. He forgot about the trap. A couple of nights later Nicky woke Kirby with a brutal dig in the ribs.

'You've got the cat!'

The howling outside the window sounded like a bull bunyip rutting. Kirby's feet hit the floor in full gallop and he was out the back before he thought about his clothing – he was in his birthday suit. Even though it was well after midnight he decided it was best to leave the light off.

Next door Trevor pulled on his dressing gown before investigating the commotion. This delay gave Kirby time to be right out in the open yard, still in the nuddy, when the flood-light came on next door. Kirby dropped to the ground and crawled along in the shadow cast by the fence. He could hear Trevor calling his beloved pet and, when Kirby reached the captured animal, his heart was thumping. In fear of detection and unpleasant court proceedings that would surely follow, Kirby quickly opened the door of the trap and released the cat, unscathed. The howling stopped and an orange flash disappeared towards his master's voice at the back of the house. When the floodlight went out and the back yards were again in darkness, Kirby crept inside and crawled into bed.

Chapter 20

THE MALLARDS OF BYAWATHA

For several years the Costerfield Field Naturalist's Club had been raising concerns about the conservation issues posed by a Mallard Duck population at Byawatha Sanctuary. Members had written letters to the local paper and a major article appeared in the edition published on the first Saturday in November.

The reporter responsible was very critical of the department because of a perceived lack of action. These animals are a legally proclaimed pest – noxious wildlife. The club, and the reporter, were demanding eradication of the Mallards at Byawatha. The species had been introduced into Australia and New Zealand and was known to cause problems when it crossbred with native ducks. The legalistic approach of proclaiming the Mallard to be noxious wildlife was designed to curtail the sexy critters ability to establish harems on Victorian waterways. The article demanded to know what the department was going to do about the problem.

The issue became so significant that senior departmental staff from Melbourne attended a couple of public meetings in the Town Hall. Reporters, members of hunting and nature clubs, scientists, wildlife officers, representatives from the local council and other interested persons were present. There was loud applause and a chorus of 'here, here' in response to the announcement of the departmental plan. Over the coming weeks the local officers would surreptitiously remove the Mallards and replace them with pinioned native ducks from a local private zoo.

Byawatha was a popular place for wedding photos, picnics and feeding the ducks. It was not an official sanctuary but it was a picturesque, passive recreation area, centred on a small lake and waterway system. Wooden bridges gave access to one or two little islands via defined pathways winding through lawns, garden beds and trees. The ducks that lived there were mostly domestic animals released by persons tired of their pets. In addition to the Mallards, Muscovy, Indian Runners and even the occasional goose made up the population of introduced species. These abandoned pets together with Native Hens, Australian Coots, Eastern Swamphens and vast flocks of Silver Gulls did very nicely on the generous handouts of leftover picnics. At times members of the public took whole loaves of bread to Byawatha, especially as food for the ducks.

With so many birds living in the confined area, nutrient build up from their droppings became a problem. Bluestone pitchers lined the edges of the waterways but the verges of the lawns next to the stone were prone to become a green, smelly and slippery sludge.

Kirby and Conrad set about their public duty not long after the official announcement about removal of the Mallards. They found one easy way to keep the problem in check was to make sure the ducks did not breed. Once a week the officers would wade out to the main island, a heavily vegetated area with no bridge and therefore an excellent place for duck nests. Here they would simply stomp on all the eggs they could find. The prospect of destroying the eggs from the other species was of little concern.

A second tactic involved obtaining two duck traps and setting these at Byawatha. These devices are illegal but this operation was official and sanctioned by the department. The trap itself had a simple cage construction with baited funnel entrances to attract the ducks. Once inside the trap the birds became caught without injury, simply unable to find the small exit holes. The officers soon discovered this method was extremely successful – for catching coots and seagulls! They did not trap one single Mallard but it only took a few minutes to get forty or fifty of the native birds they did not want.

After two weeks of the egg destruction and duck trapping program the numbers of Mallards at Byawatha had increased by about a dozen individuals. This happened through a rise in the number of releases as a publicity campaign broadcast the message that it was an offence to keep Mallard Ducks. Releasing the family pet was preferable to prosecution – or killing the children's animals. Kirby and Conrad were fast losing the war, but their first progress report to head office did not admit this. It read in part:

> 'I am pleased to report the Mallard eradication program is progressing with total organisational flexibility. Through the continuance of a responsive logistical concept and balanced contingency, the project is expected to continue until completion at the earliest opportunity.'

Kirby knew it didn't say anything but didn't think it contained any lies either. He immediately put plan B into action. Whilst Byawatha was within the town boundary there were no houses nearby. This next strategy involved obtaining permission from the police to discharge firearms in the area. The sergeant agreed to the use of CB caps in a ·22 rifle. The small explosive charges and rather insignificant projectiles would present no real safety concerns but it meant the target would need to be within a few metres for the rifle to be effective.

'That won't be a problem,' Kirby said confidently. 'The ducks are used to people. People feed the ducks and at times they even take food directly out of your hand.'

In keeping with the instruction, that the eradication program be surreptitious, shooting took place at first light. The first morning was pretty successful after some hurried explanations to a couple of early morning joggers. Seven or eight Mallards bit the mud but after that it became increasingly difficult to get close enough for an effective shot. On two or three occasions the projectile simply ricocheted off the primary wing feathers of a drake. This not only educated those particular birds but also the entire remaining flock. It was soon common knowledge among the ducks – two grown men in uniform who drove to Byawatha early in the morning were totally untrustworthy. Before long Kirby and Conrad could not get within a bull's roar of the eighteen or twenty remaining Mallards.

The situation called for decisive action. Many of the ducks were still confident enough to feed directly from small children and this convinced Kirby those birds could actually identify Conrad and himself, with or without their uniforms. Kylie was five and one lunch hour Kirby took her down to feed the ducks. Tightly clasping a sugarbag and, like a real man, he crouched behind his daughter as she held out a piece of bread and called to the Mallards.

'Here ducky, ducky.'

A small child offering food soon had a couple of Mallards within range. With all the speed he could muster Kirby lunged around and forward, grabbing the nearest duck by the neck. It was in the bag in a flash. The accomplishment caused Kirby considerable pleasure and he refused to notice the confusion and pain on the face of his little girl who continued to say, 'Here ducky, ducky.' Within a few minutes the trick had worked again, but the activity began to attract unwanted attention from nearby picnickers.

Conscious of these onlookers, but oblivious to Kylie's feelings, Kirby took her by the hand and they departed with haste. How could a little girl understand why they came to feed the ducks, but did not stay long enough for her to give out all the bread?

Kirby's retreat was out of the fat and into the fire.

'You what?' Nicky exploded when Kirby told her the story. 'That's totally unforgivable. I wondered why she went straight to her room when you got back. She'll be on her bed crying her little eyes out. Haven't you got any brains? You've probably caused deep and permanent psychological scars. She's only young you know. She's still got an impressionable little mind. For a father, or anyone in a position of trust, to deceive a child with that sort of action is thoroughly thoughtless and totally unforgivable. What were you thinking about? I'd best go and see if I can fix things up.'

'I won't do it again,' Kirby promised. 'Perhaps it won't be so bad if Conrad takes her down tomorrow?'

That went over like a lead balloon.

Back to the drawing board. Kirby and Conrad were fast running out of ideas. A few more trips with CB caps only resulted in a minor reduction in enemy numbers. Kirby and Conrad discussed their problem.

'Pity the manual doesn't have a chapter on how to eradicate Mallard Ducks in three easy lessons.'

'I've been thinking a bit about it,' Conrad announced. 'I know how to get rid of them.'

'How?'

'It will work, I know.'

'Well, tell me.'

'I'm a pretty good shot with a spear gun,' Conrad began. 'There will be no noise and if we use another car we will be able to park right there and get 'em out the car window. My new spear gun is real powerful and it'll kill 'em stone dead. We'll even be able to do it when there's people there and that will be good because that's when the ducks aren't so suspicious. No one'll know, I'll just pull 'em back in on the cord attached to the spear.'

Kirby's immediate reaction was not too complimentary, but after a while he agreed. Nothing else they had tried worked properly so next day at lunchtime, Kirby drove Conrad's yellow Torana down to Byawatha. Conrad was in the passenger seat. They planned to drive to the end of the road then turn and come back to the lawn area. Conrad would then be facing the water and the area where the Mallards congregated. From that position the officers expected to be able to tempt the ducks into range with morsels of bread.

It was a beautiful day. It was also grandparent's day at the local kindergarten and the lawn area at Byawatha was overflowing with picnickers.

'There's too many people,' Kirby and Conrad said in unison as they drove into the area.

Kirby drove past the main picnic area and there, on the opposite side of the road, were two Mallards. The drake was totally preoccupied with sex and when Kirby stopped a few metres away, the window on the passenger side was already going down.

'I'll get two in one shot,' was the boastful claim.

The spear flew true – 'til it came to the end of cord about thirty centimetres short of the mark. There was no noise as it fell harmlessly on the grass. There was only the slightest alteration to the rhythm of the ducky business at hand as Conrad drew back the spear by the cord. The spearhead had come off, lost in the grass somewhere. The metal thread on the end of the shaft looked innocuous compared to the missing cutting edges and sharp point.

'It doesn't matter,' Conrad reflected. 'I don't need the head. The gun's plenty strong enough to kill without it and I don't need the cord. No one'll see out this side, the car is between the people and the ducks.'

Conrad undid the knot and loaded the gun again. He took careful aim and fired. Again there was no noise, till the spear hit the duck. It missed the drake. There was an abrupt termination to the intimate relationship between the two lovebirds and a loud, painful series of quacks announced the calamity.

Instantly the drake flew, circled and made a beeline for the closest water. This was over the densely populated picnic area and as he fled the crime scene, the drake's tumultuous quacks were clear evidence of his panic. The entire population of the picnic area looked, first at the drake, then towards the area where the duck was making a second commotion.

The drake's trauma was nothing to the experience of the duck. Conrad's claims about being an expert shot were only partly true and his prediction about instant death was sadly wrong. The spear had hit the duck all right, but the lack of the spearhead also meant a lack of killing power. The spear hit no vital organs as it travelled through the duck's abdomen, stopping with the duck impaled about half way along the shaft. Things happened fairly quickly after that.

The water normally offered the Byawatha Mallards sanctuary from over exuberant children and wildlife officers. Like the drake, the duck also headed for the water. Unlike the drake, the duck had some real physical difficulties, including about a dozen blankets crowded with picnickers between it and its destination. Considering the handicap of the spear shaft, which added about seventy centimetres extra body width, the duck made remarkable progress across the bitumen roadway and between the picnickers towards the water. All the while the duck was trying desperately to fly, but the weight of the shaft and the injury it caused, meant its progress came only from a desperate flapping, waddling and quacking.

Kirby and Conrad were now in a wretched situation. The audience was large and intent. As the duck struggled its way towards the water and Conrad struggled his way after the duck, it became evident the duck would reach the haven of the water before the hunter caught his quarry.

Conrad grasped the reality of this about the same time the lawn changed to the last few metres of sloping, slippery, greenish mud. He tried to stop only to land heavily on his rump, continuing his momentum to the point he reached the brink. Then, as if in slow motion, he slipped over the blue stone edge and came to rest in a seated position with the water up to his neck. His uniform tie floated on the surface, pointing in the direction of the dying duck.

The inspector stood up and bravely pursued his duty. The duck was now a metre or so further out and fatally burdened by the spear and its injury. As Conrad stepped forward, the duck disappeared under the muddy water. Indecisive hands groped around for ten seconds or so but the duck did not reappear, dying with the spear tangled in some underwater vegetation.

Realising the tragic futility of the situation Conrad mustered super-human courage and bravely turned to face his audience. He resolutely walked to the shore and climbed the bluestone edge. From there he picked his way through the picnic blankets back to the car. Kirby turned around and they drove away.

Members of the public who witnessed the unfortunate incident only saw a dedicated officer performing a grisly duty related to animal welfare. Kirby knew that if anyone discovered the truth it would have taken less than two days before a complaint resulted in two vacant wildlife officer positions at Costerfield.

Chapter 21

DUCK OPENING

After the spear gun debacle Kirby and Conrad tried to keep a low profile but it was now only a couple of months before the duck season opened and the department seemed intent on highlighting the issue of ducks and wildlife officers. During February and the first part of March there were numerous press and radio statements giving warnings and advice about what would happen to hunters detected shooting prior to the official opening time. Cribbing even a few minutes would not be tolerated and wildlife officers, working undercover disguised as hunters, would be in secret locations throughout the state.

Lindsay Unger and Darren Welsford were to work at Booksby Swamp with Kirby and Conrad. Well before opening time on the first day of the season the four officers were in position, incognito, amongst two groups of hunters. Kirby and Conrad were together and Lindsay and Darren were in the other group. As Kirby and Conrad waited for the action to begin the sky changed to the lighter greys and pinks of dawn.

The shooting started. Birds began to fly en masse and in the cloudy conditions that morning it was too dark to identify targets. The intensity of the hunt increased and, as Kirby waited, he saw the silhouette of a hunter raise his gun. He heard the crack and saw the muzzle flash. It was a good shot and the bird virtually landed at Kirby's feet. The happy hunter came over to collect his duck.

He had three problems. The first was the duck – it was really a coot. These birds are one of two or three species commonly grouped together and called water hens. His second problem was the closed season and his third was Kirby.

The officer did not want to alert the other hunters to his presence and he collared the hunter as quietly as he could. Ben Boldiston was only about eighteen and Kirby seized his gun and recorded his name and address in less than a minute. Kirby handed the gun to Conrad and began the paper work associated with writing the offender up for hunting in the closed season and killing a protected species.

Before long Ben's father, Maurice, appeared out of the gloom trying to find out why his son was so long retrieving the bird. This dashed Kirby's expectations of scoring another case from the group they had infiltrated. The officer's presence became public knowledge as Maurice went into bat for his son, trying desperately to have the firearm returned.

'It's only a water-chicken. It's only a water-chicken,' he repeated. 'We've come all the way from Adelaide and now the boy won't be able to hunt any more. He's only young. It was an accident. You don't want to spoil his day do you?'

This blackmail and compassionate plea fell on deaf ears but the loud supplications alerted the other hunters in the area. The fact the officers were there, and doing their job, had a contagious effect. The shooting abruptly stopped and hunters yelled abuse at any of their compatriots who had the audacity to shoot early.

When Kirby finished the paperwork associated with writing up Ben Boldiston he and Conrad took the seized gun to their vehicle for safekeeping. The season was open now and as they moved back towards the swamp another hunter walked towards them from the left. He followed the water's edge for a while then began to wade, on an angle, towards a duck hide twenty or thirty metres out in the water. The structure was empty and the actions of the hunter were innocuous, until he raised his gun and fired at a grebe. The pellets hit the water all-round the bird. There were no legitimate target species in the area and the action had been deliberate and wilful.

'Come on, let's go.' Kirby was already leading the way out to Tony Farrugia, the man in the duck hide.

'Good morning Sir, Kirby Wellington and Conrad Holmes. We're Wildlife Officers. Please make your gun safe.'

Kirby's official request was made almost before the barrel of the gun stopped smoking. Tony obeyed instantly and unloaded the firearm.

'May I see your duck hunting licence and licence to possess the firearm please?' Kirby continued with his next question whilst the young hunter was still stuffing the unloaded cartridges into his belt.

Tony Farrugia was typical of most hunters in waders – he carried his licences in a wallet in the pocket of his trousers. He simply could not prevent his gun getting wet and his waders falling down as he undid the wader straps and his cartridge belt before reaching inside for his wallet. Even if he had managed to extract the wallet Tony would have found it impossible to sort through the host of papers and cards to find the required documents. Kirby offered to hold the firearm whilst Tony took out his wallet and searched for his licences.

'Thank-you,' said Tony not realising his gun had just been seized.

For the second time that morning Kirby handed a gun to Conrad and proceeded to write down the licence details, including name, address and date of birth. Kirby then detailed his observations about the grebe and began his questioning. As he did a second astute father arrived, demanding to know why Kirby's interest in his son included the need for a notebook.

'I am obliged by law not to discuss a case with anyone except the defendant and his solicitor. I'm sure you can understand the need to protect a person's innocence until a court finds them guilty. When I've finished my discussion with this man I will be happy to talk to you. In the meantime I'd be obliged if you'd stay out of the way.'

Kirby's lecture in jurisprudence failed to impress Angelo Farrugia. He considered the officer most ignorant and emphatically expressed that view. In the circumstances he suggested it was Kirby who should leave, and let him look after his son.

'With respect, Sir, my advice to you is to go back to your camp. This incident began without you, but on all current indications I'm about to record the names of two defendants in my notebook. Continued interjection and interference by you will be taken by me to be an obstruction of my duty. Please be advised that this is far more serious than the offence faced by your son. Obstructing an officer in his duty could result in a term of imprisonment whilst shooting at a protected bird would attract a fine at most.'

Angelo Farrugia rejected the advice outright and continued to interrupt. After a while Kirby noticed Conrad had become the centre of attention. This gave Kirby opportunity to push on with the interview. Almost subconsciously, and definitely too late, Kirby realised Angelo had asked Conrad for a look at the gun and in his innocence the young officer handed it over. This gave Kirby a good opportunity to teach his colleague how to deal with two offenders at once.

Kirby realised it was his fault – he had not been specific about the significance of actual, physical possession of the firearm.

The manual needs a bit of an update in the seizure section, Kirby thought. *Seized items become the property of Her Majesty and I'm pretty sure she hasn't given Angelo permission to have this gun.*

Kirby set about to regain control of Her Majesty's property. He tried a lecture on the law with certain advice about where the situation must eventually lead. This didn't work so he tried threats of arrest, police involvement, theft from the Crown, indictable offences and serious trouble. It was all water off a duck's back.

'Look, laddie. This gun was given to me by my late father and it's a family heirloom. If I've got to go to gaol for two years, then so be it. You're not having the gun. End of story.'

There was no way Kirby was going to get the gun so he arrested Angelo. Even then his attempts to separate person and gun were like his attempt to keep Angelo out of the debate in the first place – a total failure.

The potential for physical violence increased dramatically as Kirby and Angelo argued over the seized weapon. Eventually Kirby decided that a wrestling match was not an option. He knew Angelo had no ammunition but later realised his decision was a triumph for stupidity over good sense. The manual made it clear – he should have backed off and called for police re-enforcement.

The two officers managed to get Angelo into their car and they set off for the Costerfield police station. Conrad sat in the back with the prisoner who still held the gun. When the procession entered the watch-house Kirby found himself the subject of an official complaint to Sergeant Goldick. During the drive into town Kirby had travelled at one hundred and three kilometres an hour and Angelo wanted the sergeant to arrest Kirby for speeding. Sergeant Goldick was not impressed but it was not the speeding that concerned him. He was very uneasy about prisoners, with guns, in his police station. He did not know Angelo had no ammunition.

Suddenly several police revolvers appeared out of nowhere aimed at Angelo's head. Soon after that the Crown regained possession of the firearm and Kirby was sure Her Majesty would have been pleased. Sergeant Goldick was not!

After a few minutes of questions and answers, Angelo was released from custody and unceremoniously directed to the door with some advice about leaving town and not coming back.

As the two wildlife officers travelled back to Booksby Swamp they spoke to Lindsay Unger and Darren Welsford via radio. The other officials had moved around to the opposite side of the swamp and now asked for assistance. A number of animal liberationists had arrived and a confrontation had developed with the hunters. The two sides had aggressively incompatible attitudes with the liberationists demanding a total ban on duck hunting. This raised the indignation of the hunters who held equally strong views that duck hunting was as legitimate a sport as Aussie Rules Football.

Had it been possible to arrange a rational discussion between the parties Kirby knew they would agree that the shooting of protected species was unacceptable and the sooner it stopped the better. He suspected though, there would have been some confusion between the word conservation and the word preservation. One applied to the continued existence of Captain Cook's Cottage and the other implied sustained use of a renewable resource. Both sides knew the statement, 'extinction is forever', carried a profound message for all – not just the hunters and animal liberationists.

Kirby and Conrad, still incognito, launched a canoe in the problem area and began to paddle among the people on the swamp. As they did their attention became focused on one person who had no firearm. Kirby and Conrad were close enough to hear the conversation between this person and a hunter whom he approached.

'I am a wildlife officer,' said the person without the gun.

Kirby became very enthusiastic about being the first to ever detect a case of impersonating a wildlife officer. He alighted from the canoe with considerable haste and no concern for Conrad's ability to remain upright. After the inevitable mishap two authentic wildlife officers — one a little wet behind the ears — confronted Russell Varney. He promptly changed his story to being on assignment, working for the Australian National Parks and Wildlife Service, through working for the Melbourne Zoo, to being a veterinarian. Kirby was having none of it. He recorded what he had seen and heard and asked Russell to state his name, address and date of birth. The reply was rehearsed and confident but it was as genuine as Russell's original claim to officialdom.

'David John Modra, thirteen March fifty-two, seventy-six Bonika Avenue, Calrossie Grove.'

Kirby and Conrad were both suspicious that Russell had not been truthful about his identity and Kirby asked for a licence, or some other form of identification. Russell had nothing with him out on the swamp.

'I don't think I'll arrest him. It'll be more prudent to remain at the swamp in case there's more trouble between the two groups. I think I'll take the risk that we can find him to give him a summons later.'

Conrad agreed with Kirby's whispered thoughts and both officers knew that another arrest would mean another trip back to the police station. In reality Kirby did not want to see or speak to Sergeant Goldick again that day.

As the day wore on, hunters progressively left the swamp and no further conflicts broke out. With the end to the shooting came a halt in hostilities and eventually Kirby left for home.

Back in the office the paperwork associated with the opening weekend kept Kirby and Conrad busy. Sergeant Goldick requested a duck opening de-brief and asked the four officers who worked at Booksby Swamp to attend the police station. The sergeant drew up an agenda for the meeting with 'Armed Prisoners' the first item for discussion.

When the de-brief began the sergeant carefully explained the dangers of bringing armed prisoners into a police station. Kirby gave the sergeant a copy of his statement regarding Tony and Angelo Farrugia and explained what had happened. Sergeant Goldick remained convinced Kirby had done the wrong thing and he was not interested in why it had happened. As far as the police were concerned the real issue had been how close Angelo Farrugia had come to being shot. Kirby promised never to do it again and discussion moved to the remaining agenda items.

The wildlife officers and police exchanged information reports and one of the police documents listed vehicles that had been issued with un-roadworthy stickers. One of the cars was a yellow Volkswagen Kombi Van and the driver matched the description of the person who had given Kirby the name of David John Modra. Russell Varney from Moorabbin was the registered owner of the van. Kirby was confident Modra and Varney were one and the same person.

Two days later Kirby and Conrad drove to Melbourne to investigate the whereabouts and true identity of their impersonator. Kirby asked the local police for assistance and they obliged by sending a divisional van to help. If Russell Varney was the person who claimed to be a wildlife officer at Booksby Swamp he would be arrested and the van would transport him back to the station. The Kombi parked in the driveway gave the officers every reason to expect a smooth and quick resolution to the issue. Russell was there and he turned on a real act when the posse arrived and a worse one when Kirby put his hand on his shoulder and said, 'You are under arrest.'

Russell immediately fell limp on the ground. This was easy enough to overcome with two police officers and Kirby and Conrad each on an arm or leg. They simply lifted Russell up, stretched him out and began to march down the driveway towards the divisional van.

As they walked Russell's passive resistance suddenly changed. He developed an unbelievable wheeze, associated gut wrenching cough and a Christopher Skase inability to breathe. The prisoner's face changed colour from red to crimson and began to go blue. Everyone began to listen to his gasped requests for tablets and ventilator. A policewoman located these in his bedroom.

Russell lay on the concrete driveway whilst he had a shot of Ventolin and popped a pill or two. After a while he recovered sufficiently for the circus to move off to the police station. Russell then turned on another asthma attack, much worse than the first. He was now so convincing the duty sergeant rang the police doctor and called an ambulance.

'Who is responsible for this prisoner?' the sergeant demanded when he completed his calls. 'If he dies, you're accountable!'

Kirby didn't like the way the sergeant was looking at him. Inevitably Russell crumpled on to the floor. The colour in his face had gone very, very blue. All the police suddenly became busy with their day to day work. If this prisoner died it would not alter the statistics on deaths in police custody – this would be the department's first such blemish and nothing to do with the police. It would be Kirby's fault.

With not one police officer to be seen Kirby and Conrad knelt beside the patient. Kirby wished like crazy that he had been more attentive during the St John's Ambulance First Aid Course. Conrad appeared to have no greater qualifications but between the two of them they acted as physicians and administered life-saving advice and assistance.

'Hang on. The ambulance is on the way.'

All this medical expertise did miraculous things for Russell's attack. So complete and fast was the cure that when the ambulance arrived Russell was sitting up and breathing almost normally. After the ambulance officers checked Russell out they suggested he should go to hospital for observation. Russell refused to go. The ambulance left and Russell agreed to be interviewed. The tape contained very little coughing and wheezing and there were no other problems. A little over an hour later Russell walked out of the station, released on bail.

During his preparation of the brief of evidence for court Kirby requested a list of Russell's prior police convictions. There were a large number from nearly every Australian State and almost all stemmed from protests. From the places of his arrests it was clear many had been in remote and inhospitable country. Russell's chronic influenza did not prevent him wading around in water up to his waist at Booksby Swamp, spending time in cold mountain areas where hardwood rain forests were being clear felled or sitting in the blazing sun at mining sites in the Northern Territory. Russell was proud of his achievements bringing public attention to environmental issues.

Chapter 22

THE CLOSED SEASON HUNT

Russell Varney's court case had been in July and the remainder of the winter passed slowly. As the weather became warmer during spring people began to spend more time outdoors, fishing and hunting. Kirby's work routine began to get hectic again. Murray Stephens rang and told Kirby that Neil Lyons, the officer from Kerrisdale, was off duty for at least six weeks with a broken leg.

'You've worked with Neil in his area,' Murray said. 'I'd like you and Conrad to go up to Kerrisdale for a week or so to do something about out-of-season duck hunting. If our information is correct, and we've had a dozen complaints, it's the locals. They know Neil's off work with his leg in plaster. It's been suggested the bludgers have been at it for years and having a joke on Neil at the same time. They run an illegal book, a betting scheme, from the Bunyip Hotel. That's the old pub on the road between Neil's house and Pyamble Swamp, you probably remember it. One of the smart bludgers rings Neil at home and from the pub reports a fictitious duck shooting incident out at the swamp. Bets, having previously been taken, are won or lost depending on the accuracy of the punter's estimate of time it takes Neil to drive past in pursuit of the phantom villains. The drinkers at the pub think it's a hell of a joke but it's pretty tough on Neil – pretty bad for the department's image too for that matter.'

Kirby and Murray speculated about getting the last laugh on a couple of the rascals, if Kirby and Conrad could get into the area undetected. The two officers from Costerfield hired a small van and set off for Kerrisdale expecting to camp for a week without showing their faces in town. When they arrived in the district Kirby went directly to the reported trouble spot, arriving mid-afternoon. They drove around for a while familiarising themselves with the geography and trying to determine the most likely spots and appropriate access roads. If the shooting took place in the evening or early morning as expected, they needed good local knowledge to complete their assignment successfully.

The Kerrisdale area was in partial flood with water covering many paddocks and cutting the back roads in several places. At the most likely spot vehicle access from one direction was impossible because of the water, and from the other, there was no cover because the country was flat and open. If an illegal hunt occurred there the shooters would have to come in via the open road. Kirby knew he and Conrad would not be able to approach from that direction without being seen. They discussed their options and decided the best chance was to be on location when the hunters arrived.

'It'll be best if we stay right here for the rest of the afternoon. We could even stay the whole night if we don't do any good this evening. That way we'll be ready for the morning.'

'But we can't just stay here,' Conrad answered. 'Nobody will come here to go shooting with a strange car in the area. There's not really any place to hide for miles.'

'Oh, I'm not so sure. Everyone will think there is nowhere to hide because there is no bush and the country is so flat. But what about over there?'

Kirby pointed to a small paddock nearby. It was the location of a long gone school building or a common. It was full of thistles, monstrous dead thistles, up to two metres high and these easily hid the car when Kirby drove in. There the officers spent some uncomfortable hours til evening. Nothing happened. They spent more uncomfortable hours till morning.

Just after daylight the shooting started, but not where the officers were. It was on the other side of the floodwater and they had no option but to abandon their hiding place and drive around, cautiously approaching the area. As they neared the location of the shooting they drove a few hundred metres then stopped, listened and watched through binoculars. They zeroed in and finally saw the car, a beaten up farm utility.

Kirby and Conrad left their hire car behind a clump of peppercorn trees and walked the last two or three kilometres to the utility. As they trekked the shooting continued and Kirby was confident the hunters did not suspect the wildlife officers were there to nab them.

'I reckon the best place to hide is here, right behind their car. The shooting still sounds a fair way off but if we try to get close enough to see what they're doing we won't stand a chance. We'll just let them come to us. If we do hide here though, they'll be looking straight at us when they get back. That could be a bit of a problem so we'll have to keep our heads right down and not move. We don't want 'em to see us till they are over the fence and right here.' Kirby pointed at his feet.

Finally the shooting ended and three hunters walked around the edge of the floodwater towards the ambush Kirby had set. Each suspect carried a shotgun and they walked in single file, the last person some distance behind the first. The problems that Kirby forecast were now real. The officers found it impossible to keep a close watch on each of the hunters. If they moved out from behind the utility far enough to watch the last hunter, the first would see them. If they announced their appearance to the first when he climbed the fence, the last hunter had a golden opportunity to run. He was at least sixty metres behind and the fence, at the side of the roadway, meant Kirby and Conrad would have no chance of running him down. Besides, if they chased him the other two hunters could simply get into the utility and drive away. Kirby motioned to Conrad to keep quiet and still.

Kirby heard the wires creak and twang as the leading hunter climbed over the fence. As he walked around the rear of the utility, about to step on Kirby, the second man began to climb the fence but the third still had 20 or 30 metres to go. Kirby had no option but to stand and announce his presence and identity. As he did he closely watched the person in the paddock and was surprised to see he was wearing a necktie and suit vest. This unusual attire, the possibility of his escape and the fact he was the only one to carry a game bag, kept Kirby's total attention. The moment the ambush was sprung the hunter in the paddock surreptitiously dropped what he carried, but he did not run. Kirby then looked closely at the first two hunters – it was the Pappas brothers, Bill and Jim.

Conrad retrieved the discarded bag and emptied its contents onto the ground at the back of the utility. Five men stood looking down at two Plumed Tree Ducks and a Grey Teal. Kirby was the first to speak.

'Good morning Bill. Good morning Jim. You do remember me don't you? This is Conrad Holmes. He's a wildlife officer too.' Kirby produced his identification badge.

Conrad already had his badge out and the three hunters stood mute.

'I should have recognised that utility,' Kirby continued. 'I don't believe we've met. I've known Bill and Jim since we met one January a good few years ago. Your name sir?'

'Kieran Harper. I own the Bunyip Hotel. Pleased to meet you Kirby.'

Kieran shook Kirby's hand vigorously and spoke as if being a publican held some secret ingredient for befriending people in authority. Even without his prejudice because of the jokes played on Neil Lyons, Kirby knew he would have taken an instant dislike to the publican. The handshake continued for several seconds longer than necessary and Kirby tried to ignore the deceit in Kieran's greeting.

The Pappas brothers knew Kirby would only be interested in the feathered carcasses that came out of the bag and they took a different approach.

'We've been hunting rabbits and foxes,' Bill offered. 'With all this flood-water they can't get into their burrows and it's good shooting.'

'Where are all your rabbits and foxes then? We heard all your shooting. You must have got dozens.'

'Well we didn't actually hit one. But don't get any ideas. We found the ducks in someone's duck trap over there, didn't we fellas?'

Bill and Kieran enthusiastically agreed and Jim pointed around the flooded paddock in the direction they had just walked.

'Then these ducks will have no shotgun pellets in them then. You wouldn't have shot them in the closed season would you?'

Kirby and Conrad began to pluck the ducks and pellet wounds, oozing fresh blood, became apparent. Kirby was confident he had put paid to the duck trap conspiracy.

'Those pellet wounds would explain why the ducks looked so sick in the trap,' volunteered Jim. 'The poor things looked like they were in agony. Sure we killed them, but that was out of pity – the only humane thing to do. We felt it was our public duty. It would have been cruel to leave them there like they were, to die in misery like that.'

'I suspect you are handling the truth a little carelessly. What do you think Conrad?'

'I think you're being very polite. These blokes are hill-billy's. They're belligerent and self-centred. They've been illegally shooting ducks but aren't man enough to admit they've been caught.'

'You watch it,' threatened Jim. 'You can't just say that. We found a duck trap and if you don't inspect it and include it in your report, you'll be hearing from my solicitor.'

Kirby and Conrad reluctantly followed the hunters to an

overgrown old duck trap that had no bait, or evidence of having recently contained a duck.

'Don't come the raw prawn,' Kirby said as he inspected the trap. 'You blokes obviously think I'm a bit green but give me some credit – I'm not a cabbage. The trap's got no bait and there hasn't been a duck in it for months. If there had been there would be fresh duck crap everywhere. Look there isn't any. Besides, the entrance funnels are overgrown and a duck couldn't have physically gotten through.'

'Look, we found this trap,' said Jim. 'We kicked the holes under the netting along the sides. You can see the holes are fresh. We didn't want any more unfortunate ducks getting caught so we rendered the obnoxious trap inoperable. How could someone do such a thing? It's terrible, all the suffering those poor ducks had to go through.'

'It's pretty obvious they're not going to confess,' Kirby whispered to Conrad. 'Let's leave it be for now. It's just not worth arguing with them. I know what we've seen and heard and it will look pretty good in our statements for court. We'll just seize the ducks and their guns and tell them the matters will be reported.'

Subsequently both officers told it all in court. Under cross-examination from Charles Ralph William-Peterson, Kirby and Conrad had to admit they had no training, qualifications or experience in forensic medicine or veterinary science. In these circumstances, their opinions that the shotgun pellets would have killed the ducks, became the subject of a heated contest. The defence lawyer ignored the conclusion that must follow the evidence of no bait or fresh duck droppings in the trap. No one seemed interested in the observations of two experienced officers whose job included observing ducks being shot and the inspection of dead birds.

At the end of the day however, the Magistrate demonstrated he had been listening and had given credence to the evidence and experience of the officers.

'I have no hesitation in finding the ducks died,' he said, 'and died that day as a result of gunshot wounds.'

A person with Solomon's wisdom, Kirby thought, until the Magistrate continued.

'It is the court's job today to apply the principles of the law to the evidence before it. As I have said, those ducks were shot on the day in question but I have no evidence to shed any light on the most important question of all. Which of the defendants was a good enough shot to actually hit a duck or ducks. The evidence of the prosecution,

and I point out this was not challenged, is that there were thirty-five or forty shots – perhaps as many as fifty. The only conclusion the court can reach is that the great majority of those shots did not hit or kill a duck. On the evidence there is a real doubt whether or not all three persons shot a duck, there being only three ducks in total. The court has no option but to give the benefit of the doubt to the defence and all the charges of killing duck in the closed season are dismissed. The charges of hunting duck in the closed season are found proven.'
After court Kirby and Conrad made some vows regarding their intentions if they ever again found the Pappas brothers, or any publican, with a gun in a duck swamp during the closed season.

Chapter 23

PARROT TRAPPING

Good Friday fell on April the tenth and Kirby took nine days leave between the Easter Holidays and Anzac Day. Near the end of the leave he was looking forward to spending the last day of his break with Nicky and her parents who were visiting from Melbourne. With them living so far away the children seldom saw their grandparents and the planned family day promised to be special. Just after daylight the phone rang. Kirby answered and heard Karen Fitzgerald's voice.

'Those bird trappers are out here again,' she reported as though she expected Kirby had been waiting for her to call.

During past conversations with Karen, Kirby learned of two persons she had seen in paddocks in the Diggora area. From Karen's description Kirby suspected they were trapping birds and during that first chat he had explained that the wildlife legislation didn't cover Gold Finches or other introduced birds. He has advised that it was OK to trap them so long as there was no cruelty involved. Gold Finches were a very common species in the area but he had confided that he thought all bird trappers are worth keeping an eye on.

'You said you would appreciate a call,' Karen reminded Kirby when she called on this morning. 'Those men are back.'

'Yes, I did. Thanks for calling.'

Kirby recorded the location of the trappers and a description of their car. After he hung up he rang Conrad because he had the departmental car whilst Kirby was on leave. There was no answer and this left Kirby without official transport. He crawled back into bed and told Nicky what had happened.

'They would probably only be after Gold Finches. And after all I'm sort of still on holidays.'

'You must go. You can't let Karen down. Take our car. Dad might like to go too.'

Kirby knew she was correct. Karen had taken the trouble to ring, as he had requested, and he had to respond. After a few more minutes procrastination Kirby forced his feet back onto the floor and went in and woke Nicky's father. The two men had a piece of toast and a cuppa, then with his father-in-law as passenger, Kirby drove his private car out to Diggora.

Precisely where Karen had explained there was the car. Kirby pulled up behind it and looked across the adjacent paddock that was planted with onions. Two hundred meters away, on the other side of the onion patch, were two people crouched in hides made from thistles. There was nothing to do but walk over and determine what they were doing. Kirby climbed the fence and began to move towards the men, trying not to step directly on the onions. After he had walked about half way one person left his hide and moved a few metres, bent down and appeared to put something in his pocket. He moved a short distance and repeated the movement. Kirby did not understand but those actions were suspicious and now more important than a few squashed onion plants. He raced the remainder of the way and vaulted over the second fence. When he reached the two people they were standing near a large spring-loaded book-trap set on the ground.

Kirby did not know where to look. He glanced at the net then gaped in amazement at the men. MT Morrison and his brother Rohan! Kirby had not previously met Rohan but he did not need an introduction. The two brothers could have been twins.

'Morning Mr Morrison. What are you after?' Kirby tried to keep the surprise out of his voice.

'Gold Finches a course,' MT said indignantly.

Kirby knew he could not believe this and looked back at the book-trap. It had two leaves of netting set flat on the ground like the pages of an open book. Between these, where the book-binding would have been, was an exposed area of earth. Kirby unconsciously focused on this area.

The officer did not know that the Morrisons had pre-baited that precise tract of land during the previous week. In that way several flocks of wild birds had become accustomed to feeding right in the target area. When the day of the actual trapping arrived decoy birds in small cages further enticed wild birds into position. As he stared at the scene, almost dumbfounded, Kirby did not see the left over seed mixture that had been the bait before he arrived. All he could see was that frightful trap.

The Morrison brothers had already sprung the trap on several occasions that morning, when flocks had settled in on the grain and were eating and chatting to the decoys. At the appropriate time the spring-loaded sides of the device snapped closed, capturing the birds under the netting, as a fly trapped when a book is slammed shut.

Still overwhelmed Kirby then saw the birdseed mix spread around and saw there were two empty decoy cages and a third containing a single live Gold Finch. Feathers lay everywhere – a phenomenal number of tail feathers that were too long for the feathers from a finch.

The cruelty of bird trapping hit Kirby like a hammer as he gazed at the scene. How barbaric. He had never seen anything like it. The mass of feathers and the thought of the birds that lost them clouded his thinking. He knew he should be trying to work out what species of bird the feathers had come from, but all he could think of was the fear and pain the birds must have experienced. He reasoned that pulling tail feathers out would be something like being scalped without an anaesthetic.

Kirby imagined the birds struggling when the leaves of the trap sprang up and over the place where they were feeding. He just could not get his mind back on the job. He pictured how the birds fought vainly against the mesh and how MT and Rohan dashed out from their hides to untangle the struggling captives as quickly as they could. Their haste would be related to the need to re-set the trap for the next flock, not the relief of the hostages.

Kirby imagined the birds losing their feathers as the trappers roughly handled them. He likened it to losing teeth knocked out in a brawl. He winched with the pain and wondered if, in their terror, the birds were able to comprehend that the caged decoys and abundant food had been nothing but foul treachery. Kirby drifted back to the reality of the grizzly scene around him. MT and Rohan stood staring at him. Kirby confronted Rohan without really knowing where his questions would lead.

'Let me have it,' Kirby demanded.

It was Rohan who had moved from his hide and bent down as Kirby approached. Instinct told the officer Rohan had to have something. The bird trapper reached into his trouser pocket and pulled out a Blue-winged Parrot. Kirby took it from Rohan's outstretched hand.

'And the other one.'

Out of the other pocket came a second parrot and Kirby took that too.

'And the rest.'

Kirby continued not expecting more than the two parrots he already had. In truth, Kirby did not expect anything specific when he asked the first question, it all just happened. A third parrot emerged from the second pocket as if by the sorcery of a magician producing things from a hat.

'Come on, all of them,' Kirby said sternly.

With trouser and coat pockets turned inside out Rohan stood facing his accuser in a counterfeit gesture of total disclosure. MT did likewise when requested. He was clean.

Kirby put the parrots safely back in the decoy cages and began to interview the Morrisons. The officer went through the process feeling very uncomfortable, partly because he was dealing with MT and partly because he sensed something else was amiss. MT showed Kirby their decoy Gold Finch.

'Look we've already caught a heap a Gold Finches,' MT said. 'They're in a carry cage, in the shade, under the car. Come over an' I'll show ya. Them three parrots just flew into the trap by accident – with a mob a finches. We hadda spring the trap to get the finches and I suppose the temptation to keep 'em was too much. We're not after parrots. Come over to the car and have a look.'

'If catching the parrots was an accident, how come the parrots were your decoy birds when I came across the onion patch?'

MT did not answer and even though Kirby had no experience with parrot trappers he quickly discounted the claim about targeting Gold Finches. MT was trying to get Kirby over to the car and the officer knew that was reason enough to remain where he was.

'Oh, all right,' said Rohan, 'we changed the Gold Finches for parrots in two decoy cages but we were still after finches. There were three cages and three parrots but we didn't have parrots in all the cages did we? We kept a finch as a decoy so that proves we're after finches.'

'Shuddup,' MT hissed at Rohan before he turned and addressed Kirby. 'You're supposed to read us our rights an' tell us we don't 'ave to say nothin'.'

Kirby did not answer as he released the trap. Rohan admitted he had taken the parrots from the net and had put them in the decoy cages. MT admitted coming out to help Rohan trap birds and that he had not tried to stop Rohan keeping the parrots. This was a good case and the first time MT had made an admission of guilt about anything. This admission was one of assisting rather than being the perpetrator of the crime but MT had admitted his involvement in a very serious offence. Through his lack of experience Kirby did not ask who had pre-baited the area but, even if he had, MT would not have admitted he was the architect of the plan.

Kirby finished the paper work and packed the trap away. He almost fell for MT's incessant demands for an inspection of the finches over at the car. Somehow the multitude of tail feathers kept Kirby from climbing the fence into the onion patch and walking back to the cars parked on the road.

The Diggora area is volcanic and farmers often collected the plentiful basalt rocks and placed them in heaps around their paddocks. This farm contained dozens of rock heaps and these, and abundant dead thistles, offered numerous opportunities for concealment. Kirby began to search every possible hiding place, working out from the trap site and away from the onion patch and away from the cars. Behind a heap of rocks, about seventy metres away, Kirby found a hessian bag. He knew instantly he had found the remainder of the Morrison's trapped birds, but he was not ready for his discovery.

Under the bag he found a flat carry cage choking with more Blue-winged parrots. He carried his find back to the trappers and Rohan again admitted responsibility.

'Can I take it you helped your brother?' Kirby asked MT.

'Wot do ya reckon? I'm out here for me good looks?'

'I take it you assisted Rohan in the capture of these parrots.'

'Write down what ya want. It won't make no difference. Ya reckon I'm guilty so what's the difference?'

'It's not up to me to decide your guilt or innocence, but if you are innocent I am asking you to tell me about it now.'

MT was silent.

Over at the car Kirby eventually looked at MT's Gold Finches. He gave them a cursory glance then got back to the real job. He issued seizure receipts for all the equipment, the decoy cages and the parrots. He advised the Morrison brothers he would see them in court and sent them on their way.

With the help of his father-in-law Kirby then counted the forty-two parrots as they flew from their holding dungeon. Many were unsteady as they took flight. The decoy birds were very hesitant and scruffy looking, but they did eventually fly off. Kirby expected the trauma of being shoved into trouser pockets was responsible for their worsened condition. He reasoned though, releasing them there in their natural habitat offered their best chance of survival.

Eight days later, on the first Sunday in May, Karen Fitzgerald rang Kirby again. She made the call about 10 AM and reported the same car, on the road from Diggora to One Tree Hill this time. Kirby wrote down the registered number as Karen told him.

'It's parked on the left as you drive towards One Tree Hill,' she explained. 'You can't miss it. It's beside a great big boxthorn bush – the only one along the whole road. It's growing alongside the stubble of an old sunflower crop and if I'm not mistaken the Morrison's own the paddock. It's one of their out-paddocks and they never get rid of their noxious weeds – all the other farmers in the district have killed their boxthorn.'

Kirby picked up Conrad and they raced out to the location to find the car already gone. Kirby searched through the stubble and soon found the trap site. This time the grain bait and the feathers of Blue-winged Parrots did not surprise him. This time he was alert enough to take particular notice of the grain – it was a parrot mix and unsuitable for finches. The officers took a long series of photos and collected a number of feathers and a sample of the left over grain.

Back in town Kirby went to the police station to make sure Rohan Morrison was, as he suspected, the registered owner of the car. He was, and Sergeant Goldick assigned two officers to assist. Kirby and one of the police went to MT's place and Conrad and the other went to Rohan's house in the police car. No one was home at either house and Conrad found nothing at the farm.

Kirby discovered nine Blue-winged Parrots in an aviary in MT's back yard. The birds were timid and when Kirby approached they flew wildly against the wire of the cage. Their bloodied faces became worse with each collision with the netting. Kirby knew where they came from and decided to wait for MT to come home. Conrad joined him and they waiting about two hundred metres up the road from MT's house.

Just before dark, when the officers were beginning to despair and discuss other options Rohan's car arrived and pulled into MT's driveway in Booroopki Road. The trappers had already sold the remainder of the illegal booty in Melbourne. Conrad was driving and he pulled into the driveway right behind Rohan's car. The two officers jumped out.

Conrad immediately locked the departmental car and it blocked the driveway. He stood looking in the driver's side window at Rohan while Kirby stood beside MT outside the passenger side window. Both windows were wound up and it was impossible for Rohan to drive away. He just sat without saying a word. Kirby was about to speak to MT but the bird trapper got in first. He wound down the window and challenged Kirby.

The manual clearly cautioned against such action by an officer because blocking a suspect's car in these circumstances meant Conrad had, strictly speaking, put Rohan in custody. With Kirby standing outside MT's door he too would technically have been in custody. MT knew a bit about the law.

'Wot do ya bloody wan' now?' MT demanded. 'I'm busy. Shift ya car or I'll sue ya for false imprisonment or trespass or somethin'.'

'Hello Mr Morrison. I wonder could we have a moment of your time – and yours too Rohan? We'd like to speak to you about your parrot trapping out the road to One Tree Hill this morning. You need to know this is official and I must warn you that you are not obliged to say or do anything but anything you do say or do may be given in evidence. Do you understand this?'

'You must be off ya head.' MT spat on the ground. 'We've been in Melbourne visitin' me missus' mother. She's got cancer an I'm 'ome by meself batchin' an all you can think of is stitchin' me up for somethin' I aint done. Ya got no evidence anyway.'

'Mr Morrison, the police and I were here earlier and I already have photos of the nine Blue-winged Parrots in the aviary in your yard. They are wild caught birds and Officer Holmes and I have been to your trapping site out the road from Diggora to One Tree Hill. We also have photos of the area with the parrot-mix seed and all the tail feathers.'

'Yeah, well,' MT began. 'Them parrots in the yard was brung in for me to look after by a young kid from the local school. Jamie Askew's his name. You ask 'im. He said they was sick and I'm just tryin' ta rehabilitate 'em.'

'How long have they been here?'

'Couple a days.'

'And what treatment have you administered?'

'Just tryin' to keep 'em quiet and give 'em plenty of feed and water.'

'Did you notify the department that you had them? Officially notify anybody about your Good Samaritan deeds for the benefit of our local wildlife?'

'Don't be bloody stupid. If I'd a dun that youse blokes would a just come out, seized 'em and tooked me to court. I ain't stupid.'

'This matter will be reported. Not just your possession of the nine blue wings in the yard but also your parrot trapping earlier today.'

'Yer always gotta rub that bit in don't ya. I didn't expect a mongrel like you to let me orf but I must be gettin' too old for this, admittin' I even knew them parrots was in me yard. We've been in Melbourne and I coulda just as easy said someone left 'em there without me knowin'. I'm gunner 'ave to give the game away. It's blokes like youse that force honest men like me to give up work and go on the dole.'

'I'll bet you don't,' said Kirby. 'Give up illegal dealing in wildlife I mean. I thought you might stop after the Anzac Day episode though. If you're fair dinkum I'll see you in the office tomorrow when you come in to give me the net you used today.'

'Break it down. That net's me capital investment. Besides the blue wings aren't in Victoria all the time and me, being an entrepreneur and all, I've gotta make a quid when opportunity knocks don't I? Wouldn't wan' them Taswegians gettin' all the economic benefits just 'cos the blue wings breed on the other side of Bass Strait, would we? What happened to free trade between the states and the Commonwealth Government Anti-competition Policy?'

'I think I won the bet. What do you know about free trade between the states and the anti-competition policy?' Kirby was getting chatty and feeling pretty good about the case.

'Just because I ain't got no formal education or nothin' don't mean I ain't got no brains. I take a keen interest in politics. I knows me rights and I make up me mind on wot party to vote for on what benefits is in it for me.'

Despite how he felt earlier, Kirby began to realize that it would be difficult to get MT convicted for trapping parrots on the second day. It was obvious who was responsible but Kirby did not need to be told that the obvious was not evidence. On the way home he called in to see Karen Fitzgerald. Over a cuppa and peanut cookie he asked if she would be prepared to make a statement giving details of where and when she had seen Rohan's car. She was delighted to assist.

'Why don't you talk to Adrian Walton,' Karen suggested. 'He's been training for the marathon and I know he ran down that way this morning. I saw him. He could know something that will help.'

Adrian Walton ran the local IGA supermarket in Cornishtown and Kirby paid him a visit next day. Adrian was reluctant to make a statement.

'I don't know who it was,' he reasoned. 'How can I help you if I don't know who it was?'

'You know what sort of a car it was. With your evidence the court should be satisfied that the car you saw near the trapping site is the same one that MT and his brother were in later in the day when Conrad and I saw them. Your evidence will paint a picture and lead the court to a certain conclusion. We only want the court to know the truth. Nothing more, nothing less. It's as simple as that. What do you say?'

Adrian eventually agreed to give Kirby a statement. During his training run Adrian had gone right out to One Tree Hill and then jogged back along the same road. Rohan's car was there on the way out and still there when he ran back. It was parked beside the only boxthorn bush along the entire road. On the first occasion he saw two men carrying bags into the paddock where the sunflowers had been. His description of the men left Kirby in no doubt it was the Morrison brothers. The area where the men had gone was the same as where Kirby found the parrot feathers and left over bait. When Adrian ran back towards town he saw the two men crouched out in the sunflower stubble. His description put the men right were the trap had been.

A week later Kirby submitted two briefs of evidence against MT and Rohan. There were statements from Adrian Walton, Karen Fitzgerald the two police members as well as Kirby's and Conrad's. The officers were confident they now had sufficient evidence to get MT convicted for trapping Blue-winged Parrots on both occasions.

Chapter 24

THE BABY WEDGE-TAILED EAGLE

'They found it fallen out of the nest Dad,' Zac guaranteed his father when the lad arrived home from school carrying a baby Wedge-tailed Eagle in a cardboard box.

'Who found it?'

Kirby was looking at the white fluffy bundle Zac carried. It was a quite a bit smaller than an average chook and two big black eyes and a black beak contrasted with the white down that indicated the chick was only a few weeks old.

'Jamie Askew and Aaron Van Der Hope.' The lad paused then added quietly, 'I think.' Zac sensed he was dobbing in his classmates.

'Where did they get it?'

'They said something about a big tree in Banayeo Gorge.'

'That's way out at Diggora South. How did they get out there?'

'I think Jamie's uncle has a farm where they go and stay for weekends. I think it's his Uncle Max.'

Kirby rang Karen Fitzgerald who had recently had the phone connected. He asked if she knew of a Wedge-tailed Eagle nest in Banayeo Gorge.

'Yes. Yes. The eagles have been nesting there for years. It's right at the back end of the Morrison's farm and the local gossip has it that Rohan shot last year's chicks because they were supposed to be getting his lambs. His paddocks are always over-stocked and his sheep are always dying from starvation, or liver fluke or something. If

167

you ask me the eagles live on rabbits and they don't kill sheep. If the eagles did eat one of his lambs I'll bet it was dead before they got it. I think that horrid brother Max is back working on the farm now and I reckon the parent birds are even in danger this year. I remember those Morrison brothers from school. They used to nail bullfrogs to trees then use the frogs as target practice with an air rifle. Those two used to shoot anything that moved. They were always in trouble.'

Kirby explained his need to find the eagle nest and Karen gave him precise directions on its location and how to get there. They agreed the best chance for the orphan was to return it to the eyrie. Next morning Kirby and Conrad drove out to Banayeo Gorge and located the nest. The parent birds were still active in the area, apparently feeding a second chick, and this gave them encouragement.

'If we can get the baby eagle back with its sibling it must stand a good chance of survival,' Kirby assured Conrad as they inspected the nest tree.

The tree was tall and it had rained during in the night. The day was overcast and everything was still wet. Despite this Kirby decided to give it a go as he had served the average tree-climbing apprenticeship. What boy from a farm hadn't? The senior officer tied a thin piece of string to his belt, intending to climb the tree to the appropriate position from where he would pull up the string. Attached to the opposite end Conrad would tie strong cord and, in turn, this would lift up the eagle secure in a pillowcase. Climbing to above the nest proved impossible. Slippery, wet branches and the sheer size of the structure forced Kirby to change plans. He climbed part way down then up another limb to an appropriate height. From there he expected to be able to gently toss the chick across to the nest, and hopefully, the company of its sibling.

After Kirby climbed the second branch, the distance from his position to the top of the nest was further than he had imagined but he was still confident he could do it. Conrad encouraged his boss all the while as Kirby drew up the pillowcase. The second chick had not begun to fledge either and it sat motionless among the remains of rabbit carcasses that littered the nest.

Kirby's toss was a disaster. The little bird hit some twigs soon after it left his hands and consequently did not make the top of the eyrie. Instead it hit the side of the massive stick structure and fell like a brick to the ground. With a dull thud the young eagle lay instantly dead.

All the way back to Costerfield Kirby felt sick. In his heart he knew two things. Firstly Jamie Askew and Aaron Van Der Hope did not find the eagle fallen out of the nest and, secondly, they were far better at climbing trees than he was.

Chapter 25

JUST REWARDS

The death of the baby eagle weighed heavily on Kirby's conscience for weeks. Whenever the slightest thing went wrong he seemed to be thinking about the little bird and feeling guilty. He often debated with himself about what he should have done. Many times he wished he had not climbed the tree to try to get the chick back in its nest. He could have asked Karen Fitzgerald to raise and rehabilitate it, or he could have taken it to the zoo like he did the baby koala. Kirby knew that was not an option at the time but now wished he had talked more to Karen about hand raising as an alternative. Kirby had failed the baby eagle in the worst possible way. If only his plans had worked out. If only he had managed to climb the limb to above the nest. If only.

The Morrison parrot trapping court case was only a few weeks away and as Kirby continued to feel miserable about the eagle he began to worry about the court case too. He thought he would never be able to face Karen Fitzgerald or Adrian Walton again if MT got off. Kirby was not eating or sleeping properly and had snapped at Nicky when he had no reason to. When Adrian agreed to give evidence against MT, Kirby had every confidence in the prosecution case. Now he was not so sure. The intensity of his doubts increased as the case drew closer.

When MT and Rohan were summonsed to court for trapping the Blue-winged Parrots they immediately went to see their solicitor, Charles

Ralph William-Peterson. MT's instructions were clear – he was not guilty. The lawyer and the two brothers had a long discussion and they decided it would be best if Rohan pleaded guilty. They hoped this would take the heat off MT and keep him out of jail.

Kirby was sitting in the office, thinking about the baby eagle again. The phone rang. It was Charles wanting to discuss the prosecution of his clients. Kirby hoped the call would shed some light on the defence tactics. He hoped they would plead guilty as that would relieve him of considerable stress. Instead of discussing tactics Charles simply introduced himself and stated bluntly that he considered the charges against MT were outrageous and scurrilous.

'Our conversation is without prejudice of course,' Charles continued.

'Naturally,' Kirby agreed. 'But I suspect you and I will have to agree to disagree about the merit of the charges against Mr Maxwell Morrison.'

'It appears to me that we could save a lot of time on this one. It would be in everyone's best interest if Rohan pleaded guilty. In the circumstances you wouldn't be pushing for a conviction against the other brother, will you?'

Charles' last two words changed the tone of the conversation. They were a demand, not just a strongly obnoxious request.

'I'm not too sure about that. What exactly do you mean?'

'It's obvious from my instructions. Rohan is the responsible one. I imagine you'd be happy to discuss the possibility of a withdrawal of all charges against Maxwell. We would not seek costs if you withdraw now. If, on the other hand, the court dismisses your charges against Maxwell, that will be a different proposition when it comes to the question of costs.'

'I beg your pardon. The department decided to prosecute both men and I've got no power to just overturn that decision. I wouldn't want to anyway. I recommended prosecution of them both and so far you haven't given me the slightest reason to change my mind. I'm not intimidated by your threat about costs. If you win, naturally we'll pay the costs awarded by the court.'

'If this case goes to a contested hearing in court it will last for three or four days. It could go a whole week. Think of all the taxpayer's dollars you could save by simply walking away from the second defendant. Justice will be seen to be done because Rohan will plead guilty. I can't imagine the court will do anything but convict him, and fine him heavily.'

'No way! Is there something else I can help you with?'

There wasn't.

When Kirby put the receiver down he realised he was annoyed. He was not thinking objectively and, as usual, the subjective became personal. Kirby knew the call from Charles Ralph William-Peterson was no coincidence. The officer smiled wryly to himself as he remembered the end of the case where MT was charged with the possession of the bird's eggs.

Back then the Magistrate had said, "If you appear back at this court I suggest you remember the advice I'm about to give you. If you are charged with any offence that has a jail term as a possible sentence, your great number of prior convictions will leave the court with no option but to incarcerate you. If you do come back in such circumstances I strongly advise you to bring your toothbrush".

Kirby knew the solicitor would be worried about the very thing that was now making him smile. Even though it would be a different Magistrate this time Kirby also knew that MT would probably go to jail if found guilty of the charges relating to the trapping of the Blue-winged Parrots. He also knew that Charles Ralph William-Peterson would be up to his old tricks trying to get MT acquitted. Kirby sat for another half an hour and went over, in his mind, the details of a couple of Charles' defence tactics. Kirby recalled the detail of one zealous objection the moment he had identified some Red-browed Finches he once seized. The objection had been on the basis that Kirby was not qualified to identify any wildlife.

The court over-ruled the objection but during that cross-examination it became clear the defence was based on a claim the birds were actually a species of wax-bills indigenous to South Africa. Kirby had readily admitted Red-browed Finches were commonly called waxbills and as that cross-examination intensified, he wished he had taken identification photos – just like the manual suggested. On the occasion of the seizure of the finches though, Kirby had taken the easy option rather than go back to the office to get a camera.

After all, he remembered thinking at the time, *Red-browed Finches are common and I am familiar with them.*

As Kirby sat thinking he recalled the detail of Charles' cross-examination about the finches.

'You're familiar with the schedule in the legislation are you?"

'Yes I am.'

'You know the birds and animals listed in it I presume?'

'Yes.'

'Can I assume you are an expert on the legislation?'

'I know how it works if that's what you mean.'

The lawyer opened up his copy and read from the schedule.

'Well what species is *Emblema bella E. guttata*?' he asked.

'That's not one species, it's two.'

'Are you sure? Don't forget it is you who claims to have this good knowledge of how the legislation works and you are the one making the accusations against my client.'

'Yes, I'm sure.'

'Well tell the court what they are,' the lawyer demanded.

'Emblema bella is the Beautiful Firetail Finch and the E. guttata is an abbreviation for Emblema guttata, the Diamond Firetail Finch.'

Kirby remembered how positive his answer had been and how luck had been on his side. He recollected how Charles Ralph William-Peterson had broken the golden rule of cross-examination when his questions had apparently highlighted one of Kirby's strengths – the use of scientific names to identify wildlife. What was worse for Charles, he had also asked one question too many. Kirby again smiled to himself because he knew the lawyer had been too nervous to continue. He would have shown the officer's wildlife identification skills to be severely lacking had the next question asked for the scientific name of a magpie, or any one of a hundred other common birds. It was just luck that Kirby knew the scientific names of the two finches Charles chose to read from the schedule.

Kirby knew he could not rely on luck to win the parrot trapping case and as he sat thinking he realised the defence may not be too interested in the truth about the Blue-winged Parrots. He understood they would probably attack the credibility of the civilian witnesses and he hoped he had not pushed Karen or Adrian into something they would regret. Kirby anticipated all the prosecution witnesses would have to withstand some form of defence attack but he was concerned most for Karen and Adrian. Perhaps Charles would defend MT on the basis that the birds were Elegant Parrots and not Blue-winged Parrots. The two species were very similar in appearance and their range overlapped in the Diggora area. Kirby momentarily hoped Charles would use this defence because that should mean the evidence given by Karen and Adrian would not be challenged.

What could they be up to? Kirby wondered. *If Rohan pleads guilty the identification of the species can't be the issue.*

Four days later Kirby received a letter from the solicitor. This included official advice that Charles acted for Maxwell and Rohan Morrison and it was boldly marked "Without Prejudice". Kirby read

it but could not understand how it could be used to defend MT.
Kirby read the letter a second time, out loud to Conrad.

"Persons throughout Australia can
be licensed to keep, inter alia, Blue-
winged Parrots and other indigenous
species. Various governments, in their
wisdom, have seen fit to facilitate the
legitimate hobby of aviculture upon
payment of appropriate licence fees.
This recognition by governments
over the years acknowledges the
responsible wildlife management
practices carried out by aviculturists.
Some Australian species (E.g. the
Princess Parrot) are now more
plentiful in captivity than in the wild.
This fact must be attributed to the
unselfish actions of people like the
Morrisons.

In this matter the defence propose
that Rohan Morrison plead guilty to
all charges on the understanding that
the prosecution withdraw all charges
against Maxwell Morrison. This is
put in the light of the Morrison's
aforementioned contribution to the
conservation of Australian wildlife.
Implicit in the government acceptance
of legitimate aviculture is the need
for hobbyists to get new blood lines
so that healthy populations can be
maintained in captivity.

It is clear to the writer that the only
real vice on the part of the defendants
was a failure to obtain a licence. In
the circumstances outlined above,
with the principal offender pleading
guilty, vigorous prosecution of both
men cannot be justified by your
department".

'They've certainly got some front,' Kirby said. 'What would they know about conservation – and you can't even get a licence to trap Blue-winged Parrots. What's more Princess Parrots aren't indigenous to Victoria!'

'They're pretty worried if you ask me,' Conrad observed. 'If that's the best they can do we're in like Flynn.'

Kirby rang Murray Stephens and they discussed the case and the letter. Murray decided to prosecute himself and this took some pressure off Kirby.

'Don't worry about the defence tactics,' Murray comforted. 'Most Magistrates know Charles and know how he operates. We've got a good case and I reckon having Charles Ralph William-Peterson acting for the Morrisons actually gives us an advantage.' Murray emphasised Charles' hyphenated family name. Kirby chuckled.

'Mr Charles Ralph William-Peterson isn't really very clever with the law if you ask me,' Murray continued. 'If he trots out that letter I reckon it will sink MT. Don't you worry, he can't get MT off this one.'

Murray's confidence helped calm Kirby but he and Conrad still spent hours going over their evidence in the days before the case began. On the morning of the court Kirby woke around 4 AM and could not go back to sleep. He got up and read through the brief again. He was at court 45 minutes early and met Karen Fitzgerald and Adrian Walton when they drove into the car park. They chatted and Murray, the police officers and Conrad soon arrived. The senior officer went over a few minor points including the order in which the witnesses would be called to give evidence. Kirby was to be first and Adrian last.

MT, Rohan and Charles Ralph William-Peterson arrived about two minutes before 10. Kirby saw the clerk look at his watch and frown when the defence procession walked into the court foyer. The court began on time and after a couple of applications for restitution of driver licences the Morrison case began.

MT pleaded not guilty to all charges. Rohan pleaded guilty to the charges for the first day and not guilty in relation to the second incident. Murray frowned across at Charles.

'The offer of a guilty plea was on the basis that the prosecution would drop all charges against Maxwell,' Charles whispered. 'Don't come that stunt with me. You know how it works.'

'How many witnesses for the prosecution?' the Magistrate interrupted.

'There are two departmental witness, two police witnesses and two civilian witnesses. A total of 6 Your Honour.'

'And if called on for your defence Mr Peterson, how many witnesses do you intend to call?'

'The defence will not be calling any witnesses Your Honour.'

Instead of standing and facing the Magistrate, Charles only rose slightly off his seat in a display of indifference.

'The defence case is based on the inadmissibility of the prosecution evidence,' he continued. 'In relation to the charges alleged to have occurred on the earlier date we say the inadmissibility relates to the defendant Maxwell Morrison. For those charges alleging offences on the second day the defence will argue that the prosecution evidence is inadmissible against both of the defendants.'

Charles flopped audibly back into his chair with a melodramatic sigh.

'There is no jury here for you to play up to,' the Magistrate growled. 'Your antics do not impress me. In fact, quite the opposite is true.'

Murray opened the case for the prosecution and produced the regulations and several certificates. The first two related to the official appointment of Kirby and Conrad and the others showed that the Morrisons held no licenses. A certificate from Vic Roads showed Rohan to be the owner of the vehicle. Kirby entered the witness box and gave his testimony without the need for Murray to ask one question by way of clarification. Charles rose and began his cross-examination. He pulled the chair out from the bar table and put his right foot on it, leaning on his knee.

'Now let's start with the incident you say took place near an onion patch,' he said. 'It is true, is it not, that Mr Rohan Morrison admitted he caught the parrots that day?'

'Yes.'

'And he has pleaded guilty to those charges here at court hasn't he?'

'Yes.'

'It is also true, is it not, that Mr Maxwell Morrison told you he was there to catch Gold Finches?'

'Yes.'

'And in fact he did catch a large number of Gold Finches?'

'Yes.'

'And that was a quite lawful pursuit.'

'That is a statement, and a statement of law,' the Magistrate interjected before Kirby could answer. 'If you have a question ask it. I trust I don't have to remind you though, questions of law are for the court, not the witness.'

'The department has not laid any charges relating to the trapping of Gold Finches near the onion patch that day have they?' Charles asked. He knew his point was now framed in the form of a legitimate question – nevertheless a question so obvious it annoyed the court.

'That's stating the obvious,' the Magistrate scoffed spontaneously.

He could have been speaking to himself but Charles Ralph William-Peterson knew better. So did everyone else in the room.

'Mr Maxwell Morrison insisted you look at the Gold Finches he caught that day didn't he?'

'Yes.'

Kirby was not at all concerned. He trusted Murray's skills as a prosecutor and knew that during re-examination the prosecutor would bring out the truth – MT had been trying to divert attention from the hidden parrots when he insisted Kirby go to the car to look at the finches.

'You did not see Mr Maxwell Morrison trap any parrots?'

'No.'

'And you did not see him in actual physical possession of any parrots that day did you?'

'No.'

Charles began to think he was on a roll.

'And I put it to you,' Charles said forcefully. 'Mr Maxwell Morrison's actions on that day were consistent with him only trapping finches. What do you say to that?'

'That's absolutely untrue,' replied Kirby. 'As I said before there were hundreds of parrot feathers in and around the trap area and there were only two men there. It is incomprehensible to me that Max Morrison was not involved. There was only one trap and both men were in hides watching that one trap. The general area was baited with a parrot seed mixture, not a finch seed mixture. Then when I challenged their claim that they were targeting Gold Finches when they had Blue-winged Parrots in the decoy cages Rohan said "we changed the finches for parrots". Even before he used the term "we" I was convinced the two men were acting together, helping each other. It is true that Maxwell Morrison kept asking me to go over to their car to look at the finches but I was, and still am, convinced that was his way to get me away from where the parrots were hidden. Later when I found the carry cage full of parrots I specifically asked Maxwell Morrison about helping his brother.

> "I said: Can I take it you helped your
> brother?
>
> Max Morrison said: Wot do you reck-

on? I'm out here for me good looks?

I said: I take it you assisted Rohan in
the capture of these parrots.

Max Morrison said: Write down what
you want. It won't make any difference. You reckon I'm guilty so what's
the difference?"

'Maxwell Morrison did not deny his involvement and that
conversation in particular left me with the distinct impression both
men were involved. I gave Max Morrison every opportunity to deny
his involvement then and there at the scene. He admitted being there
to trap birds and admitted that he did not try to stop Rohan keeping
the parrots.'

'But,' Charles quickly pointed out. 'There was no conversation
or admission to the effect that; "yes I'm helping catch parrots", was
there?'

'No.'

Charles took Kirby to the second day and without trouble gained
Kirby's agreement that there were no direct observations or admission
in relation to either brother actually in physical possession of any
parrots.

'Now,' Charles continued. 'These nine parrots you say were in Mr
Maxwell Morrisons yard. There was no-one at home when you first
arrived was there?'

'No.'

'And when the Morrison's did come home where did they tell you
they had been?'

'Maxwell Morrison said they had been to Melbourne to visit his
wife's sick mother. I don't believe Rohan Morrison said anything.'

'You have no evidence that either of the Morrison's knew there
were parrots in the yard do you?' Charles challenged. 'You said before
that Maxwell claimed to be looking after them for one of the pupils at
the school but that's simply untrue isn't it? You made that up because
you knew you had no case without some sort of admission?'

'Now wait a minute,' the Magistrate snapped. 'That was two
questions in one but my real problem is your attack on Inspector
Wellington's credit, Mr Peterson. I hope you have something to
support that allegation. You told the court before that the defence
was not calling any witnesses so where is the basis for your personal
attack on the officer?'

'Those are my instructions Your Honour,' Charles responded.

'That is not at all helpful Mr Peterson,' the Magistrate observed. 'Unless there is to be some testimony to support it I intend to ignore that part of the evidence. You don't have to answer the allegation Officer Wellington.'

As the cross-examination dragged on Kirby was surprised Charles did not challenge his evidence that the parrots had, in his opinion, been recently wild trapped. Eventually Kirby's ordeal in the witness box was over and he felt the prosecution case had come through in pretty good shape. He began to relax and feel confident. When Karen and Adrian gave evidence about what they saw at the trapping site on the second day Charles did not challenge it. Kirby was now very confident.

At the end of the case for the prosecution Charles made a submission that MT had no case to answer on the first day because all the evidence was against Rohan. The court promptly rejected this.

Charles then began his legal arguments in relation to the second set of charges. He submitted that all the evidence of conversation at MT's residence should be ruled inadmissible. This was on the basis that the moment the officers had pulled into the driveway behind the Morrison's car they had locked the departmental car.

'This had the effect, in law, of placing my clients in custody,' Charles argued. 'They were physically prevented from leaving because of the locked car. I am not arguing the officers actually, physically, arrested my clients but I do say they placed them in legal custody. All persons in custody must be read their rights, not just cautioned. This was not done. In the circumstances all conversation should be ruled inadmissible.'

The court did not agree, but to be fair, some courts may have backed the defence submission on that.

Charles then submitted that all the evidence of observations at MT's residence should be ruled inadmissible. This was on the basis that MT was not at home when the officers alleged they found the parrots. In these circumstances, Charles argued, it was too dangerous for the court to assume MT had knowledge of the birds.

The court accepted Kirby's evidence that MT had made an admission he was responsible for food, water and keeping the parrots quiet.

'I find all the charges proven,' the Magistrate eventually concluded. 'Are there any prior convictions?'

Murray asked MT to stand whilst his long list of convictions was detailed to the court.

'Now,' said the Magistrate. 'What are the penalty provisions and the costs Mr Prosecutor?'

Murray had prepared for this question and had his notes ready. He had no notes or arguments in relation to costs if the charges had been dismissed. Murray expected to win. He stood, eager to respond and as he spoke he glanced at the open pages on the bar table. He enjoyed being centre stage in these circumstances.

'The two charges for possessing the parrots are under section 47 in the Wildlife Act,' Your Honour. 'This carries a maximum penalty of 50 penalty units or six months imprisonment or both the fine and the imprisonment. There is an additional penalty of five units for each head of wildlife in respect of the two offences. If my arithmetic is correct, and given there were 42 parrots from near the onion patch, I believe the maximum fine is therefore $215,000 for that day. Based on nine parrots, the penalty is $50,000 for the second day. As I said, Your Honour, the option for incarceration for up to six months on each charge can be applied in addition to the fines.'

Murray watched and when the Magistrate had finished making notes he continued.

'The other charges, for trapping the parrots illegally, are under section 47D. This carries a maximum penalty of 240 penalty units or 24 months imprisonment or both. There is no additional penalty for these charges. In summary the courts' sentencing options on the four charges are to a maximum aggregate fine of $313,000 with or without imprisonment for up 60 months.

The Magistrate raised an eyebrow and looked to the other end of the bar table.

'Mr Peterson,' he said coldly. 'I expect I do not have to tell you that I consider that the only real option for the court is to impose a considerable term of imprisonment. If I were you I would concentrate your plea on reasons I should not impose a very substantial monetary penalty as well.'

Despite a long and repetitive plea from Charles Ralph William-Peterson the court sentenced MT to imprisonment for a year. Rohan was fined $20,000.

When the officers walked out of court Kirby knew he should not let his personal feelings show. He did not want Mrs Morrison to see he was smiling broadly, very happy that MT was now in jail.

'Congratulations,' Murray said, shaking Kirby's hand. 'Well done. Half the officers in the state have tried to close MT down. I've been trying myself for over twenty years. Ever thought about coming back to Head Office as my replacement when I retire?'

'No, not really,' Kirby answered.

'Well you've got three or four years to make up your mind before I retire,' Murray confided. 'You'd be good, bloody good. A fair bit of policy work but you could do it on your ear. The manual needs updating in a few places. Actually I'm going to ask you officially to write a whole chapter on bird trapping. I want the usual, you know, what evidence to look for, how they pre-bait an area and that sort of thing. But I want this chapter to be different. Better. I want it to show the conservation damage caused by trapping wild birds. This won't be just about parrots but they'll be an important part. What do you think? You'll give it a go?'

'I'd need to know a bit more,' Kirby mused. 'This has come out of the blue and it sounds like a lot of work.'

'Sure there's a bit of work,' Murray continued. 'You'll need to get some statistics and population dynamics. Get figures for the number licences issued and the number of different species reported to be held under licence. Keep to the endangered and notable species and those most in demand. Have a look at the dates the blue wings turn up on licence holder's official books. See if there's a correlation between this and when MT moved back to Costerfield – or when the birds return to Victoria from Tasmania.'

'Sure,' scoffed Kirby. 'I should be able to get that done by the end of the week. What about all my normal work?'

'I'll get you all the relief you need,' Murray agreed. 'I'll send a couple of the new recruits up here for a week or two at a time.'

The senior officer paused. He was obviously thinking.

'Hang on a minute,' he said. 'I've just realised MT may not have been the ringleader – just like Charles told the court. There probably isn't anything in MT's shift back to Costerfield – I reckon Rohan may have been the source of most of the illegal parrots in Melbourne for years. MT was probably just the middle man – he wouldn't have the brains to be the boss.'

'Maybe.' Kirby was not convinced.

'Well I suppose it doesn't matter,' Murray said. 'This chapter in the manual can point out that several species are officially classified as endangered directly as a result of the illegal take from the wild. Find out the truth about the Princess Parrot. How come it is more plentiful in captivity than in the wild? Look at the plight of the Golden-shouldered Parrot and the Gouldian Finch and relate their population dynamics, in the wild, to their abundance in aviculture. Is there a correlation between the decline of the Princess Parrot and the decline of these other two species? What do you think? You'll give it a go won't you?

'Neil Lyons once told me it was an honour to get to write a chapter for the manual,' Kirby answered looking at his watch. 'Of course I'll do it. I'd love to.'

It was just after 3 PM.

'I've got a bit of private business,' Kirby announced, unexpectedly changing the subject. 'I'm not going back to the office now and I'm rostered off till Monday. See you then.'

Kirby called out his thanks to Karen and Adrian as he hurried away towards the car park. Murray and Conrad glanced at each other and both shrugged their shoulders. Neither had any idea what their colleague was up to.

'It's my shout,' said Murray. 'Who wants a coffee?'

He led the way across the street to the Court House Café.

Before going home Kirby visited Nicky's best friend, Gayle, and arranged for Zac and Kylie to sleep over. He then used his mobile phone and called the motel at Mafeking Bay. He booked a room with a spa bath and a window table for two in the restaurant. The restaurant overlooked the harbour and Kirby knew the setting sun would give the evening meal a fantastic atmosphere. After dark the lights around the general bay and town area should be just as spectacular.

'Did you win?' Nicky asked as Kirby walked in the door.

'I'll tell you on the way to Mafeking Bay. Gayle is looking after Zac and Kylie for a couple of nights and we're booked in at the motel at the bay. You pack and I'll drop the kids off as soon as they get home from school. Come on, you've only got 15 minutes. Take your new pink outfit to wear at dinner tonight.'

Nicky stood with her mouth open as Kirby scurried around getting the children's things together. Gayle had told him what to pack and Nicky soon realised Kirby knew exactly what he wanted. She did not argue.

Chapter 26

ARE YOU A BUSHRANGER, MISTER?

Next spring Ronald Orney, head master from Zac's school, rang the department's Costerfield office and spoke to Kirby.

'Two of my pupils have found a baby eagle that fell out of its nest,' he explained. 'They rescued the poor bird so they've done the right thing there but they've brought it to school. It can't stay here – we don't have the resources to look after it. It's an awful distraction to other pupils too. Besides, I'd have thought this was more your department's responsibility than mine.'

Kirby remembered the disaster twelve months previously but said nothing on the phone. He went to the school and picked up the bird, a wedge-tailed chick about three weeks old. Its primary wing and tail feathers had just begun to appear as dark lines in the white down that blanketed the baby eagle. Kirby asked to speak to Ronald Orney and began to pry into the origins of the bird. He simply explained that it was policy to find out where sick, injured and orphaned wildlife had come from.

'I can only tell you what the play-ground gossip is,' Ronald advised. 'If that's anything to go on the eagle fell out of a nest in Banayeo Gorge out near Diggora somewhere I think. It was found, and rescued, by Jamie Askew and Aaron Van Der Hope.'

'I'm afraid it's is not quite that simple,' Kirby said soberly. He was convinced the head master knew nothing of the previous incident. 'Young eagles don't just fall out of nests. Anyway they're built a bit like Buddha and if they are not well fledged they are far too heavy to survive a fall of even a metre or so. Unless a baby eagle had fully formed primary wing feathers, and tail feathers, it's impossible for it to even glide, let alone fly. I can tell you from bitter experience they hit the ground with such force the impact kills them instantly.'

'What are you saying?' Ronald asked. 'Where did Jamie and Aaron get a baby eagle then?'

Kirby explained what had happened the previous year – not pulling any punches about the persons he believed responsible.

'Oh, dear,' said Ronald. 'That puts a different perspective on things doesn't it? What do you suggest we do?'

'Well I'd like to come up to the school and talk to the pupils, probably in two age groups, the senior school and the junior school. The lesson could be about conservation values and the environment generally, not specifically about the eagle, but specific enough that most of the students will get the message.'

'That will certainly be arranged,' Ronald agreed. 'If this has happened before wouldn't it be best if you spoke to the boys directly?'

'Yes,' said Kirby explaining his intended course of action. 'I will do that but I think it's best with their parents present. Perhaps that should happen at home and not at school anyway.'

Ronald agreed and Kirby soon left with the eagle in a banana box, open at the top and sitting on the front passenger seat of departmental car. He called Karen Fitzgerald and she agreed to try to raise and rehabilitate the chick. Without going back to the office Kirby drove out to Diggora South and as he neared Karen's home the little eagle became restless. It circled in the box then suddenly raised its backside, easily clear of the top of its temporary home. It then let fly with the force of a fire hydrant. The height the young bird effortlessly propped its back-side amazed Kirby and he gained first-hand knowledge of how Wedge-tailed Eagles keep their nests completely clear of excreta. Not a single drop went on the banana box! Kirby later found out how difficult it is to clean eagle white wash off car seats, air vents, dashboard and floor.

Back in the office Kirby made two appointments – the first to see Aaron Van Der Hope with his parents and the second to see Jamie Askew with his parents. The interview with the Van Der Hopes went smoothly and Kirby was sure Aaron would hear, and perhaps feel, more from his father later. The appointment to see the Askews was two days after that and in the meantime Aaron told Jamie what to expect. Jamie's little brother, Stuart, heard and partly understood that Aaron and Jamie were in deep trouble over the baby eagle.

Kirby rang the Askew's doorbell about five minutes early. It appeared no one was home despite the appointment. Eventually the door was opened by Mrs Askew. She carried a newborn baby and a bright-eyed Stuart peered around from behind her dress.

'Sorry,' she said as she opened the door. 'I was changing the baby. You must be Kirby Wellington.'

'Yes, I am, but please don't be sorry.'

'Come in Kirby. I'm Robyn. Stan is out the back with Jamie. They're feeding the ferrets.'

Robyn Askew swung around and walked away down the passage carrying the baby. Stuart's cover had disappeared and he stood there in the middle of the doorway staring wide-eyed at Kirby.

'Hello. Do you help Daddy look after the ferrets too?'

There was no response. Stuart's big blue eyes did not blink. The young boy gazed intently at the officer.

'I guess Daddy and Jamie can look after the ferrets by themselves can they? You'd help Mummy and Daddy with other jobs wouldn't you?'

Kirby expected his attempts at conversation would fail. He was wrong.

'Are you a bushranger Mr?' the little fellow eventually asked.

The question was totally sincere and the logic was brilliant. It stunned Kirby. Stuart, aware of his brother's trouble, knew the ranger was there because of the baby eagle. He had seen rangers on TV but Kirby's uniform didn't look like the one he'd seen before. Who then could Kirby be, except a bushranger?

Seated around the kitchen table Kirby explained why he was there. Jamie's frank admissions about two eagles came as a shock to his parents. The officer felt sorry for them when he realised they were genuinely astonished to hear this was the second bird. Stan promised Jamie he would not be visiting Uncle Rohan on the farm for six months, despite considerable protest at the prospect of not being able to try out a new ferret.

Kirby wondered if Robyn and Stan know about the trouble between the Morrisons and the department. He concluded they must know something. He contemplated how much negative influence Rohan Morrison must have already had on Jamie Askew and Aaron Van Der Hope. Rabbits, being pest animals, did untold damage that adversely effected the rural economy so a weekend ferreting was a good thing for the boys to do. Unfortunately their taste for fun out on the farm may already have been poisoned by stories about shooting bullfrogs and exploiting wildlife for personal pleasure or gain.

A week or so later Conrad stood in for Kirby and spent two afternoons up at the school talking to the pupils. During question time at the end of the talk nearly every student wanted to ask at least one question. Jamie Askew, Aaron Van Der Hope and Zac Wellington were silent. Conrad knew why the first two did not speak but he did not understand that Zac was worried Jamie and Aaron would suspect he dobbed them in. They had no idea.

The young eagle survived and thrived. It grew into a beautiful bird and Karen, with help from members of the local Field Naturalist Club, put the young eagle through hundreds of hours of rehabilitation. The eagle was eventually released in the gorge where it had been born and for several months its human benefactors taught it to search for naturally occurring food. At times when this was not plentiful Karen and the Field Naturalists made sure the eagle found a meal before it became too hungry.

Everything appeared to be a sensational success but the Morrison's sheep were still dying from starvation, liver fluke or something. One day the eagle was no-where to be found. Karen and the Field Naturalists drove every road and back track for fifty kilometres without success. In desperation Karen rang Kirby and reported her suspicions. Kirby agreed to speak to Rohan and the next morning visited the farm. Rohan was working in the yards at the shearing shed. He was marking wormy, skinny lambs and he protested his innocence the moment Kirby mentioned the eagle.

Kirby knew Rohan had shot the bird but he had no evidence. As he drove back to Costerfield the officer began to think about how people simply accepted that Jamie Askew and Aaron Van Der Hope found the eagles fallen out of their nests. He thought about the super efforts of Karen Fitzgerald and the Field Naturalists when they rehabilitated the second eagle chick. His mind went back to the first baby eagle and how it had died. Kirby still felt immensely guilty. He remembered the phone call he received early in his career when a lady found an echidna lost in the bush and took it back to suburban Melbourne in a heart breaking, but ignorant, effort to try to help.

The eagle stories were typical – the wildlife had plenty of legal protection and many volunteers gave enormously of their time and talents. Those eagles were both now dead and time marched on regardless of that or election promises or government policy. Kirby felt all his efforts were not making any difference. His work was no different from any job, just a means to an end, a way to gain material possessions and gratification for self. These things were all that seemed to matter in a lot of ways.

Kirby made some personal judgments about the irreversible harm MT had done over the years and how much public time and effort had been expended before he was eventually sent to jail. Did that help or make any real difference? Rohan just stepped up a cog and took over MT's illegal enterprises. Or, as had been suggested, was Rohan the Mr Big all the time? Kirby did not know. All he could hope for was a change in public attitudes and he knew the efforts addressing school children was vital if this was to be successful.

As he drove Kirby wondered how he would react if I he were ever again confronted by the story of an eagle that fell out of its nest. He expected he would not be too benevolent and perhaps, by comparison, Australia's most notorious bushranger would be a gentleman.

Acknowledgements

Hundreds of photos of cute and cuddly critters enhance my memorabilia collected through my work with sick, injured and orphaned wildlife. I have pictures of young kangaroos, gliders and possums, a baby koala, a few parrots, owls and wild ducklings. To these, and a host of other creatures, great and small, I owe a debt of gratitude. If no animal ever needed help I would not have had so much satisfaction from my work.

Strangely enough, the people I caught breaking our conservation laws also deserve some credit for providing me with experiences that added spice and variety to my work. Unfortunately this thank-you is the silver lining on a black cloud of environmental vandalism.

I would also like to acknowledge my many work companions for various contributions; you gave special depth to my experiences. Your efforts gave me the ideas for many of my tales and I congratulate you for your part in the important work of conservation. Those of you who were my original workmates made your contribution at a time when working conditions were poor and remuneration was abject. Back then very few people used the word conservation and even fewer understood it.

Our cherished emblem was a black-and-white platypus. Bill Lynch was the Chief Fisheries and Wildlife Officer, Geoff Clarke was the Assistant Chief and Phil Rhodes was the Senior Inspector. Working with them in head office were Fisheries and Wildlife Officers: Lachlan Bracken, Bill Bate, Peter (Buster) Brown, Peter O'Riley, Tony Meakes, Bob Timms and John Adams. Stationed on Port Phillip Bay were Campbell Cox and Rod Hasthorpe.

Bill Kelly was at Mildura, George Hardwick at Kerang, Jim Pope at Echuca, Owen Thomas at Horsham, Ian May at St Arnaud,

John Clements at Ballarat, Joe Morris at Hamilton, Jim Davidson at Port Fairy, Tim O'Brien and Bob Jackson at Geelong, Gill Foster at Alexandra, Jim Crosier at Shepparton, Pat Sherridan at Wangaratta, Jack Rhodes at Wodonga, Bob Eames at Cowes, Arthur Roberts at Traralgon, Bob Austin at Yarram, Kevin Street at Bairnsdale and Graeme Whitham was at Mallacoota.

I also acknowledge the enormous encouragement given by Diane Inchley. Her enthusiasm for my original manuscript was contagious and much appreciated. The advice I received from Sarah Endacott, *edit or die*, has been invaluable and her assistance has made my work a book. Thankyou Sarah.

Finally, to my wife Anne, I say the biggest thank you. You put up with me, married to a job when you were busy making our two daughters into beautiful people. You saw that my experiences were worth a yarn or two and lived through all the time I spent at the computer putting this book together, then revising it over and over again.

About the Author

Robert Pietsch was born in Warracknabeal, Victoria, in 1947. He spent his childhood at Pomonal, a tiny hamlet, twenty kilometres west of Stawell. A number of Pomonal farmers, including Robert's father, were orchardists who protected their livelihood by shooting parrots, kangaroos, emus and any other animal that caused damage to fences, pasture or crops. Sometimes the shooting was done under permit; sometimes it was not. It was never done for pleasure – farmers could not afford ammunition for sport.

Today the Pomonal orchards have all but gone, mostly sub-divided into small holdings with the majority of the population perceiving conservation and wildlife issues from a very different perspective than farmers did in the 1950s and 60s. Today, however, farmers everywhere still compete with nature for their economic existence and they sometimes see "greenies" as out of touch with reality.

In 1970 when Robert joined the Fisheries and Wildlife Department terms like greenie, environmental protest, animal liberation and even conservation were never heard — these terms hadn't yet entered every-day use. Like most fisheries and wildlife officers, Robert had some understanding that the bush and our wildlife were far more important than most people then understood, but there was so much to learn. The public debate about environmental issues had not yet begun in earnest. Today, schools teach conservation and its principles and terms like natural resources, pollution, biodiversity, sustainable use, re-cycling, habitat, endangered species and extinction are all household words.

There are still mountains to learn, and do, in the area of natural resources and the environment. But while the public debate about conservation still rages there is hope. The fact that there are two sides with aggressively incompatible attitudes should be good in the long term. Once we become complacent the battle may be lost.

In 1970, during the reign of Alfred Dunbavin-Butcher as Director of the Victorian Fisheries and Wildlife Department, Robert received a letter from the departmental head office at 601 Flinders Street Extension, Melbourne. It read, in part:

> "You have been appointed to the posi-
> tion of Fisheries and Wildlife Officer,
> Grade One, without additional salary".

The "without additional salary" bit didn't mean much at the time but the first departmental pay-packet ended any thoughts of returning to life on the farm where money from shooting and trapping rabbits paid for petrol, entertainment and a Coca-Cola on weekends. This changed financial situation happened at the same time as a mutation from Robert to Bob – from mere mortal to Fisheries and Wildlife Officer.

After several years in the job the truth about officer's salaries became evident. Compared to other public servants and equivalent officers in other states, Victorian fisheries and wildlife officers did not receive fair compensation – even though it was better than the earnings of those who shot and trapped rabbits for a living. Employment conditions compelled work on 40 weekend days in each year. In addition officers were on-call 24 hours a day, seven days a week. There was no such thing as overtime.

Bob married Anne in 1972 and the birth of Heidi in 1975 meant they really were a one-income family. Donna was born in 1977 and in 1979 the family purchased its first home. From then until Anne went back to work in 1994 the "without additional salary" bit had real meaning.

When he received his letter of appointment, Bob's job expectations were either blatantly ignorant or blissfully innocent – he has no idea which. No one had any idea how economic rationalism would shape the officers jobs, especially in the latter years. Expectations were based simply on a love of nature and a couple of specific childhood experiences.

The first of these related to the re-colonisation of the koala back into the Grampians where they had died out since white settlement. It involved the local fisheries and wildlife officer, George Hope from Horsham, and Bob Austin his young assistant from Melbourne. In 1953, on their way to release koalas at Halls Gap, the two officers called at the Pomonal State School where Robert was a pupil in one of the lower grades. He was fascinated by the caged koalas and when they took a mother out of its crate and showed the kids its pouch, with a baby inside, ecstasy showed on the faces of every pupil – the whole 24 of them. This show-and-tell session demonstrated how the little mite attached tightly to its mother's teat.

A couple of years later, when he was eight or nine years old, an experience with his father helping George Hope and Ian May, the fisheries and wildlife officer from St Arnaud, became the second incident. The officers were catching trout with mesh nets in Lake Fyans as part of the Fisheries and Wildlife Department's salmonoid breeding program. It was early spring and the soil around the lake was totally saturated after an exceptionally wet winter.

George had driven off the track and bogged the departmental Land Rover in a bottomless slush. The quagmire reached halfway up the doors, pushing them tightly closed. The officers could not get out and the vehicle was still sinking. Eventually the two officers escaped through a window and walked for help. The local farmers all knew about the murky, sloppy mud that bogged every vehicle that travelled the back road between Pomonal and Lake Fyans during winter. No one was willing to risk the farm tractor going to assist.

The Pietsch orchard was not the closest to the action but Robert's Dad had a grubbing machine – a torturous piece of equipment incorporating a long lever and a series of cogs and pulleys which worked a winch cable onto a drum. It was made mostly from cast iron – heavy, black and sinister. Even the main lever was so heavy all a young boy could do was pick up one end and drag it – so long as the going was downhill. Through the principles of levers and pulleys a man could, single headedly, wrench quite a large tree out of the ground with the grubbing machine. The cogs and levers were kept well-greased – in an attempt to make the thing easier to use, not to stop it wearing out. Somehow the grease always managed to get all over the operator and his clothes every time one walked anywhere near it. Robert's Mum and Dad both hated the grubbing machine.

The grubbing machine, an old tractor, a crosscut saw and more than one axe were used after World War II to clear the land that became the Pietsch farm and orchard.

George and Ian walked for help and found the farm closest to the bogged Land Rover. This was owned by Robert's Uncle Dave who listened to their woes then, scratching his head under his hat, mused, 'I reckon if you want the car back before summer, your only chance is with Ed's grubbing machine.'

He directed the officers up the road to the Pietsch place.

Robert tagged along with his Dad, uncle and the two officers as they man-handled the machine and its bits and pieces towards the half-submerged Land Rover. The grubber itself was the most difficult. Its heavy cast iron frame and puny wheels bogged, and bogged again and again. The men took it in turns to pull and push the thing but progress was painfully slow. It took more than two hours to move the grubber the several hundred yards from the safety of the road. All but one of the components of the machine was too heavy for the young boy to lift but, he wanted desperately to help his mates.

When he began to carry the smallest pulley his Dad yelled out, 'Git outa the way!' Dejected and hurt Robert stood and watched from the road.

The men put two planks on the ground to form a makeshift pontoon. This gave them an opportunity to haul, push and shove the grubbing machine a few feet at a time. Two more planks placed in front and used the same way, allowed the next few steps of progress. Finally, by re-placing the planks and repeating the steps several more times, the machine with its assorted cables, levers and attachments, was in position. With the anchor cable secured to the base of a huge red-gum tree nearby and the drag cable attached to the rear of the Land Rover all four men took turns working the lever. Clank-clunk, clank-clunk, clank-clunk, went the sounds of the anti-reverse ratchet as it worked on the cogs. The drum gradually took up the slack and the cable became so tight it began to creak. The tension eventually moved the vehicle, though only an inch or so with each torturous crank of the lever.

It was mid-morning next day before the vehicle was back at ground level and sitting safely on the road. Then everyone travelled down to the lake where the officers prepared their boat to go out and haul the nets.

The hurt of the previous day was nothing to the bitter disappointment Robert felt when he was told he could not go in the boat. It seemed forever before George and Ian eventually arrived back at shore but, when they did, the trout they had caught became vibrantly and permanently etched in the boy's mind. He was only a lad and the fish were undoubtedly larger than life in his memory.

Ian and George sorted the fish and prepared the equipment needed for the egg stripping and insemination. This was fascinating, and in his youthful ignorance Robert thought this was what the Officers did all the time. There certainly was no understanding that it was only a small part of the work done by fisheries and wildlife officers, even back then. Ian explained that only the biggest trout were used because these had the best genes and represented those fish best able to survive. He went on to explain that virtually all trout in the lake had been spawned in the same way, reared at the Snobs Creek Fish Hatchery and then released by the fisheries and wildlife officers. Even at the age of eight or nine a boy could understand this. Big fish mean big appetites and feeding fish are the only ones anglers catch. There had to be a direct relationship between insatiable appetites, large fish and good catches.

It then dawned on Robert that the Fisheries and Wildlife Department's manipulation of Mother Nature in this way had to be for the good of all. He wanted to become part of the action.

The intimacy of the trout-breeding program then commenced. A needle attached to a bike pump was inserted into the abdomen of a female trout. Ian held the fish over a stainless steel bowl. With a gentle pump or two George artificially bloated the gut cavity and forced the eggs to spurt out into the bowl. This was the actual stripping process. Fertilisation then took place with milt stripped from males in the same way. It was fantastic — Robert's first sex — he was allowed to stir the eggs and milt mixture with a spoon! That night he dreamed of being part of all that he had seen and heard.

In retrospect the koala incident at the school kindled a desire to become a fisheries and wildlife officer. The experience with the grubbing machine showed a job that could involve hard work. The biology, genetics and physiology of the trout-stripping episode fanned the spark into flames and kept them burning.

In 1970, when Robert received his offer of employment, the trout-breeding program no longer involved fisheries and wildlife officers in the stripping and insemination of fish. This change in work practice denied considerable anticipated pleasure, but it did not dampen the young officer's enthusiasm for his new career.

Fisheries and wildlife officers were the shopfront of the department then. At the time Bob had an ambition of becoming officer in charge at a country station and he still feels fortunate to have achieved this, in 1975, at Geelong.